ALONG THE MERCHANT WAY

The Maiyochi Chronicles
Book Four

PHILLIP L. JOHNSON

Black Rose Writing | Texas

ISBN: 978-1-68513-535-5
PUBLISHED BY BLACK ROSE WRITING
www.blackrosewriting.com

Printed in the United States of America
Suggested Retail Price (SRP) $21.95

Along the Merchant Way is printed in Book Antiqua

*As a planet-friendly publisher, Black Rose Writing does its best to eliminate unnecessary waste to reduce paper usage and energy costs, while never compromising the reading experience. As a result, the final word count vs. page count may not meet common expectations.

ALONG THE MERCHANT WAY

The Maiyochi Chronicles
Book Four

PROLOGUE

Giorgi carefully made his way through the dark, narrow streets of 'south wall', taking pains to avoid the refuse strewn carelessly in the path of all who chose to travel thereabouts.

In addition to the waste thrown from doors, windows and carriages, there were occasional piles of feces, both large and small, coming from horses, cattle, pigs, goats, and possibly even humans. It seemed all who traveled this part of Gunjunson, admittedly the dregs of the city, felt free to use anywhere they tread as a depository. And these streets, where some of the poorest of the city lived, were rarely, if ever, cleaned. The filth lay in place, slowly becoming an accepted part of the surroundings, kicked and trampled and flattened into another layer of the streets and alleys that its residents strode daily.

Despite the surrounding squalor, Giorgi's mood was light. His stride and carriage spoke not of a man picking his way through refuse, but of one almost giddy with anticipation. He was heading to a special place, alive with good food, fine drink, and finer company. That it was necessary to lift the hem of his robe, to keep it clean as he walked, was hardly even an inconvenience. He counted it a small price to pay for the night that awaited him.

As he continued toward his destination, he once again mused on the events that had made this night possible.

It was seven nights past when his fortune had so quickly changed.

Giorgi was employed at the docks of the Manchess river, the waterway flowing south past the western walls of the great city of Gunjunson, the capital of Cantor. His designation was 'bargeman'.

A good bargeman worked all aspects of the job, even unto building a custom barge if the load to be carried was more than the usual vessel could hold. Once a barge was judged sufficient, the bargemen then loaded the goods or livestock, careful to leave enough room for themselves and the few belongings they would need for the journey downriver.

It took the better part of three days for a barge to ride the current downstream to the ancient port adjacent to the city of Wroughtmire, the capital city of the nation of Rayine. The bargemen worked in shifts to ensure that someone was always awake and alert should the river choose to *complicate* their journey.

Once at their destination, the bargemen got to work unloading the goods, now with the help of the locals employed by the purchaser. This made their job considerably easier and allowed them to conserve their strength for the task of disassembling the barge so that the planks could be loaded into carts pulled by teams of horses. In this way, the barge and the bargemen were returned to the city of Cantor and to the docks outside the South gate. After an all too brief visit with their families, the bargemen would again head down to the docks where the cycle would begin anew.

The bargemen were paid six pieces of silver for their labors, more if a custom barge had to be constructed.

It was the custom of the bargemen to ask for their pay prior to the beginning of the work. If he was foolish enough to wait on his pay, he could be run off at the port of Wroughtmire without a coin to show for his labor. It would then be his word against that of the bargemaster as to what, if any, he was due. If he was inclined to take his pay at the beginning and disappear prior to the completion of his work, the bargemaster would place a bounty on his head that would ensure he could no longer work, nor even be seen, near the ports of Cantor, Rayine, Byrne, or anywhere along the Manchess river.

Seven nights ago, Giorgi and his mates were close to finishing loading a barge when six horsemen dressed in gray robes led their mounts onto the docks. Without dismounting, they approached the bargemaster, their features hidden deep in the shadow of the hoods pulled over their heads. All had heard stories of 'The Robes' and all activity on this part of the dock ceased as the men looked to each other and back to the robed riders with anxious glances.

As they spoke to the bargemaster, no words could be heard, even by the bargemen standing nearest. It was only by the attentive stare and occasional nod of the bargemaster that anyone could tell instructions were being given. When the instructions were both given and understood, one of the Robes passed to the bargemaster a pouch, and all waited as the bargemaster called together the six men who were to work his barge on the trip down river. Not one to parse words, he got right to the point.

"We'll be hauling additional cargo," the bargemaster said, after the men had gathered close. "Two of the robed men behind me will be coming with us to Rayine. I need you to reload the barge to make room for these men, their belongings and their horses. For your part in this, the Robes," he cast a cautious glance their way at having used this common name in their presence, "have demanded your complete silence as to what be happening here this night. For your added work, your promise to see the two safely to Rayine, and your still tongues, you will earn two gold coins apiece."

These last words had brought a gasp of surprise from the assembled bargemen. It would take five trips down river to earn silver equal to a single coin of gold. And the Robes offered two! Seeing the truth of the offer on the face of the bargemaster, the men hurriedly agreed to the extra work, and the required vow of silence. As was custom on the docks, the master approached them one by one and placed two gold coins in each hand, the weight of which brought instant smiles to the faces of those so blessed.

"Bend your backs now!" the bargemaster spat as the last palm was filled. "Get to it! We'll still be launching within the hour!"

With hurried thanks and assurances of their silence, the men jumped to the task of making room for their new charges. Once the load had been reconfigured and the two robes, their belongings and their horses were in place, it was clear that there would not be enough room for the six bargemen. One would have to stay behind. The other five agreed that Giorgi would be left.

Cursing his lost fortune, Giorgi approached the four remaining robes who, still on horseback, had been watching as the bargemen reconfigured the load and saw the two robes safely aboard. His outstretched hand held the two gold pieces he was most certainly loath to part with. To the surprise of all, a voice from deep within the hood simply reminded him of his vow of silence and waved him away. The remaining bargemen, who moments ago had snickered at Giorgi's misfortune, stared after him in envy. He was to be paid his full wage, plus two gold coins, and his work was done.

Giorgi smiled to himself as he remembered the looks on those faces. They had thought to do him dirt and instead had bestowed upon him a boon! He remembered making his way back toward the south gate and thinking how surprised his wife would be when he walked in the door of their shack nine days early and carrying pay for over ten trips down river. She would be so happy! The things she could do with the extra coin!

But at the thought of turning over all of his newfound wealth to his wife, as was his normal way, the smile had disappeared from Giorgi's face. He wanted to keep some of this good fortune for himself alone. He felt he deserved it.

But to give only a portion to his wife was to call down her wrath upon his head!

His wife was shrewd, and at times seemed to know him better than he knew himself. Even if he kept a small portion, what would he do with it? He would have no opportunity to spend it, nor could he be seen to bring goods into the house that he could not explain. If he did, she would know. She would watch him like a hawk and he would find some small way to unknowingly signal his deceit.

No, he would have to turn over every cent to her.

That was when Giorgi began to formulate his plan; a plan so simple, yet so foolproof, that his wife would never have to know, and he alone would get to enjoy the blessing of the two gold coins!

Giorgi smiled to himself as he again reviewed the plan that he was now eight nights into.

His wife, good woman that she was, would not expect him back from a trip downriver for nine nights. So, he would take a trip... a short trip to the far side of the city, near the east gate, to visit with his cousin, Falfo.

Falfo was unmarried and lived in a shack much worse than his. For a single piece of silver, he could convince his cousin to let him sleep there for the time he would normally be downriver.

And he was sure that a second piece of silver would buy his cousins' aide and silence concerning the rest of his plan.

Giorgi had always been poor and, being poor, had gone to work at an early age. His wife too had been poor, and they had married young. He had never enjoyed the freedom that seemed a rite of passage for many young men, and could only listen in jealous silence at the many bawdy stories he heard from others who manned the barges on the long, slow trips downriver.

Resting in the inner pocket of his dirty tunic that night had been the means to end that jealousy and make his many dreams come true!

Right then and there, Giorgi had come up with the plan to use this windfall at the kind of place he had always heard about but had never been. He would spend his coin at one of the many taverns near the east gate! He would feast and drink and come to know the tavern wenches he had heard so many stories about over the years. And on the evening of the ninth day, he would return to his wife with six silver coins in his hand and she would be none the wiser!

It had taken more persuasion than he thought to secure the aide of his cousin, but three silver pieces, along with the promise of a night of food and drink, had done the trick. That had been last night, and Giorgi had used the time he and Falfo had spent feasting and drinking to scout the many options available to him now that he had the means. What he soon learned was there were taverns and *taverns*.

Those taverns closest to the gate, referred to as 'Inns', were by far the finest, but a single gold coin would barely get one such as himself in the door. At first this had been disheartening, but persistence had paid off in the form of a brightly lit but much less pretentious place located down the road a piece, south of the east gate. The food was rich, the drinks ever flowing, and the wenches were comely beauties, though not as cultured as those of the Inns. He had treated Falfo to a meal and flask at reasonable cost, and had plenty of coin left over for a solitary visit the next night.

For this reason, the filth of his present surroundings was of no thought to Giorgi tonight. He knew he would soon be free of the dwellings of the 'south wall' and onto a better, cleaner part of the city. Then he would make his way to the comforts that awaited him at his newly discovered haven.

He found himself smiling anew as he made his way toward The Milkmaid's Rest.

CHAPTER 1

Lucius arrived at the campsite well after the midnight hour.

The camp was located in a sparse patch of woods surrounding a shed used to store farming implements during the winter. It was located south of the walls of Gunjunson and far enough from the main roads that none would be expected to stumble upon them. The small fire was built on the far side of the shed so its glow would be more difficult to see from the walls of the city. It was a quiet, secluded place where no one would expect anyone to be this time of year.

As he stepped into the small clearing, Lucius looked around at the faces revealed in the sparse light thrown off by the flames.

Jared, the dutiful soldier from the South Gate of Stronghold, squatted beside the fire and nudged it with a long stick to coax more flame, more light, and more warmth on another cold late winter night.

The young priest Petri was not far from him, sitting sideways to the fire and holding what appeared to be a small scroll at such an angle as to maximize the effect of the firelight.

Leaning against a tree at the boundary of the ring of light stood Hendric, newly appointed Captain of the Citadel Guard and the leader of this group that was sanctioned by King Ammon IV to pursue, capture, and return to Stronghold, the Harbinger of the Fourth Prophecy.

Lucius let his gaze linger on the captain's face, both hidden and revealed by the flickering firelight. It had certainly changed, as had all their faces, since the beginning of their quest. The polished and clean-shaven officer who had led them from the base of the high stone cliffs above the Ninum Valley was now a nondescript ruffian with thirteen days of dirty beard clinging to his face. His eyes had changed, too. Now they were hard; much harder than when the pursuit began. This was due to the weight of his mission and the many unexpected complications that had sprung up between Stronghold and Gunjunson.

Upon seeing Lucius, Hendric pushed off the tree and stood erect in expectation of his sergeant advancing to deliver a report.

That is exactly what Lucius did.

"Hail, Hendric," Lucius said in greeting as he started across the clearing toward him. As he covered the distance, he allowed his eyes to further sweep the clearing, spying the brothers Ishmed and Fevor, native trackers attached to the garrison of the South Gate, sitting close together in conversation just outside the ring of firelight.

"Lucius," Hendric said in reply, motioning him further into the shadows. "Have you word on the whereabouts of our quarry?"

"I do, M'lord," said the sergeant. "A contact spoke to me of six robed and hooded figures, those of the *gray robes*, leaving the city through the south gate last night. They headed for the river Manchess. He said, though six left the gate, only four returned. I believe the Harbinger and his acolyte commissioned transport there and are now headed downriver toward Wroughtmire."

This made sense to Hendric as the Harbinger had been linked to the gray robes by their attack on the Golden Lantern, the tavern where he and his acolyte had sought shelter. Although there were no witnesses who could swear to what occurred there, all evidence pointed to the Harbinger and his acolyte leaving the tavern with the gray robes, mysterious figures that were thought linked to Gunjunson Palace. It was in the palace of King Moton the IX, well beyond their grasp, that both Lucius and Hendric had guessed the Harbinger to be held.

Though the report was given in a whisper, still Hendric looked up; allowing his eyes to search the clearing to assure that none had overheard the naming of their quarry. Satisfied that the identity was still a secret, Hendric again turned his attention to Lucius, only to be interrupted by the sounds of more men entering the clearing. Lucius also turned to see who had come, and watched as Sergel and Blige, the two soldiers who Commander Galin had ordered to wait for them near the Gates of Stronghold, strode into the camp and up to the fire. Lucius felt that something was amiss but, before he could pose a question, Hendric spoke.

"Where is Tomar?" the captain asked. "Did not he accompany you to the tent city?"

The two looked startled as they quickly snapped their heads around toward the shadows from which Hendric's voice had emerged.

"We rode there together," said Blige, usually the quieter of the two, "but after we reached the tents Tomar begged off, saying his leg was a bother. He went off somewhere to rest and we never laid eyes on him again. We thought him to have come back here."

Sergel said nothing, only staring in wide-eyed confusion and bobbing his head in agreement with the words of Blige, as Hendric stepped from the shadows and approached them.

Lucius followed Hendric, his face reflecting a concern much greater than the fact of Tomar's failure to return to camp should have provoked.

Sergel saw this look… saw it mirrored in the eyes of Hendric as he turned to glance at Lucius, and even caught a glimpse of it in the expression on Jared's face as he looked up from the fire.

"I'm sure he's on his way back even now," Sergel said quickly, eager to establish that he and Blige were not at fault. "He probably lay down with a flagon somewhere comfy and nodded off. Surely, he's slept it off, and should be here directly."

By now, even Petri and the brother trackers were staring at the two late arrivals, and the looks on everyone's faces spoke clearly of something more than the simple tardiness of an injured soldier.

Ever alert, Lucius saw the growing question in the eyes of the two and stepped forward to defuse the tension that was beginning to be felt in the camp.

"It's no problem, M'lord," Lucius said to Hendric, but loud enough for all to hear. "If he's not back by morning, I'll go for him." Then he sidled up to the fire, slapping Sergel on the back and asking if the two had spent time in the tents of the dancing girls.

Hendric watched as the tension dissipated and everyone returned to whatever had previously held their attention. He understood what Lucius had meant by his words and he hoped that Tomar really was sleeping off a drunk somewhere. If he was still absent at sunup, it could well be his last.

Hendric arose in the gray between darkness and dawn.

Immediately, he began searching the camp for Tomar and found no sign of the injured infantryman. On a whim, he left the small clearing and walked the short distance downwind to where the horses were tied. There he found Lucius tightening the cinch on his horse before mounting.

"Lucius…" Hendric spoke in a loud whisper as he approached, saying no more as the sergeant, and right hand to Commander Galin, turned to look at his current commander.

There was no surprise in Lucius's eyes. He had heard Hendric's footfalls. Neither was there an explanation or apology offered, and the two men simply stood quietly, their eyes locked one with the other. Hendric, the much bigger man, looked down at Lucius and broke the silence.

"Do you plan to bring him back?" the captain asked.

"Only if he is to be found coming off a drunk near the tent city," Lucius replied. "If he is not there, I will find him…" Lucius spoke these words as he stared unflinchingly into Hendric's eyes.

No more needed to be said between them.

Hendric knew in his heart that if Tomar was not accounted for, everyone remaining in camp…that is, everyone who knew about the chest of gold coins buried at the stables south of Stronghold… would be reeling with the thought that the injured soldier had abandoned them to go after the treasure.

Discipline would erode.

It would be the beginning of the end.

He had been tasked with returning the Harbinger, the name some called the warrior-priest Hanshee, to the Royal House and the protection of King Ammon IV. Because of the plans that the Monarch had already put into motion, it could be said that Hendric, the current Captain of the Citadel Guard, held the fulfillment of Usaid's Fourth Prophecy and the future of the Pithian Empire in his hands. It was an awesome responsibility and Hendric felt every bit of its weight pressing down upon his broad shoulders. He could not fail. He had to hold this command together, no matter the sacrifice. As much as he loathed what Lucius was preparing to do. He recognized that it had to be done… for the good of the Empire.

"Damn gold and the way it twists' men's souls!" he spat under his breath, as he watched Lucius mount his horse and expertly turn the beast in the direction of the Merchant Way. In this moment, another thought occurred to him.

"Lucius!" Hendric called out, and watched as the sergeant turned in his saddle to face him once more. "I will need proof. We will all need proof."

A slight nod of his head is all the acknowledgment Lucius gave as he again turned his horse away. Hendric watched him clear the sparse woods before turning back to the campsite and the remaining men.

As he approached, the noise from the campsite told Hendric that his men were beginning to rise even before the first rays of the sun could show through the peaks of the distant mountains. Entering the clearing, he saw that Petri was the only one still on his bedroll. The others were up and about, engaged in the small tasks that early morning seemed made for. The brothers, Ishmed and Fevor, were busy stoking the remains of last night's fire.

"There'll be no need for that," Hendric said to the trackers. "Give a piece of last night's bread to every man and be quick with it! We leave for Wroughtmire before the sunrise.

CHAPTER 2

It was about midmorning when the barge carrying Raymond and Hanshee managed to dock at the riverport just north of the eastern gate of Wroughtmire. The temperature this far south was much milder than the highlands of Stronghold, or even the northern plains of Gunjunson, and Raymond was glad that King Moton IX had outfitted them accordingly.

Hanshee and Raymond had decided to continue their travels in the roles of wandering priest and loyal acolyte, a ruse that had served them well to this point. To that end, when being supplied by the King's outfitter, Ray had been sure to seek robes of the plainest sort for *his master* and himself.

Hanshee wore a plain gray robe of coarse cloth. Underneath the robe he wore the leather that Ray was familiar with; the sling made of soft leather, the loin covering made of much more durable leather, and the harness on which he carried his sword, sheathed to his back, and his knife, sheathed to his chest. Hanging on his left hip was what Raymond referred to as his 'magic pouch', so named because of the variety of powders, salves, ointments, tools, and even coins that Hanshee stored within its sturdy leather confines. His boots, recently taken from the dead feet of the assassins at the Royal House, had seen him through the rigors of their escape down the eastern wall of Stronghold valley, and the journey to Cantor. They were now replaced with the sandals that Hanshee wore when he first pulled Ray from the 'River of Dreams'.

Raymond also wore a plain robe; his of a dull brown color. Underneath, he wore baggy leggings that tucked into the tops of a worn pair of leather boots. The leggings, usually worn by laborers in the stables, the docks, or the fields, were the closest thing to trousers that could be found. Raymond felt more comfortable in them than in the tunics and robes worn by most men in these lands. He did wear a tunic, which covered his upper body, over which he also wore a leather harness similar to the one worn by Hanshee, though made thousands of miles distant. On this harness, which hung from both shoulders and crossed his torso both front and back, he wore a finely worked sword of the best iron, sharpened to a razor's edge. It came with the harness; the pairing being salvaged from the dead body of an assassin.

And now Raymond wore his own pouch of heavy canvas which, similar to Hanshee's, hung beside his left hip. Inside was his purse containing the remaining gold he had taken from the chest at the stables south of Stronghold, and two sets of papers bearing the personal Seal of King Moton IX, Monarch of the Nation of Cantor. These documents, mounted impressively on finely worked wooden scrolls that bore the Seal of Cantor, granted the bearers unrestrained passage throughout the width and breath of Cantorese territories. Not satisfied with simple papers of transit, King Moton made sure the documents mentioned 'Hanshee of Dula' and 'Raymond Covington' by name.

Of the clothing taken from the dead assassins to assist their escape in the high mountain cold of Stronghold valley, only the fur cloaks remained. The cloaks were used to bundle the rest of their supplies and were tied to the backs of the horse's saddles. Those bundles now included a bow and a quiver of arrows for Raymond.

Hanshee had been teaching Ray archery as part of his training while at the Citadel. A bow of his own meant that there would be no need to pass the one Hanshee carried back and forth. Hanshee's quiver had also been replenished with new arrows and a supply of loose arrowheads.

As soon as the barge was tied down and the ramp was in place, the barefoot dock workers converged like ants on a pile of sugar, doing everything short of climbing over one another to unload the goods that had just arrived. Raymond and Hanshee, located in the rear of the bottom cargo section of the two-tiered barge, could only wait patiently. When most of the cargo had been removed, a good many of the workers were hustled on by their foreman to the next task, leaving a much smaller crew to aid the bargemen in completing the unloading. Only then could the travelers find the space to lead their horses, already saddled and loaded with their gear and supplies, up the ramp and away from the vessel.

Ray thought that Hanshee might feel slightly uneasy amid the hustle and bustle of the crowded port. This many workers, packed together and working so franticly, probably put someone like Hanshee, who was raised in a mountain village in the high forests of a foreign land, ill at ease. The activity here was much more hectic than that of the tent-city at the east gate of Gunjunson. Therefore, Raymond took the lead off the barge, signaling Hanshee to stay close as he wound his way between the comings and goings of the workers and cargo until they reached the end of the dock.

After stepping from the wooden dock onto dry land for the first time in three days, the pair found themselves in the center of a large market. Here, much of the cargo from the many boats and barges docking daily was bought, sold, and traded. Vendors could be found in rickety wooden stands, solid, well-built sheds, and large elaborate tents.

The barefoot workers still came and went, ensuring that the merchants had goods to sell, but now they were joined by the many shoppers attracted to the riverside market for first choice of the newly arrived goods, at what they hoped were the best prices.

Raymond heaved a sigh of exasperation when he saw their dilemma. After a quick glance backward to ensure that Hanshee was holding up, he led his mount south, hoping that the direction they were bound to travel was also the quickest way through the market.

As they made their way, Raymond peered into the different stalls and tents, noticing that they lacked the variety of wares for sale that he would have imagined in a riverport market situated just outside a major city.

Most of the merchandise seemed to be agricultural products. Hay and grain were plentiful. It had been the main cargo aboard the barge on which he and Hanshee had arrived. Most of it would be used to keep the local livestock alive and healthy during the last days of late winter-early spring. There was also a large variety of seeds that were moving quickly, purchased by the farmers with an eye toward the coming season of planting and of the harvest beyond. There was a much smaller market for winter vegetables, some local and some from upriver, along with dried and preserved produce and nuts, probably from the lands much further south.

What caught Raymond's attention was the large market for metals; especially farming implements or building and household tools. Everything from plows, shovels, picks and hoes, to handheld drills, saws, mallets, knives and scissors was being sold, and almost every vender claimed his stock was made from good Pithian iron molded in the forges of Stronghold. Though Pith was certainly a hated enemy, the quality of their ore and the craftsmanship of their blacksmiths insured that the output from their forges was highly prized.

As they pushed through the crowded market, Ray noticed the languages he heard were very similar. Apparently, the proximity of Rayine to Cantor, and the close ties they had established so many centuries ago, meant that they spoke essentially the same tongue.

Raymond had first overheard the Cantorese language from Laretha and Meesha, the two young women assigned to their needs while guest of the Temple of The One Spirit and the Royal House, in the Pithian capital. He had learned to speak it from the boy Kellen, and from mingling with others along the Cantor Road. Ray had first been exposed to aspects of the merchant tongue in the Citadel also, but he was emersed in it when among those in the temporary tent settlement outside Cantor's eastern gate.

His gift for languages, an unexplained phenomenon since his arrival in this strange land, had served both he and Hanshee well in the past. They had learned many secrets as Raymond feigned ignorance of the common tongue, thereby encouraging those around them to speak freely amongst themselves. It was a valuable practice they both decided should be continued.

Several glances behind him had assured Raymond that Hanshee was not as ill-at-ease as he had first imagined, and so they made their way through the market at an unhurried pace until reaching its end at the base of a slight incline about a hundred feet from the main east/west road that led to the east gate of Wroughtmire. Here Raymond paused, allowing Hanshee and his mount to come up alongside him.

Hanshee had what Raymond could only describe as a wry smile on his face as he met Ray's eyes before surveying the road that lay before him.

Raymond couldn't help himself.

"Alright, what did I do… or what didn't I do that I should have done?" asked Ray, expecting another lesson of some kind from his erstwhile teacher.

"You took the lead," Hanshee said. "You are no longer a stranger in a strange land."

If Raymond could have blushed, he was sure he would have. Instead, he just smiled at what he saw as a rare compliment from his friend. A fleeting thought then caused him to speak.

"You probably held back as some kind of test to see if I would go first, didn't you? It was a test to see how I'm now feeling about my situation here, right?"

Hanshee arched his eyebrows in consideration for a moment, turned to Ray, and posed a question.

"If it was," he said, "how would you access your actions?"

"Well…," Ray began, now a little unsure of himself "… I did … good…I guess… didn't I?

'Poker face' was the description that came to Raymond's mind as he studied Hanshee's expression and waited for a response. Hanshee studied Raymond's face too, and apparently having seen what he looked for, turned away and led his horse up the incline and onto the Wroughtmire Road. Raymond, now wishing he had never asked the question, had no choice but to shrug his shoulders and follow.

After gaining the road, the pair paused to look west toward the towering eastern gate of Wroughtmire before guiding their horses east in the direction of the distant Merchant Way. Neither felt the need to mount up yet, preferring to let the horses find their legs after two and a half days and three full nights of standing in place on the barge. The men welcomed the chance to stretch their legs, too.

At this point the road was paved with bricks fashioned for the express purpose of road building, with the pavement continuing up to the bridge that crossed the Manchess River as it continued its course south. The bridge itself was a wide and sturdy affair, its foundation made from granite blocks that were cut, sunk, and fitted one atop the other, on the river bottom. The granite blocks, placed so that there were four on each side of the bridge, protruded about seven feet above the current waterline and provided the foundation for the huge wooden posts upon which the load carrying portion of the bridge was built. Each post, hewn from a single tree, was three feet square and at least twenty-five feet tall. Twelve of those feet towered above the bridge as it gently sloped across the leisurely flowing waters below. Near the top of each post was a large lamp - actually more of a glass covered torch - that was lit every evening before the sun set beneath the western horizon and extinguished as the sun rose again over the Ursal Mountains.

Raymond and Hanshee walked their horses across the bridge which, by some coincidence, had no one else trodding its distance at the time. As they had the bridge all to themselves, they took their time in their crossing and stopped at its peak to look down into the murky river water that ran deep at this central point. The same stones that made up the road continued across the surface of the bridge, ending only when they reached the other side. There began the type of dirt road that Raymond and Hanshee had become accustomed to outside of a city.

Even while making their observations, their last exchange was still banging around in Ray's head. After moving down the road a short way, he couldn't hold it in any longer.

"Hanshee," Raymond began, "I know sometimes I over-think things…and sometimes I don't quite think things through. Traveling with you, even after all that you have done for me, I feel as though I am always being tested, watched, and weighed.

"I feel anxious," he continued. "It's like I'm making progress, learning from you and dealing with my surroundings …my situation …, and then something happens like just happened back there," Raymond motioned with his head to indicate the exchange back up the road, "and then I'm left wondering if I've made any real progress at all."

Here Ray paused in his words, not knowing if Hanshee understood what he was trying to say, and not sure that he had expressed himself in the best way.

Hanshee did not immediately reply. He let Raymond's concern linger in the space between them while he searched for the words he thought Raymond needed to hear at this time.

"When we train the young hunters," Hanshee finally began, "we keep them close and watch their every move. Our methods are simple; we show them what we want and tell them why we want it. Then we watch to see that they do as we instructed. When they do, they are praised. When they do not, they are corrected. The young need praise. This is the way they learn, and why they always seek approval. It is a good way... for the young.

"We watch, and we see them grow their skills, find a thirst for knowledge, discover a need to push further, understand the difference between recklessness and true courage. We then change our methods. Now praise becomes rare. We still instruct and correct, but a hunter must look more to his deeds and to himself when wondering if he has done well. He must learn to look within for his praise. He must learn to please himself, while never selling his pleasure cheaply. This is how confidence is nurtured and belief is achieved.

"Know this Way-mon," Hanshee concluded. "No matter his strength, speed, stamina, skill, knowledge, or cunning, without belief, the hunter will always fall short when the need is most dire."

Hanshee had delivered this rare monologue as they had continued to move steadily down the road, his face always forward and his eyes always searching for the next obstacle or opportunity. Now he turned his face to Raymond and held his eye.

"If it *were* a test, Way-mon," Hanshee asked," how would *you* access your actions?"

Raymond let this question, asked at the end of what he recognized as a lesson, sink in. Though Hanshee had asked emphatically, Ray knew that no response was expected.

****

Continuing down the Wroughtmire road took them past farms whose fields appeared chaotic in their unplowed states, and pastures on which herds of cattle, horses, goats and sheep scrounged for any morsel that could still be scratched from its surface. Occasionally there could be seen a cluster of animals gathered around a pile of hay that had recently come in at the dock they had just left.

There were also several small townships spread out along the road. These usually occurred at a crossroads and one could see many of the services needed in such communities; a farrier, a leather worker, maybe a butcher shop and a small market, maybe a tavern, all clustered around an intersection. There were what appeared to be personal dwellings spread round-about, and the whole thing made Raymond think of the small rural communities of his home.

Being secure in the belief that they had placed considerable distance between themselves and any pursuit, they did not mount their horses until late afternoon. Still, they reached the Merchant Way with about two hours to go before sunset and decided to press on a bit further after turning to follow it south.

Though well worn, the road was not teaming with traffic. Looking behind them, there appeared to be no sign of anyone approaching from the north, and only a small cloud of dust in the far-off distance spoke to the presence of a traveler ahead of them and moving south.

They made good time on the road and before long found themselves 'eating the dust' of what appeared to be three wagons that, although moving briskly considering what they were, could not match the pace of two horsemen traveling light. Quickly tiring of the dusty rear view, Hanshee and Raymond prodded their mounts forward so to go around the wagons. While doing so, they took the time to get a look at the wagons and their drivers.

The first wagon they passed was the largest of the three and was pulled by four sturdy horses. It had plank sides about three feet high. A canvas was tied to the planks at that point and this extended up and over the contents, before being tied down to the planks on the opposite side. Raymond thought it looked somewhat like a covered wagon from the old west, but much longer and lacking the curved slats to support the canvas laying in direct contact with the heavy load it carried.

The wagon was driven by a young man about the same age as Raymond. He appeared fair of skin, lean and tall, and handled the team deftly and without apparent strain. He looked over toward Raymond and Hanshee as they passed, nodding his head in greeting so as not to unhand the reins. Beside him sat a dusky hued, dark-haired beauty, holding tight to his arm as she looked across his body at the strangers who had pulled up beside them. Both Raymond and Hanshee nodded in acknowledgement as their horses slowly made their way past the wagon.

The middle wagon, unlike the one behind it, was all wood and had the appearance of a rectangular shed on wheels. It, too, was driven by a young man. He appeared shorter than the other driver, with a deeply tanned complexion under dark hair, and piercing eyes under heavy brows that looked suspiciously toward Raymond and Hanshee as they passed. Beside him sat a young woman, somewhat fairer of complexion and with hair that Raymond would describe as dirty-blonde. She sat taller than the driver and leaned back slightly, looking at them with curiosity from behind his head. Raymond and Hanshee nodded acknowledgement here also; a gesture only the girl returned.

The third wagon, leading the three down the road, appeared much sturdier than the second and reminded Raymond more of an RV than a shed on wheels. It was decorated with paint and markings that appeared to be a written language that neither Hanshee nor Raymond could read. To their surprise, a woman drove this wagon. She appeared compact and sturdy with a dusky complexion, the muscles in her tanned arms visibly writhing as she bent the two large horses pulling the wagon to her will. Beside her sat the twin of the driver of the middle wagon. Well, he could have been a twin had he been twenty years younger, twenty pounds lighter, and had a surly disposition. As it was, he smiled brightly upon seeing the riders, lifting a hand and even calling out a greeting to them.

Raymond recognized the language. It was the language spoken in the city-states that surrounded the eastern shore of the Great Inland Sea, known in the upper kingdoms as the merchant's tongue. He had heard bits of it while at the Royal House in Stronghold, but had really picked it up in the tent city outside Gunjunson. He waved and returned the older man's greeting in his own language. This brought an even bigger smile to the man's face and he began a frantic waving of his hands toward Raymond and Hanshee. At first it was undecipherable, but then Hanshee leaned toward Ray and spoke.

"I believe he wants us to move our horses to his side of the wagon," Hanshee said, and when Ray looked back toward the man, this made perfect sense. After first looking behind them, they decided to ride beyond the wagon, cross the road, and allow the wagon to pull up beside them where they could then match its pace. Hanshee encouraged Raymond to ride on his left side, closest to the wagon, for obvious reasons.

Once beside the wagon, the man stared intently at both riders before speaking.

"You look like you could be from my homeland!" he said enthusiastically, while pointing at Raymond. "And you," he said, pointing at Hanshee, "could be from the Southern Shore and the lands below. Am I correct?"

The man's eyes burned with an intense glee at the prospect of finding more of his kinsmen this far from home. Ray was loath to disappoint him.

"My companion and I are not from your homeland, good sir," Ray said and watched as the light faded from his eyes.

Almost as swiftly, the man recovered his enthusiasm.

"Still, you speak our language. There must be a connection. We will stop soon to make camp and enjoy a meal. Please, dine with us this evening."

Ray was about to open his mouth to tactfully refuse the invitation but, for some unknown reason, paused.

"Are you in such a hurry as to pass up the cooking of my lovely wife?" the man continued in the pause left by Raymond. "Many have paid to feast in our tent before the gates of Gunjunson. I offer you the same experience for no coin at all!"

First raising a finger to induce a pause, Raymond replied.

"Sir, your offer is most generous, but I must first ask my master if it is his desire to partake of your hospitality."

The face of the man now assumed an expression of puzzlement as Raymond quickly turned to Hanshee and explained what had been said.

"…and as your acolyte, I could not take it upon myself to accept or refuse. I must leave that to you," Ray finished.

Before Raymond could sit back and enjoy the moment of exasperation he expected his explanation would bring, Hanshee shot him a response.

"Tell him 'Yes'."

Raymond half turned in his saddle, expecting to tell the man that they would be moving further on this night, but had to catch himself as he swung back around to look at Hanshee with questioning surprise. Hanshee simply smiled his 'joker' smile, knowing he had turned the prank around on Ray.

I'll never figure him out, thought Ray, with a slight shake of his head. Then he turned back to the elder man and spoke.

"My master is both honored and grateful to be invited to share your meal this evening," he said, embellishing Hanshee's stoic response.

"Good," bellowed the man before turning to his wife and directing her to guide the wagon into a stand of trees up ahead. Then he rapped hard on the wagon wall behind him and smiled at Raymond as a small door opened and the head of a young girl, the image of the young woman in the last wagon, only several years younger, popped out.

"Yes poppa?" she said before looking over at Raymond and Hanshee with wide eyes, obviously taken by surprise.

"Go and tell your brother we make camp now," the elder man ordered before turning back to Raymond.

"Your master will greatly enjoy my wife's cooking," he said with a big smile.

Hanshee and Raymond sat beside the fire in a state of blissful satisfaction while Delno Menowin looked from one to the other, beaming with delight.

As he had promised, the meal had been extraordinary, especially considering it had been prepared in a grove of trees over a camp fire. Delno's wife, Valda, had prepared a stew of greens, both wild and domestic, and potatoes. She seasoned the mixture with spices from her homeland, wild onion, and bits of smoked pork. Just the aroma of the stew had Raymond and Hanshee salivating as they waited for it to be served. When it was served, it was accompanied by slices of roasted white-meat pork and hot bread freshly prepared by her daughters, Lakshmi and Flora. Once the men had finished building the fire, preparing the area, and tending the animals, they had only to clean themselves up and sit, impatiently awaiting word that the meal was ready to be served.

While they waited, Danior, the eldest son of Delno and Valda, and Galid, the husband of Lakshmi, pulled instruments from their wagons that put Raymond in mind of a guitar and a clarinet. Although both were of simple construction, the melodies that the two men coaxed from them were enough to make the spirits of the weary soar with hope and joy. Soon Delno pulled out his skin, containing red wine of the very best, and made sure all were served. Then he pulled out what appeared to Raymond to resemble a harp and joined in. Though the younger men were amazing in their own right, the trio reached new heights when Delno took the lead on a tune, playing with such precision and emotion as to make his guests almost forget about the sumptuous meal that had been causing their mouths to water.

Almost.

At a signal from Valda, the instruments were put away and the food brought forth. As they ate, Raymond, and Hanshee through Raymond, alternated in complementing both the food and the music that had preceded it. The young men nodded their heads in appreciation as they ate, while the women, much more cultured than their men, actually pause in their eating to speak their thanks for such lavish compliments. Delno seemed to take his joy from watching the faces of his guests as they ate and drank with gusto.

After the meal was done, the women collected the bowls while the men again reached for their instruments. Accompanied by the youngest son, Vano, on what appeared to be twin drums played with fingers and hands, they took up a song that soon had everyone moving and dancing around the campfire. Even Raymond and Hanshee were pulled to their feet by Valda and Flora and led around and around until they were both dizzy and delighted.

When the music came to an abrupt stop, all collapsed on the blankets and logs that they had reclined on prior to the meal, laughing and cheering the music and the night.

"That was to help the digestion," Delno chuckled as he took his seat atop the log beside which they had chosen to build the fire.

Now Hanshee spoke and Raymond translated for their hosts.

"My master says that you and your family are indeed great hosts, serving a meal fit for a warrior and music to delight a warrior's soul."

"Tell me, Raymond, about you and your master," Delno asked.

Raymond first turned to Hanshee and relayed the request. Hanshee spoke briefly to Raymond and then nodded his head in consent, encouraging Raymond as he launched into the very same story that he had spun for two servant girls in the sanctuary of the Temple of The One Spirit, in the capital of Pith, not so long ago.

This time, Raymond greatly embellished the 'famine of his people' and his long trek in pursuit of game to feed them. He went even farther describing the greater pilgrimage his master, a warrior-priest of Clan Dula, had endured from the western slopes of the Blue Towers to a land well beyond the Ursal Mountains, in search of holy atonement. When it came time to place his hands on his head to mimic the horns of the 'great elk' he had pursued so far, Ray took a quick glance at Hanshee. Hanshee was looking on in wide-eyed anticipation; ready to erupt into full throated laughter should Ray make the motion. Raymond was almost ready to burst into laughter himself, but decided not to take the tale that far. He finished the story, ending with Hanshee fishing him from the 'River of Dreams', after which he pledged himself as Hanshee's acolyte as was the custom of his people.

Delno and his family were enthralled by the tale and one of the young men, Danior, immediately asked if he could make a song of it. Raymond asked Hanshee and, after hearing his lengthy reply, turned and spoke to Danior.

"My master says he would be honored, as would I, if you chose to tell our story in song. He also says that he now knows who you," he motioned with his arm to include the entire family, "are."

Raymond then told the story of their arrival at Gunjunson and their walk through the tent city at dusk. He spoke of the sounds and aromas emanating from the many tents there, and of being particularly enthralled as they paused to listen to the music, and admire the beauty of the dancers in one special tent.

"My master means no disrespect and wishes only to convey his deepest appreciation when he says that we were first pulled in by the haunting music. Once at your door, we were captured by the grace of your daughters and the aromas of your hearth. He says that, had we not been on a mission of importance, we would have stopped then and spent much coin to enjoy your hospitality."

At hearing this, Delno burst into laughter, slapping his knee to accentuate his mirth, while the others gathered around laughed and smiled at the compliment.

Galid then spoke up.

"Tell your master that, in our culture, it is never disrespectful to acknowledge beauty. I..., we...," he waved his hand to take in all the women present, "have been blessed with beauty in abundance."

At this the other men roared with appreciative laughter, the women giggled in modest acknowledgement, and Galid bowed his head as if overcome by the depth of his own words... before raising it and joining in the laughter echoing through the night woods.

CHAPTER 3

A pall hung over the heads of the men in Hendric's command. In some, it was fueled by speculation at the absence of Lucius, and in others by what they felt was being left unsaid in the camp.

As promised, Hendric had indeed broken camp before full sunrise, but was careful not to push his men hard down the Merchant Way toward Wroughtmire, capital of Rayine. He doubted they would respond to the crack of the whip now. What they truly needed was for the current situation, with Lucius and the missing Tomar, to be settled.

They made camp that night in a grove beside a stream not far off the road, arising early the next morning to continue their trek south. It was not until close to sundown, just after camp had been struck, that Lucius again joined them.

Lucius had a haggard look about him as he bypassed the tether rope and rode his horse directly into camp. Guiding Tomar's horse by its reins, he moved between and around the other men and their bedrolls, approaching the center of the camp, near the freshly crackling fire before which Hendric stood.

Here, Lucius stopped his horse but did not dismount.

His comrades could only stand and stare open-mouthed as all could see that he rode into camp alone. They had hoped to see Tomar trailing him, and looks of questioning resignation were now plain on their faces. No one spoke, and the only wandering eyes belonged to Sergel and Blige. They looked from

Lucius to their other comrades and back to Lucius, all the time wondering what everyone else seemed to know that they didn't.

It was Hendric who broke the silence.

"Show me," the captain said.

Wearily, Lucius reached for the cord of a burlap sack that hung from his saddle, struggling somewhat as he attempted to untie the knot. Finally, the cord came loose and the bundle fell to the ground with a heavy thud, rolling slightly to one side as the load it contained found its balance. Lucius followed the sack to the ground and all continued to stare as he opened it, reached inside, and produced the severed head of Tomar. He then approached his captain and after first spreading the empty sack on the ground at his feet, propped the severed head upon it so that the dwindling light could reveal to all the 'what' and the 'who' of the object staring back at them.

Petri was the first to make a sound, a small squeak from deep in his throat, but Sergel was right behind him with words. Moving to stand before his captain to be sure of what lay upon the sack, and followed closely by Blige, he spoke.

"He's dead?" Sergel stammered while pointing down at the head of Tomar. "Dead?" he repeated, before raising his eyes to Lucius. "Why?"

Although Lucius' carriage spoke to his fatigue, his eyes were clear and his face emotionless. He made no effort to respond to Sergel, but instead looked to Hendric. When all other eyes had followed his and rested on Hendric, the captain moved, bending down to take a fistful of the hair atop the lifeless head, lifting it high for all to see.

"Take a look!" Hendric spat while holding the head aloft. "This is what we have come to!"

In that moment, no one dared to speak.

Acknowledging their silence, Hendric continued.

"This is the result of the secret we share, the bond we've forged…, and the oath we took," Hendric said, his voice trailing off as he spoke the last.

Blige and Sergel shared looks fraught with startled confusion before again turning back to Hendric, who now lowered the head even as he again raised his voice.

"But not all here partook of that oath," Hendric said, as he looked toward the two newest recruits. "Sergel and Blige," Hendric motioned toward the two, "wonder now what knowledge we share that they don't. They wonder how a man can find aid, comfort, and camaraderie among us and, at what seemed the slightest gaffe, have his head removed from his shoulders."

Hendric spit the last words in disgust, adding the weight of shame to an act already reeking of a casual and unnecessary cruelty.

Having been called by name, and identified as outliers, Sergel and Blige were now on alert. They continued to look to Hendric, but also cast quick glances around the camp, even as their hands stealthily sought the handles of the knives nestled in their belts.

"You can turn lose your blades," Hendric said, having noted their growing fear. "You are not yet a part of this… but you soon will be. You will be because I wager the two of you are just like the rest…, willing to sell your very souls for gold!"

At the mention of gold, both their eyes went wide with surprise. Hastily they jerked their heads around so they could see the faces of the others and, to a man, they saw their surprise was not mirrored in their comrades' expressions. Again, they turned their eyes toward their commander, eager now to hear what he had to say.

"Now I see the curiosity in your faces," Hendric almost gloated. "A curiosity fueled by greed…, soon to be wholly replaced by greed. You see what became of Tomar," Hendric nudged the lifeless head with his boot, "and still you stretch your necks to hear the secrets that will bind you, like him, to the rest of us? Very well."

"Before you two joined us," Hendric began, "we happened upon a fortune in gold coins. Enough gold to make each and every one of us wealthy men! Each man held claim to a share and some wanted to take theirs right then. Because we are on a mission sanctioned by King Ammon himself, they were..." Hendric rested his hand on his hilt, "*persuaded...* to wait until we had completed our duty before indulging their greed. And so, an oath was taken, and together we hid the gold until such time as honor was satisfied and we could return to divide it among us."

"Tomar was among us when we hid the gold and made our oath. It is an oath that had the result of binding all here," Hendric waved his arms to encompass his command, "in what amounts to a death pact. Tomar should have known that he could not leave..." Hendric let his gaze sweep over the men standing on the perimeter, "...that none who know the treasures' location can leave!"

Hendric had been speaking to the camp when he said these words. Now he focused again on their two newest members, Sergel and Blige.

"And now you, also, are bound with us and cannot leave until you fulfill your duty or are taken by death."

"You can't hold us to that!" blurted Blige. "We never saw any gold! We don't know where any gold is hidden!"

"You know enough!" countered Hendric. "And if one fine morn one or both of you is missing from camp, we would have to assume that you pried the secret from someone here and had gone to claim it for yourselves.

"But you do have a chance. You could leave now... right this second! And never again show your faces to this gathering. Only then could we be assured that you had no knowledge, and therefore, no designs on the treasure."

At Hendric's proposal, all eyes shifted to the two latecomers. As the silence grew, each waited for Sergel or Blige to react. And as the moments passed and the two made no effort to leave, all who surrounded them knew the dye was now cast.

Hendric continued to let the silence build as he locked eyes with first Sergel, then Blige.

Neither looked away.

With his next words he confirmed the curse under which the two, by their inaction, had chosen to live.

"That," Hendric said to all, while pointing to the 'newly damned', "is the power of the spell… the spell that gold has ever cast upon men."

As the echo of Hendric's words died out, no other sound was heard save for the crackling of the fire. Sergel and Blige were now fully fledged members of the pursuit, unable to step away for fear of death. The unblinking eyes of Tomar, his severed head resting atop a burlap sack, bore silent witness to this fact and drove home the point better than any additional words could.

After a while, Lucius broke the silence.

"I'll bury his head, captain," he said as he stepped forward to claim the proof that Hendric had demanded. Then Lucius paused… turned… and addressed the rest of the camp.

"Tomar was a fool!" he said. "He was impatient. His injuries were too grave for swift travel. He thought to hide until we left Gunjunson, then journey back for the gold. Let that be a lesson to us all. Your surest path to riches is to hunt down and capture the escapees. Your surest path to death… is to abandon this pursuit."

Hendric noted that Lucius stuck to the lie put forth to conceal the truth about the Harbinger. Only the two of them, and the young priest Pitri, were to be privy to that secret.

"Take your rest," Hendric called out as the men turned back to preparations for the night's camp. "Tomorrow, we rise early and move swiftly."

That night Hendric lay awake well after the midnight hour wondering what was to become of his command. Looking back, it seemed that this pursuit had been cursed before it had gotten underway.

I would have been much farther along had I been granted a squad of the Citadel Guard hand chosen by me. Men who I could count on…men who knew their duty and could be trusted. Instead, it seemed everyone from the Temple, to the Court, to the Commanders, to the King himself, found a way to get their man attached to the squad.

At that thought Hendric chuckled to his self.

I can't really accuse Ammon of tampering, can I? Not when the Kings man leads the squad.

Still Hendric worried that he was losing control of his men. He had known the discovery of the gold would lead to complications. He thought that his solution, of hiding the treasure for whoever returned from the pursuit, was sufficient to push that issue to the side. But he was no fool. He knew that the promise of riches so near always hovered close to the surface of a man's thoughts. He just had not expected those thoughts to breed such confusion… such fear and distrust…

At least not so quickly.

Lucius was right. The only way that any of the men would be allowed to see their share of the treasure was through the fulfillment of their duty. Hendric hoped that they realized this and awoke with a newfound sense of purpose. He planned to push them hard on the morrow. He would make good time while driving the thoughts of the last two days deep into their minds. He felt that they would focus now. What else could they do? Even *they* must eventually realize that allowing thoughts of treasure and newfound wealth to linger close was to lessen their readiness and invite them to indulge in foolish fantasies. Fantasies of just how easy it would be for them to slip away unseen.

They would hardly be missed until they were long gone, Hendric imagined them thinking.

Fantasies of how swiftly they could cover the now fifteen-day journey back to the stables outside the southeastern wall of Stronghold.

They would ride like the wind itself!

Fantasies that would no doubt get them killed.

I've done all I can do for this night, thought Hendric, *and anything else must wait until morning.*

With that, Hendric lay his head down on his blanket and tried to get some sleep. But sleep remained elusive, as there was yet another concern that kept him staring at the night sky.

Lucius.

What kind of man is he?

Hendric had witnessed firsthand the many traits that no doubt endeared Lucius to Galin. The man thought and acted quickly, was well versed in languages, and very intelligent. He had a certain way about him that allowed him to fit in and quickly gain the trust of strangers, ferreting out their secrets without them knowing secrets had been shared.

As a soldier the man appeared well versed, able to take orders or give them as the situation demanded. His loyalty had been instrumental in persuading the others that it would not pay to make an issue of the gold when it was first discovered. And had he not offered, without being asked, to 'do what was needed' had Tomar been unable to travel after suffering at the hands of the Harbinger?

That was part of it, Hendric thought to himself.

Lucius seemed able and willing to fulfill whatever role had been needed on this journey, not shying away from hardship, espionage, or bloodshed, even when the bloodshed had been directed at a comrade-in-arms. Surly these traits should only serve to reinforce his value to the pursuit.

Then why should I feel such unease about him?

Hendric knew.

It was because the man seemed to be able to anticipate what was needed, what *he* needed, before Hendric himself could be sure. Twice now… no, three times… Hendric had almost felt as if Lucius was in charge, and not him. Lucius had not waited for orders but had quickly stated what was needed and then waited for Hendric to catch up. Although Hendric had not admitted it at those times, he had taken an uneasy feeling away from their interaction. He knew he was in command here and Lucius had not shown the slightest instance of insubordination, but still the captain could not shake a feeling about the man.

Is it my unease with this command and the situation that has developed, or is Lucius much more than he seems, if that could even be possible?

Pondering this last thought, Hendric finally closed his eyes and drifted off into a fitful sleep.

CHAPTER 4

The time of the counting was almost complete.

Much of the tent city had been dismantled by the time Seenio and Nola made their way along the last miles of the Cantor Road, toward the imposing gates of Gunjunson.

With the huge crowds now dispersed, the guards at the gate were not so numerous nor so formal. A more relaxed atmosphere prevailed. No questions were asked by the few guards that remained, though they still laid careful eyes on any who entered the city.

Seenio had a naturally intimidating demeanor and so garnered his share of suspicious looks. As he and Nola passed the gates, he spoke to the guards in their native Cantorese, putting them at ease with his eloquence and lack of an accent.

Had Nola not been beside her father she would have gotten more than her share of looks too. Her beauty was obvious, even concealed in the traveling garments she wore; garments more suited for a man than a woman. Some may have even mistaken her for an extraordinarily handsome, though slightly effeminate, man. Those that recognized a woman under her clothing thought her to be the woman of the menacing fellow at her side.

The sun was just about to dip behind the western horizon as they made their way south, away from the large and fancy inns that surrounded the gate. These palaces were still flush with the coin they had accumulated since the beginning of the counting.

They would be some of the last places to feel the effects of the dispersal of the crowds and even now a bawdy cliental was making its way through their portals a few at a time.

Both Seenio and Nola remembered the instruction they had been given late one night, in the quiet town of Sandledge, by the blacksmith Suleski. They were on the lookout for a smaller and more subdued tavern that lay a piece south of the gaudy inns. It was called the Milkmaids Rest and would be readily identified by its distinctive banner.

Nola was the first to spy the tavern. It was a three-story structure of sufficient size and appeal. It was painted a creamy white, with red doors and shutters, but still much more modest than the palatial inns that beckoned when one first entered the east gates. If there were any doubt as to whether this was the correct tavern, the sign above the door served as confirmation.

It was a large sign that hung down from an extended beam high above the door so it would be visible from a distance to those approaching from either direction. On both sides were carved the same image; a young barmaid whose smiling face, framed by flowing locks, eagerly beckoned all who set eyes upon her to chance a visit inside. Her arms were spread wide with one hand clutching a handled urn while the other held a goblet overflowing with the rich foam that formed the head atop a goodly serving of ale.

And it was easy to see why her arms were spread so wide.

The ridiculously ample bosoms that her colorful low-cut dress was straining to contain would hardly allow her to carry the urn and goblet any closer to her body. The words 'The Milkmaids Rest' were carved into the lower portion of the sign and snuggled underneath her charms as if needed there for extra support. Taken together, this sign, and thus this tavern, were difficult not to notice.

If the outside of the Tavern was lighthearted and gay, the inside was a bit more subdued. The barmaids were comely enough, though not as advertised on the sign above the door. The food was good and your purse would certainly be empty before your drinks ran out. Still, it seemed that only a few of the many inhabitants wore giddy smiles on their faces.

Seenio noticed this from the table they chose in one of the taverns darker corners. This was a tavern frequented by regulars, with only a few novice patrons on any given night. Most of the tables were taken by gruff men who had seen their share of life's hardships and so arrived regularly at the Milkmaids Rest, either to drink away their troubles or celebrate a rare turn of good fortune. The barmaids flitted between the tables with platters of food and pitchers of drink, avoiding the grasping hands when possible, ignoring them when not.

Not long after they sat, a brightly smiling barmaid sashayed over to their table to offer the two strangers the Milkmaids hospitality. Her smile dimmed slightly upon realizing that Nola was a woman and her walk seemed to have lost some of its sway when she turned to go and fill their order of a bowl of stew, a loaf of bread, and a pitcher of hot spiced wine.

This was Nola's first visit to a tavern and she had to hold back her laugh at how the women displayed themselves and sauntered about for the obvious delight of the men who frequented this place. She watched in fascination as hungry eyes followed each of the tavern wenchs when they passed. Even her father had an eye for one or two of the girls and looked on unashamedly, even after Nola let it be known that she was watching him.

It wasn't until the serving wench returned with a platter covered with bread, stew, and their order of wine, that Seenio removed his leather gloves. He did this in as casual a way as he could while being sure to flash the heavy gold ring that he wore on his left middle finger. The serving girl was quick to notice, her eyes temporarily going wide and just as quickly feigning disinterest, as she unloaded the contents of her platter onto the table. Another big smile signaled her taking her leave, but both Seenio and Nola noticed that she made a beeline directly to the barkeep. A few whispered words and a slight not of her head in their direction let them know that the ring had been noticed. All that remained now was to enjoy their meal and see who would approach them.

As they dove into their hot stew and fresh bread, Seenio noticed the steady traffic of tavern girls leading patrons up and down the stairs that were situated not far from the end of the bar. These stairs led upward to the second and third floor rooms. The rooms of the third floor were reserved for those who needed a place to bed overnight. The second floor was reserved for commerce.

As Seenio watched, one girl led a stocky and roughhewn fellow down the stairs and over to a table next to their own. There the fellow was quick to order another flagon of ale, but loath to turn loose the girl so she could fetch it. It was clear that he was having the time of his life, and the smiling serving wench planned to keep him in the mood so she could siphon off every last coin that he still managed to carry in his purse. Giggling her feigned delight, she managed to pull loose and sashayed toward the bar, the fellow following her every move with his eyes. After she stopped at the bar, he turned and looked toward Seenio and Nola, flashing a drunken grin. He was just about to speak when someone caught Seenio's attention from the other direction.

The barkeep had approached as Seenio was distracted by the new arrival. He now stood halfway between Seenio and Nola and cleared his throat to gain their attention.

"A pleasant evenin' it be," said the barkeep. "Are ye satisfied with yer stew?"

Seenio first looked the barkeep up and down, glancing behind him to see if he had approached by himself, before answering.

"It's a good stew."

"Especially when ye be fresh from the road," the barkeep probed.

Seenio looked over at Nola and smiled before turning back to the barkeep.

"How could you tell?"

"Oh, ye have the look" the barkeep replied. Then turning his attention to Nola, he said. "I'd not noticed from a distance that yer wife accompanies you. Good evenin' to ye, ma'am. How is yer spiced wine?"

Nola lifted her goblet and nodded her head in appreciation and the barkeep smiled in delight.

"Ye let us know if we can be gettin' anythin' else fer ye." He turned to leave and caught himself before again turning to Seenio.

"Will ye be needin' a room fer this night?" he asked.

"We could," Seenio said, as if considering the offer. "If we do, who should we ask for?

"Just holler out for Wiley," the barkeep said. "Holler out and I'll find ye."

Seenio watched the barkeep as he turned away and headed back to the bar. Nola watched too. She was seated so as not to have to turn her head to see the bar and so noticed when the barkeep motioned to one of the burly men who stood off to the side watching the room with a disinterested scowl. He came over and bent down so that the barkeep could whisper into his ear. Whatever the barkeep said, it caused him to cut his eyes toward their table before he nodded his head and walked off in the direction of a group of men much like himself.

Nola passed all that she saw on to Seenio before the two settled in to finish their meal, enjoy their spiced wine, and make their plans.

Seenio and Nola ordered two more pitchers of wine, most of which found its way through the floorboards on the side of their table opposite the bar, with the tavern staff none the wiser. The crowd at the tavern was now about half of what it was upon their arrival. The fellow at the table beside them had been whispering and giggling with the tavern wench for a good while before the two of them again took the stairs to the second floor. It was then that Seenio looked up and saw Wiley approaching with yet another vessel of wine.

"The two of ye must have worked up quite a thirst," the barkeep beamed. "I've brought ye another, on the house."

"Many thanks!" Seenio replied enthusiastically, as he reached for the offering and showed his teeth in a drunken grin. Nola joined in, smiling broadly and holding her goblet out for more.

"That's an impressive ring yer wearin'," Wiley said, pointing to Seenio's left hand. "I'm not sure I've seen it's like before."

Upon hearing this Seenio burst into drunken laughter, spilling half the wine in his goblet onto the table and floor. Regaining his composure, he looked at the barkeep from the corner of his eye and spoke.

"You may have seen it on the hand of a certain blacksmith across the border in Pith, eh?" he said, and again burst out laughing.

Now Wiley joined in and the three of them appeared to enjoy a good laugh before Wiley asked the inevitable question.

"How did ye get that thing off ole Suleski's hand...?" he asked, still chuckling, "...last I saw t'was on so tight it threatened the flow of blood to his finger!"

"It looked painful, let me tell you!" Seenio said and everyone laughed anew. "He stuck his hand in a vat of grease... and worked it until it bled!

The three of them exploded into great belly laughs at this description and it took a few moments for the mirth to subside to the point where Seenio could continue.

"He...heh, heh... he said...heh, heh...that this ring... would be the only way that you would talk to me."

Seenio finished the last of his statement with a somewhat straight face and an expectant stare straight into the eyes of Wiley.

Now Wiley's laughter faded as he saw the look in Seenio's eyes. He chanced a quick glance to Nola, and again back to Seenio.

"Not here" he said, meeting Seenio's stare straight on. He cast his eyes about the main room of the tavern before turning back to Seenio.

"Follow me."

Seenio and Nola both rose from the table on unsteady legs and carefully paced after Wiley as he led them to a door at the end of the room opposite the main entrance. Three of the burly men who worked for him stood before the door and moved aside as he led the two through the portal and into a separate room about half as wide as the main room and not nearly as deep. Walking past a high bench table and a few stools, Wiley approached another door that opened onto a landing illuminated by the light of a single oil lamp. The landing interrupted a flight of stairs that ran up to the floors above and down to the cellar. Here he paused.

Yer woman must wait here," he said to Seenio.

Seenio looked behind him and saw that the three guards that were on the outside of the room had followed them to the inside; two of them now stationed in front of the door Wiley had led them through. The third had followed along as Wiley led him to the door opening onto the landing. Seenio shot a quick glance toward Nola, noting the assurance in her eyes, then he followed Wiley out the door and onto the landing. The third guard followed and closed the door behind them. Then the three proceeded down the stairs that led to the coolness of the cellar.

The cellar was deep, and another landing was required so that the stairs could continue downward. Once past that landing the darkness closed in. By the time they reached the hard packed earth floor of the cellar, Seenio could barely make out the two rows of large barrels that extended out before him into the darkness. Obviously knowing his way around, Wiley did not hesitate as he stepped onto the dirt and moved off between the rows of barrels. Seenio had no choice but to trust in the barkeep and followed his lead. On a whim Seenio turned to mark the progress of the third guard and was not surprised to see that he had paused on the last landing. Now turning back toward Wiley, Seenio saw that his guide had completely disappeared into the darkness.

Trusting his ears, Seenio followed the footsteps that came from somewhere in front of him. On the periphery of his vision, he could barely discern the outlines of the huge barrels most likely filled with the fermenting spirits that were served on the main floor, as well as grains, beans, potatoes, spices, and other of the perishable ingredients needed to handle the appetites of the clientele of the Milkmaids Rest. After three more steps, even the barrels were obscured by the dark.

Seenio now froze in place, allowing his ears to tell him what his eyes could not. Ahead of him the retreating footsteps of Wiley seemed to increase in speed, as if the barkeep was intentionally putting distance between them. Then they came to a stop and for a moment all was silent.

Seenio knew that he was somewhere between two of the huge barrels and reached both arms out to confirm his position and his distance from them. Listening intently, he heard the slightest movement, along with the slightly labored breathing of excitement. Both sounds emanated from the darkness to his right, but he could not be sure from which side of the barrel they came. He chanced a glance backward and could see no one behind him, but the faint glow from the stairwell let him know that, from up ahead, Wiley could clearly see his outline against that dim light and so mark his position.

Carefully Seenio took a step forward. So careful was he that he knew he did not give away his position by this movement. He took another step… then another… and…

"Now!"

It was Wiley, calling out Seenio's position for those waiting in the darkness to attack.

Seenio threw his back against the large barrel to his right even as he reached to his belt and filled his hands with two razor sharp blades. Holding his position, he clearly heard two sets of feet begin to move; one to either side of the barrel that braced him. Giving them time to better reveal their position, Seenio hesitated for a heartbeat… then another… and then let loose with both blades in powerful backhand thrusts to either side of him. Satisfaction washed over him as he felt both blades find a home in the bodies that had so recently been crouched in the shadows beside the barrels.

The blade in Seenio's left hand seemed to meet minimal resistance as it slid in just above the collar bone and severed the windpipe before lodging in the front of the man's spine. The impact stopped his forward progress, causing him to stagger backward until he fell against the wall, thrashing about and trying desperately to find a breath that would never again come.

The blade in Seenio's right hand struck heavy resistance, but the force of the blow ensured that the blade penetrated the guard's leather tunic and the massive chest underneath it. Fortunately for the guard, the blade missed his heart. Unfortunately, it sunk deep into his left lung. This, however, did not stop his momentum and he burst from the space between the barrels still searching for a body in which to imbed the blade of the short-handled fighting axe he held in his right hand.

Seenio felt the continued momentum and gave a mighty pull, yanking his blade free of the guard's chest while simultaneously turning the guard in his direction. As soon as he felt the blade tear free, Seenio dropped his body into a low crouch. He first heard the axe blade cut the air above his head before he felt the blade imbed itself into the barrel he crouched against.

Now feeling the intense pain of his wound and having difficulty breathing, the injured guard tried desperately to free his hand axe from the thick wood of the barrel, even as Seenio rose from his crouch and stood chest to chest with him. Reaching out with his left hand until he found the guards head, Seenio grabbed a handful of hair and violently pulled the head forward while dipping his chin to his chest and launching his own head into the oncoming face. Stunned from the force of the head butt, the injured guard released the handle of the trapped axe and drop his arm to his side. Now knowing the precise position of his opponent in the darkness, Seenio drove the blade still clutched in his right hand under the guard's sternum and up into his heart. There he leveraged the hilt up hard, cutting into the cartilage of the sternum and doing massive damage to the already punctured heart. He then pulled his blade free and tossed the body aside by the handful of hair he still gripped in his left hand.

Having dealt with the first two assailants, Seenio again became still. He was sure he had heard a shuffling before he had moved forward. He knew another attack could be coming from behind the barrel to his left; the one he had stepped past.

"He's down! He's down! Did ye strike true? Is he dead?"

It was Wiley. From his position deeper in the cellar, he was able to see the silhouettes of those locked in battle against the dim light coming from the stairwell, but apparently was unable to tell friend from foe.

Still frozen in place, Seenio listened as Wiley's words brought movement from the far side of the barrel on his left. Turning his head, he used the dim light from the stairwell to mark a shape emerging from the space; the shape of a man, weapons down and moving forward so that now his entire silhouette was framed in the glow.

As he saw this shape turn toward the darkness, toward him, Seenio took a two-handed grip on his knife and moved in low. He rose up as he struck, driving the blade into the center of the guards' unprotected torso, lifting the guards' feet off of the hard packed earth with the force of the thrust. The guard made a croaking, gurgling sound when his body came back to the earth, and dropped into what would soon become a lifeless pile of flesh as Seenio pulled his blade free.

Once again, Seenio waited. He was expecting one more attack; the guard who had paused on the landing above. But instead of movement on the stairs, Seenio heard the striking of a flint and a torch flaming to life. He turned to see Wiley starting down the aisle toward him, weaponless, torch held high, the better to survey the death that littered the cellar floor.

Seenio smiled a wicked smile as he began to advance upon the smaller man.

Even seeing that it was his thugs that lay about the cellar, Wiley still spoke as if he had the upper hand.

"If ye be wise, ye'll stop in yer tracks!" he spat. "Though probably not through with their fun yet, if I but holler a word my men will kill yer woman!

Nola watched the door close after the third guard had gone through, leaving her alone in the room with the two who guarded the door she had entered through. She cast a glance in their direction and could see they already had smiles on their faces as they stared at her.

Nola considered the look that Seenio had given her a moment ago, just before stepping through the opposite doorway. That look told her that, if treachery arose, he would kill all that accompanied him. He was trusting his first-born and only daughter to do the same. Nola felt herself slipping into the mindset of a Reaper.

She turned away from the men and walked toward the opposite door. Still feigning drunkenness, she allowed a sway to her hips as she had seen the tavern wenches do. When halfway to the door she leaned her back against the wall on her left and again glanced at her guards. Hunching her shoulders and folding her arms under her breast as if to ward off the cold, she worked each hand into the loose sleeve of the opposite arm. Then she hugged herself tightly and waited.

Almost immediately one of the two guards stepped toward her.

"Look at her," he said to his comrade as he advanced. "She looks to be cold. I think I can warm her." Then he laughed a hearty laugh.

The guard continued forward until he stood in front of her. There he paused, smiling down at a face that was more lovely than he first thought, now that he had closed the distance between them.

Nola still leaned against the wall, hugging herself and looking up into the eyes of the guard whose intentions were more than clear. She was tall for a woman, but he towered over her. Still, she appeared unconcerned.

The second guard, who had stayed by the door, started forward, speaking words to egg his partner on.

"Look at her. She looks calm and ready. She's surely done this before…" he said with a lecherous smile, "…probably many times."

The first guard looked to his friend and smiled, before turning back to Nola and reaching for her shoulders.

When Nola had slipped her hands into her sleeves, she immediately grasped the handles of the two six-inch blades she kept sheathed to her upper arms. When she saw the guard reach for her shoulders, she moved like lightening, whipping her arms free and slicing into both hands with the same motion. The guard gasped in surprise and drew back his hands so fast that he witnessed the very beginnings of the torrent of blood that now poured from twin gashes.

But Nola wasn't through.

Now stepping inside his still spread arms, she struck him six times in rapid succession in the center of his chest; six blows delivered so fast as to almost mimic a beating drum; six lightning-fast blows, each launching six inches of sharpened iron into the center of his chest; six blows that forced the burly guard to take one, then two steps back in surprise, even before he felt the pain in his chest.

Then, with a sneer of disdain, Nola stepped into a vicious kick to his midsection.

Rendered defenseless by the trauma inflicted on his body, the guard was sent staggering across the room. He crashed into a table as he fell, coming to rest among the broken stools, his heart fighting to keep beating while blood poured from the many wounds to his hands and chest.

In a state of shock, his partner rushed over to his side and squatted down to examine him. He instantly saw that his comrade was dying and rose to face the woman who had ended him. But, as he turned toward her, she was there… in his face… with her blade at his throat!

And he dared not move!

Now Nola spoke for first time.

"You were right," she sneered "… I have done this before… many times."

Before either of them could again speak or move, the door to the landing swung open and the third guard, alerted by the crashing furniture, stepped into the room. There he froze, stunned at the sight before him.

The surprise of the opening door caused Nola to whip her head in that direction. The guard with her knife at his throat saw his opening and took his chance. With all the speed he could muster, he reached for the hand that held the blade to his neck.

Fortunately for him, he grasped it before the distracted Nola could drive the blade home. Unfortunately for him, Nola had two hands… and two blades.

No sooner had the guard grabbed Nola's right wrist than she brought her left into play, driving her second knife up through his lower jaw and into his skull. The shock and pain of the blade caused the guard to release Nola's right hand, which she then used to slash deeply across his jugular even as she turned her body toward the far door and escape.

All of this happened while the third guard was still frozen with surprise but, as Nola turned toward the door, he came alive and swiftly moved to beat her there.

But Nola's movement was a feint.

She took two rapid steps toward the door but, on her third step, she planted and pivoted, changing directions and meeting the guard in full stride.

Having been focused on reaching the door first, the guard was taken by surprise and lashed out with his arm to knock Nola aside. Nola ducked under the awkward blow even as she dropped the knife in her left hand and grabbed a handful of his shirt. Then she swung herself up and onto his back, wrapping her legs around his torso. Her motion and weight threw him off balance and he spun into the wall with Nola still clinging to his back. Now, as he pushed himself away from the wall, Nola locked her ankles and looped her left arm under his chin, grabbed her right arm, and applied a chokehold. The guard's first instinct was to pull the arm from his throat but, by having grabbed her right arm, Nola had the left arm locked in place. Releasing her left arm, the guard began swinging his arms wildly as he twisted his body, hoping to dislodge this wild woman as would a bucking horse.

This played right into Nola's hands.

Now able to free her right arm, she filled her left hand with a handful of his hair. Then she leaned back and began plunged her blade again and again into the ribs below the guards thrashing right arm. The man was forced to raise his head as he screamed in pain, allowing Nola to wrap her left arm around his neck once more, getting an even tighter choke hold this time, and all the while working her right arm like a piston, driving her blade again and again into his exposed right side.

Blood was now frothing around his mouth as he reached again for the arm around his neck, this time with both hands. But now he was in shock and struggling to breathe due to his severely punctured lung. As he fought to grip the arm around his neck, his knees buckled and his body began its descent to the floor. Forced to release her choke hold, Nola rode the toppling body to the ground, coming to rest atop his lower back as he sprawled face down on the floorboards.

Reaching forward and grabbing a handful of hair, she stretched his neck, and ended his struggles by slicing his throat.

As the echo of Wiley's threat died, Seenio found himself focused on another sound; a slow drip that could be heard falling in the darkness off to the side. Wiley heard it too, and had a puzzled look on his face.

Seenio just smiled.

"What sound could that be, Wiley" Seenio taunted. "Go, take your fire and look. I'm sure you will find it is blood, dripping through the floorboards above your wine cellar."

Wiley turned an annoyed look to Seenio, but just as quickly looked perplexed as he continued to hear the drip… drip… drip coming from somewhere off in the darkness to his right.

"Do you have more men, Wiley? You will need them. The six you began with are now dead; laid low by me and 'my woman'."

Seenio chuckled as he stepped forward and snatched the torch from Wiley's hand. Grabbing a handful of the barkeeps collar, he forced him into the darkness and the spaces between the barrels that he kept there. After a short while he guided the now blood covered barkeep back out, past the corpses laying on the dirt of the cellar floor, up the stairs and through the landing door, pushing him onto the blood-soaked floor where his trio of dead guards lay.

Nola had retrieved her second blade and was poised to further defend herself until she saw The Beast at the door, shoving the hapless barkeep before him.

"Now," said Seenio as he settled onto one of the few stools left unbroken, "we shall try a different way."

After coming to terms with the futility of his situation, Wiley had become as pliable and accommodating as any royal manservant. Sitting on the floor of his back room, among puddles of blood still seeping from the corpses of his henchmen, he confirmed to Seenio and Nola that he was indeed a conduit for local information.

"Most everythin' that happens between the eastern gates and the castle walls finds its way into me tavern and me ear," the tavern master now boasted.

Seenio considered that this could be the flailing of a man who had played out his gambit to no avail and now lay at the mercy of he to whom he'd raised a hand. He also considered that the blacksmith, Suleski, truly feared him and would not have passed on the name of The Milkmaids Rest and its proprietor had he not thought it would be helpful.

At Seenio's suggestion, Wiley called for a serving girl to bring soap, water, and a change of clothes. Nola stopped the girl just outside the door, taking the requested items and shooing her away. Once Wiley had cleaned himself up, a table away from the regulars was arranged for himself and his guests. He saw that Seenio and Nola were treated with roast bird, fresh bread and a fresh urn of cool watered wine. As they ate, Wiley called his girls over one at a time to share what information they had pulled from their customers over the last few nights.

The third girl that sat before them proved to be the jewel of the group.

Her name was Dalphine and Seenio recognized her as the wench who so delighted her customer at the table beside theirs when they first arrived. After motioning the girl to a seat, Wiley instructed her to answer any questions they might have for fear of punishment.

Several minutes into her questioning, Seenio was of a mind to dismiss the girl. She sat stiffly before them, her gaze locked on hands kept tightly clasped in her lap. She was trying very hard to recall every detail related to the questions, for fear of punishment, but it was all for naught. She seemed to know nothing of two tall dark strangers, one of a darker complexion than usually seen in the plain's kingdoms.

As he was prepared to wave her away, Seenio felt a touch on his arm and turned his face toward Nola. She had sat quietly as Wiley and her father pressed the first two girls, and now this third, for what they might know. She now found her patience was wearing quite thin.

"Father…if I may…" Nola spoke in their native tongue, "You question her as if she were a man."

An arched eyebrow above a half smile accompanied Seenio's reply.

"And how else should I question her?"

"*Talk* to her, father… talk to her like she is a woman," was Nola's reply. "May I…?" she asked in response to Seenio's now quizzical expression.

"How is your Cantorese?" Seenio questioned.

Nola gave a warm smile and spoke to the serving maid with words also meant for Seenio and Wiley.

"If the men would allow," Nola said gently and in perfect, though heavily accented, Cantorese, "I would like to speak with you for a moment."

Pausing after she spoke, Nola instinctively rose from her seat beside her father, who sat across from Dalphine, and moved to sit beside her. Instantly the serving girl's expression changed from one of quiet anxiety to guarded relief.

"Of course, M'lady," Dalphine said formally, as she shifted in her seat so she fully faced Nola.

As Seenio and Wiley listened, Nola first questioned the serving girl about the tavern and her duties there; the boisterous atmosphere; the patrons who could alternate from rough, ill-mannered and stingy, to cultured, kindly and generous, and all things between. The girl first answered Nola's questions cautiously, casting quick glances toward the men as she measured her words. But before long, the two women were leaning in and giggling conspiratorially as Dalphine described the colorful types that frequented the Inn and what brought them there.

"I 'ave a customer," Dalphine said, "a little freer than most. 'E'd gone an told 'is wife some story, said she didn't 'spect 'im back for a time. Says 'e was working on the docks of the Manchess some nights ago, when the Robes themselves approached!"

She said this last in an awed whisper, still surprised she had spoken to someone who had actually seen the mysterious figures in the flesh and that they were real men, not spirits passing swiftly in the night.

"They purchased passage on a barge headed for Wroughtmire for two of their own, their 'orses an all. With the extra cargo, someone 'ad to stay behind. 'E said the bargemaster kicked 'im to the side," Dalphine leaned in closer, her eyes now wide, "but they paid 'im two gold coins for 'is trouble…and 'is silence!"

Seenio and Wiley had been growing bored with the snippets of the conversation they could make out but, at the word of two robed strangers secreted on a barge for Wroughtmire, both men came to life, their intense gazes locked onto the two women who seemed to share some secret bond across the table from them.

"Where is this man?" Seenio cut in. "Where can he be found? Do you know how to reach him?"

Happy that what she shared had piqued the interest of her employer's friend, Dalphine eagerly answered.

"Why e's upstairs asleep."

Seenio stared at the serving girl, puzzlement furrowing his brow.

"Oh, I've kept 'im 'appy 'ere for two days," Dalphine said with a wiggle and a smile. "I fancy e's still got a few coins left!"

****

Later that night, Seenio and Nola found themselves on the eastern docks of the Manchess, watching as Wiley paid the bargemaster fare for the two of them to travel downriver to Wroughtmire.

In the interest of privacy, Seenio and Nola had gone to the bedside to awaken the hapless drunk personally. Thinking it was his sweet Dalphine eager for more fun, Giorgi nearly choked on his own saliva when he saw the strange burly man who had shaken him awake and now stood threateningly over him. Of course, he spilled everything to them, reprising the story that Dalphine had already told. When Seenio pressed him on whether he had seen either of the two travelers, he fairly panicked.

"No, sir," Giorgi stammered, his head still spinning from strong drink and a rough awakening. "They wore those silvery robes that covered them from head to boot. Even their faces were but shadows in the deep hoods. The only things uncovered were their hands."

"And did you see their hands...the two who boarded the barge?" Seenio pressed, his eyes flaring with his impatience.

"I did" Giorgi nodded and swallowed hard, unable to move his eyes away from Seenio's face.

"Was one of them of a darker complexion?"

"It was late in the night, M'lord," said Giorgi, "but by the torchlight the back of the hand of one did appear to be darker...or mayhap he could have worn gloves."

That had been all Seenio Masscus needed to hear.

With the negotiation and payment now complete, Seenio turned to Wiley.

"Be glad, barkeep. You are about to be free of us. Unless..." Seenio leaned closer to the frightened tavern master, "...you have arranged for some mishap to occur on the voyage to Wroughtmire... or you betray your vow of silence about our presence here."

"Oh, I would never..." Wiley began before Seenio quickly cut off his words.

"Because if any misfortune, of any kind, should befall us on our journey to Wroughtmire..." Seenio held Wiley's frightened eyes with his own, "...you will see us again."

The panic that welled up in Wiley's eyes was palpable.

"M'lord," he gushed. "Know that ye and yer woman are forever welcome to warm yourselves at my fire and partake of my hospitality. At no charge! Had I but understood from the beginning..."

"You would have six fewer corpses to dispose of when you return to your tavern," Seenio finished his sentence.

Struck speechless, Wiley could only watch as Seenio turned to lead his horse toward the barge with Nola close behind him.

As they approached the ramp leading onto the vessel, Seenio paused and turned back to the tavern master.

"Catch," Seenio said as he tossed something to Wiley. The tavern master caught it without thinking and then looked in his hand to see what it was.

"When next I pass through Sandledge, I expect to find Suleski in good spirits and with that ring again welded to his fat finger."

Without waiting for a response, Seenio and Nola led their horses across the ramp and onto the barge. Wiley did not dare move until the vessel had drifted free of the dock and found the strong current that would, on the third day, release them onto the banks of the river Manchess in Wroughtmire, the capital of Rayine.

CHAPTER 5

Raymond and Hanshee spent the next day and a second night camping with Delno Menowin and his family. Traveling with the Menowin clan was never boring. Delno thoroughly enjoyed the company and was quiet the story teller. When he was not enthralling Raymond with tales of his homeland and the great inland sea, Vano, his young son of about eight years, was playing games with Raymond and Hanshee, and playing tricks on everyone. He grew particularly fond of Raymond and spent a good part of the day riding on his horse with him.

In the early afternoon of their third day together, the group came upon a roadblock.

This section of the Merchant Way skirted the base of the western foothills of the Ursal Mountains for several leagues, on its way to the southern border of Rayine. The roadblock began at the northern end of a bridge that crossed a small river flowing southwest out of the Ursals. There were several wagons stopped there and, with nowhere to pass, the party had no choice but to bring their three wagons to a halt as well.

Being wary of their position as pursued men, Raymond and Hanshee were hesitant to move forward to see who blocked the road and for what reason. Before they could make a decision, Hanshee spied the back of Delno's head as he moved between the wagons and horses, seeking information from all he passed.

When he returned, he called his family together with their guests to share his knowledge.

"The soldiers of Rayine have set up a roadblock here on the order of their King," Delno began. "The stretch of road beyond this bridge, and running down to the southern border of Rayine, has become rife with thievery. Several travelers have been killed, their goods stolen, their women defiled. In order to combat these crimes, the King ordered a garrison built on the banks of this river and has decreed an armed escort must accompany any who wish to proceed past this bridge.

"A company of soldiers is about to form up and escort those chosen down to the border. Those escorted will reach the border after midday tomorrow. Those not chosen must wait until the return of the soldiers the day after, before they are allowed to cross the bridge."

Delno's words were greeted by expressions of aggravation on some and concern on others. Delno himself showed disgust at having to postpone his return to his beloved homeland, the first emotion other than joy Ray had observed in him.

Ray took his cue from Hanshee who never seemed to let adversity beyond his control affect his mood. The pair sat calmly on their horses as the solders at the barricade on the northern riverbank directed wagons and riders across.

When the bridge was again closed Delno's party was second in line behind a family with two wagons. They appeared to be citizens of Rayine who were leaving their nation, which had been struggling for some time due to drought caused by the seemingly never-ending expansion of the great desert that lay to the west.

As with the other kingdoms that lay between the Blue and Ursal mountains, Rayine had an agriculture-based economy. The land was level and water had been plentiful, with rivers beginning in both mountain ranges running through it, and some that flowed south from the northern wastes. For thousands of years, the peoples who had settled here found life less challenging because of the richness of the soil and the plenty that it provided. It was said that this began to change about a thousand years ago, right after the passing of the nomads from the west… the Pith.

Though obviously not of their making, the Pith were blamed for catastrophic events to the west and northwest, the results of which diverted the course of several waterways, actually causing the waters of some rivers to flow underground. Weather patterns also changed, with the decrease in surface moister resulting in less evaporation and less rainfall. This was especially true along the middle and southeastern slopes of the Blue Towers. Over the years these dry lands at the base of the mountain became desert and over the centuries the desert had expanded.

The spread occurred mostly in the south and so had a much greater effect on the lands of Rayine. Fully two-thirds of what used to be farmland to the west of the city was now unusable. It was the type of catastrophe that could cripple a nation such as Rayine, depriving them of the type of future that they had always envisioned.

As Rayine continued to collapse in land, wealth, and prestige, the people that many sought to blame – because, of course, someone had to be blamed - suffered from an embarrassment of riches. In the minds of many in Rayine, their demise as a great nation was directly related to the rise of the Pith.

The nomadic tribe of Pith, saved from total destruction by the afore mentioned "catastrophic events," was now a mighty nation.

Only by their longstanding alliance with Cantor, spurred as it was by the arrival of the Pith, was Rayine still itself a nation. It was their strife that had fueled their encroachment into the Ursal Mountains so many years ago, in an ill-fated attempt to duplicate the good fortune of the Pith. It was an encroachment for which they had paid dearly and were saved only by the intervention of their ally to the north.

By one ill-considered act, Rayine had launched itself into second-class status as a nation, while the Pith had cemented their claim to the Ursals and their status as a rising power. Now it was said that they even claimed 'empire'!

The exodus away from the western lands of Rayine was a result of failures of both man and nature. For generations its inhabitants had watched as year after year the amount of land capable of sustaining a crop dwindled in size. There had been talk of irrigation projects, redistribution of unused land hoarded by the nobility, even centering the economy of Rayine away from agriculture. The incursion into the western Ursals had been a heavy-handed attempt at the latter. As for expensive irrigation projects and redistribution… well… both would require sacrifice by their rulers; one of treasure, the other of land, so none were surprised when these ideas came to naught.

The family in line ahead of the Menowin was one of many who had endured for as long as they could. Now, having loaded all their remaining possessions into their two wagons, they were set to find a better life somewhere to the south. And as the morning progressed, it appeared that their fortunes had changed somewhat for the better.

About two hours after the first escort company of over thirty mounted soldiers departed, taking with them nineteen waiting wagons, a smaller company totaling seven foot-soldiers led by a captain, arrived and stated their willingness to escort one family to the southern border.

Hanshee and Raymond looked on as their captain strode boldly across the bridge toward the barricade while his helmeted men formed up at the other side. Reaching the side where the wagons waited, the captain first had words with the sergeant of the men on barricade duty. Once the barricade had been raised, he approached the travelers.

"In his generosity," the captain said, "King Hessgard of Rayine has release an additional squadron of men to help in escorting merchants and pilgrims across these badlands and to the southern border."

"We are ready to go!" Delno shouted in a heavy accent from his place standing upon the seat of his wagon.

The captain looked to the merchant and the three heavily laden wagons he commanded, then to the family in front of him in line. For a moment he seemed torn, but then he spoke.

"These people stand before you and will have first choice on leaving now," he said. "Perhaps another patrol may show up soon to escort your wagons."

"You were sent to us by King Hessgard?" a feeble voice asked of the captain. It was the grandmother of the family in the front. She had heard the commotion and was leaning her frail frame from the wagon where she had been huddled beneath a blanket for warmth.

The captain approached her with obvious concern showing on his face.

"Your King cares deeply about all of his subjects," the captain told her. "He has indeed sent us," he gestured toward his men on the far side of the bridge, "to guarantee your absolute safety from this spot until we reach the southern border, if it is your wish to precede that far."

The captain's words brought a visible expression of relief to the old woman's face.

"That is good to hear, mum, is it not?" a middle-aged man said as he coaxed the woman back to a comfortable position inside the wagon. Then he jumped down and turned to the captain.

"Please, sir, give us a moment to collect our belongings and check our animals and we should be prepared to follow you through hell."

The captain smiled and slapped his back.

"There will be no hell under my watch" he said with a laugh.

Soon after, Raymond, Hanshee, and the Menowin clan watched as the farmers from western Rayine coaxed their wagons across the bridge where the newly arrived squadron formed up on either side. It wasn't long before the dust of the wagon wheels settled, leaving no sign of the pilgrims or their escort to those watching from beyond the bridge.

Being first in line would normally bring a smile of anticipation to the waiting faces but, in this case, the travelers knew that the main company of soldiers was not scheduled to return until the afternoon of the day after tomorrow.

With this in mind, Delno had his sons strike a small camp on the side of the road beside his wagons and the family settled in for a two day wait. Others who waited behind them followed suit and after a while an atmosphere of familiarity developed. Several families were now preparing their evening meals on fires built on the roadside and the aromas that wafted along on the evening breeze wet appetites up and down the line. Even the soldiers on the barricade began looking jealously toward the stewpots that now lined the road.

Needing a distraction until the meal was prepared, the Menowin men broke out their instruments and soon had a small crowd gathered round while they played and sang. Every so often one of the Menowin women would take a break from cooking and dance in the circle made by the onlookers while they cheered encouragement. Soon others from other families were joining in and the drudgery of waiting was transformed into a festival of music, soon to be followed by food and drink.

The next afternoon brought some of the monotony that had been warded off the evening before.

Seeking a distraction after the noon meal, Raymond and Hanshee decided to walk the short distance to the makeshift tavern that had been erected outside the walls of the barracks so that the soldiers stationed here could enjoy what little down time was afforded them.

The tavern was a single rectangular room with a stone fireplace centered on the northernmost wall. A makeshift bar had been thrown up beside the hearth, from which the tavern keeper served drinks and hot stew, the ingredients of which was anyone's guess. Though hastily constructed, the building was none-the-less solid, holding three tables with several chairs for each, and a few extras chairs scattered here and there.

All the tables and chairs were occupied when Raymond held the door open for Hanshee and the pair ended up standing near the end of the bar. Hanshee was satisfied with this, as their position provided an unencumbered view of the entire room.

Ray first tried to order in Hanshee's native tongue.

This was a test, done simply to see if anyone present would be versed in the language. Raymond knew it was doubtful, but it was better to be sure.

Upon hearing the strange language, the tavern master leveled a scowl in his direction and a glance around the room, convincing Raymond that none present could decipher his speech. Once this was clear, Ray used hand gestures to order watered wine for himself and his master. This accomplished, the pair settled in to enjoy the wine while Ray kept an ear open for anything that might be useful.

Hanshee being Hanshee, there was very little that escaped his senses. So it was that he mentioned to Ray that the men at the table farthest away looked familiar. Ray's first instinct was to brush this off.

"Really," he said. "You've been to Rayine before? You've been here before?" Ray waved his arm as if taking in the whole of the small encampment.

"My journey through Rayine was swift," Hanshee said. "I first came through the Great Desert and into these lands. I did not linger, nor show myself to any."

"Well," Ray continued, "we've been around a lot of soldiers recently. You probably just recognize the type."

Hanshee responded with a sideways glance but said nothing more. Raymond's curiosity was now piqued and he looked over to the table in question, and at the men seated around it.

There were seven men sitting or standing around the table. As they all wore simple clothes, Ray could not be sure they were soldiers in the military of Rayine. Those seated at the table were huddled close together in discussion and paying hardly any attention to their spirits. The men that were standing leaned over the table to better hear what was being said.

Ray was thinking how different they looked from the other rowdies in the tavern, when a man in military attire, obviously a soldier, approached their table and said a few hushed words. Now the men who were seated stood and the entire group filed past the bar and out the door. One of the men, a stocky, heavily bearded fellow, allowed his eyes to linger on Raymond and Hanshee as he passed. Rather than draw any unwanted attention, Raymond looked away as he and Hanshee continued to enjoy their wine.

Much later, as Raymond and Hanshee walked back toward the wagons, they were met by a boy who was leading two horses. First spying them from a distance, the lad perked up when he recognized them and, clucking encouragement, coaxed the horses into a trot until pulling them up beside the pair. After looking from one to the other, the lad finally decided on the master and spoke up.

"Good sir, the man whose wagons you followed has been offered safe passage." Not sure if he was being understood, the lad nevertheless rushed on with his message. "The soldiers are pressing him and he asked me to find you and bring you your animals."

Raymond looked to Hanshee and received a quick nod of his head. Then he answered the boy in the language he had spoken; Cantorese.

"My master does not know your tongue boy, but I thank you on his behalf for bringing our mounts. Now tell me, how long since the soldier's call?"

"They are just now leaving," the boy said. "If you hurry, you may be able to join them."

As quickly as Raymond translated, the two were mounted and trotting their horses toward the bridge. They arrived just in time to see the company of eleven soldiers form up on either side of the three wagons of Delno Menowin, the last of the soldiers looking back toward Hanshee and Raymond as they marched away.

"Hold!"

It was the sergeant of the barricade.

"There will be no more passing this day. You'll have to await the next escort."

Raymond knew that to speak would reveal their deception, but there was no need. The soldier's posture, along with the barricade now back in place, told the story. The two could only watch in silent concern as the Menowin family was escorted toward the distant border.

CHAPTER 6

Raymond had been following closely behind Hanshee for the better part of three hours. It had taken them that long to reach their current secure location.

They were now south of the barricade and well above the road, having carefully worked their way through the heavy brush and unstable footing, treacherous for both men and horses.

As they continued forward, Ray could not help but think again about what had put them on the path they now followed.

As he and Hanshee had watched the Menowin family and their escort begin their trek to the border, both took notice of the soldier in the rear who briefly turned their way before falling in with his comrades; a stocky heavily bearded fellow.

When they had retreated to a place out of earshot of the other wagons, Hanshee spoke.

"The men from the tavern who looked familiar," he said, "are the foot soldiers who yesterday led the two wagons before us down the road beyond the barricade."

"That can't be," Raymond had shot back. "Those men are still on their way to the southern border of Rayine. If it's a two-day trip on horseback, it's at least three days on foot."

"They are not, Way-mon," Hanshee said, "for even now they walk with Delno and his clan."

Hanshee did not say this as if it were simply speculation. He said it as fact. No embellishment or emotional punctuation was needed. He then locked his eyes on Ray and waited for him to catch up.

It took a moment, but finally recognition dawned on Raymond's face and he met Hanshee's stare.

"If those are the same soldiers" Ray said, "then what happened to the family they led off yesterday? Do you think they released them to another patrol and returned to help those next in line?"

Raymond put this question to Hanshee in earnest, but was met only with a blank stare, a stare that continued to drag on until Ray's mind naturally filled in the silence.

"You think that something isn't right... that they're up to something," he said.

Hanshee's expression didn't change, nor did he nod or shake his head. His eyes did his speaking now and Ray could see in their depths that he was now thinking along the same line as Hanshee. Still, for some reason, he felt he wasn't grasping the whole situation. In his mind something was still missing.

The pair had been walking their horses north on the Merchant Way, away from the line of wagons waiting for a southern escort. Now Hanshee released Ray from his stare and glanced back toward the roadblock, confirming that they had rounded a bend and passed from the view of both the soldiers and waiting travelers.

"Come with me, Way-mon," Hanshee said as he dismounted his horse, took the reins in hand, and led the animal into the brush to their right.

Ray had no choice but to follow.

After a few yards the ground began to rise and continued rising as long as they climbed. The trees and thick brush, the rocks and odd footing, made the trek uphill an ordeal. Several hundred feet above the road, Hanshee finally found what he was looking for and the duo turned south along what appeared to Raymond to be a faint trail. Hanshee planned to use this trail to bypass the roadblock at the bridge and continue on toward the southern border of Rayine.

It hadn't taken long for them to reach the cold waters of the river upstream from the bridge and the barricade. After crossing, Raymond figured they had trekked the difficult brush for another two miles - *two thirds of a league in this place,* he thought - before Hanshee guided them back down to the Merchant Way. They were now well beyond the river and the soldiers of Rayine who blocked the bridge there. Any patrol now on the road should be approaching them from the south, and not coming up from behind.

The sun was hanging slightly above the western horizon and the marks recently made by horse drawn wagons and soldiers afoot were clearly visible in the dust and gravel of the road. As always, Raymond trusted Hanshee to set their course and pace, and he paid little attention to the road or the tracks that covered them. So it was that Raymond was taken completely by surprise when Hanshee peeled his horse away from Raymond's side, veering toward the far left of the road and into the tall grass at its border.

Pulling up on his reins to bring his horse to a halt, Raymond watched as Hanshee leaned slightly from the saddle as he slowly guided his horse further into the brush and studied the ground.

"Do you see something?

It was the first Raymond had spoken since they left the road to bypass the roadblock and he was puzzled that Hanshee had chosen this time and place to pause. In his opinion, they ought to be picking up speed to catch up to Delno and his Rayine guard escort.

Hanshee did not speak in response, instead turning toward Raymond and, with his head, motioned him forward. When Ray had pulled his horse alongside, Hanshee leaned toward him and spoke in a whisper.

"We follow the wagons of Delno on the road," he said. "His mark is easy to see. But there are other tracks, hidden tracks, leading into the brush."

Raymond craned his neck and inspected the grass and shrubs where his horse now stood. Some of it appeared to be bent and broken, as if something had recently passed this way. As he continued to look, he noticed an indention near the patch of grass that his horse had chosen to graze. He sat up and looked at Hanshee.

Having again caught Raymond's eyes, Hanshee motioned to the beginnings of the forest they now faced. Again, leaning into Raymond, he pointed out more evidence.

"See there… saplings bent and broken."

Raymond cast his eyes into the forest and noticed several young saplings broken and leaning. They were situated between two larger trees that were just far enough apart to allow a wagon to pass between them

Now Raymond looked back at Hanshee with an alarm in his eyes that his voice dared not sound. He leaned forward, prepared to whisper his fears, but was cautioned by Hanshee's hand on his forearm. Shaking his head from side to side, Hanshee anticipated the question and shared his thoughts on what they both saw.

"No, Delno's wagons did not pass this way," Hanshee began. "The marks are too shallow and too close together. See there?" Hanshee pointed toward the saplings. "The trail has been brushed and covered. The saplings have been straightened."

At the prodding of Hanshee, Raymond now saw what ordinarily he would have missed. Some broken saplings had been propped up against those that were sturdier. And though covered in sticks and leaves, the forest floor there looked a little off; a tad different from that which surrounded it.

Raymond now understood why they had stopped. He again caught Hanshee's eye and motioned with his head toward the interior. Hanshee nodded once and slowly began to dismount. Raymond followed suit and, after guiding their horses further into the brush and securing them, the pair silently made their way along the trail so carefully concealed by someone unknown.

The trail led straight up through the woods toward the foothills for about two hundred feet and turned to the right just past a grove of young trees as the ground began to rise. At the end of that curve, in a small clearing among the young trees, the questions boiling up in Raymond's mind found their answers.

They first came upon the bodies.

Stretched out on the ground a short distance behind the wagon, the farmer and his wife, his adult son and the son's wife…even the old woman… had reached the end of their journey here in the woods beside the Merchant Way. All were stripped of their clothing to varying degrees, the two wives being completely naked. Lying as they were, their condition was clear, their wounds readily visible.

The farmer bore a nasty gash where something had hacked into him between his left shoulder and neck. His salt and pepper hair was darkened and matted with dried blood, signaling some type of head wound. Several other wounds, mostly stab wounds by their appearance, could be seen on the front and sides of his torso, with what could be bits of intestine protruding from deep slashes in his abdomen. The son bore wounds only to the front of his torso, in the upper abdomen and near the center of his chest. Both of the men's shirts and boots had been removed, and their leggings had been loosened to reveal their undergarments.

The old mother too was partially disrobed, her small, pasty, wrinkled form appearing more like an apparition in the forest shadows of the late afternoon. Her robe had been opened, whether torn or cut was not readily apparent, and pulled down until it gathered around her boney legs. Her undergarments were gone.

The two younger women were totally naked and the bruises from the handling they endured stood in stark contrast to the pale almost bloodless skin that lay motionless in the dirt of the small clearing.

All three of the women had long, deep slashes across their throats and pools of now congealed blood surrounded their heads almost like a corona. Their eyes remained open, punctuating the looks of fear, shock and pain on their faces at the instant of their horrible deaths.

Raymond took all of this in and felt the bile in his stomach begin to rise into his throat. He caught himself before retching, and somewhere in the back of his mind hoped this was not a sign that he was becoming accustomed to seeing butchery, blood, and death.

Hanshee was the first to speak.

"The men and the old one were stripped in search of valuables. The women too were searched, before being taken… and killed."

Raymond had no clue how to respond to what lay before him. He registered Hanshee's words, but the coldness that had suddenly washed over him left him unable to reply.

"Their attackers searched the wagon," Hanshee continued, pointing to the goods and clothing, most of it torn or broken, strewn about the small clearing. "These travelers possessed two wagons. The attackers took the other and what valuables remained, leading it and the animals out the way they entered before covering their trail."

Raymond took note of the clinical, almost detached way Hanshee described the scene and what likely took place here, and felt a sudden rage well up within him. He wanted to lash out at his friend; remind him that before them lay the remains of good people… decent people… a family… who surely did not deserve the fate they had suffered or the cold description of their end that he offered.

But Raymond recognized this for what it was; his awkward attempt to deal with the brutal and casual nature of violence in this strange world that he now inhabited. He knew Hanshee meant no disrespect in his description of the dead and what had befallen them. He knew that Hanshee's ability to keep his composure, no matter the circumstances, was the only reason that they were both still alive. These rational thoughts slowly whittled down the rage that had begun growing in Ray, his breathing began to return to normal and he again found himself calm enough to speak.

"Who…?"

He had begun his question just as he tore his eyes away from the scene before him and turned toward Hanshee, but now he saw that Hanshee was staring directly at him with an intensity that silenced Raymond after a single word.

Before Raymond was not the look of detachment of which Hanshee's speech had hinted, not the look of a man to who wanton slaughter was of no particular concern. The look that flashed across Hanshee's face was a look that Ray had only glimpsed once before; their time of capture in the Southern Ursals, the instant before Hanshee had launched himself from the rock to rain punishment and judgment upon the giant Botha.

Hanshee made no apology for the way he had first broken, and then killed, Botha. He felt his actions were completely justified. Raymond considered the explanation Hanshee had given after those events.

How had he described Botha?

"He had no soul."

Raymond's thoughts were interrupted when Hanshee spoke again.

"This was not done by bandits," he said. "This is the work of the soldiers of Rayine…those who claimed to provide safety."

Hanshee was staring hard at Raymond as he spoke, waiting for him to reach the conclusion that Hanshee had only suspected as he had watched Delno's wagons set out along the southern stretch of the Merchant Way.

"Those same soldiers," Raymond spat, his eyes now wide, his words jumbling together in his rush to speak them, "that you saw in the tavern… that are now escorting Delno and his family?"

At the recognition, Hanshee spun around and began to retrace their steps back to the horses. "Leave all as it is," he said regarding the slaughter that lay about them. We must catch up to Delno… quickly!"

Raymond again found himself following Hanshee as he crept through heavily wooded hills just after sundown, and now his mind wandered back over the last hour or so since they left the slaughtered farmers.

After retrieving their mounts, they had traveled south down the Merchant Way. Knowing the head start that the wagons had, Raymond was prepared to push their horses hard to make up the distance.

Hanshee, ever shrewd, viewed things differently.

If this were the work of the soldiers of Rayine, as he suspected, they would not travel so far down the Merchant Way as to possibly meet another patrol, or not be able to make it safely back to their barracks beside the river in good time. Hanshee noted that they had not taken the farmers too far down the road before veering off into the brush and killing them. He did not think they would take the Menowin clan much further. For this reason, he led Raymond at a careful pace, keeping their horses on the softer footing of the shoulder of the road so the sound of their hoofs would not alert any up ahead of their coming.

Knowing the fate that awaited Delno and his family… that to his mind could have already befallen them… Raymond found it almost impossible to not send his horse barreling down the road in pursuit of the caravan. Only his trust in Hanshee, a trust now built over many months together and what seemed a lifetime of adventure, kept him following behind no matter how his insides twisted with pent up frustration.

After walking their horses for another half league, Hanshee signaled a halt.

The moon had crested the Ursal Mountains to the east almost as soon as the sun had set, causing the tallest trees to cast a shadow over the road at this point. It was in this shadow that the pair sat, remaining silent and motionless by the roadside and allowing the cool evening breeze to confirm to both what it had already hinted to Hanshee.

Again, Raymond found himself fighting the curse of inaction, resisting the urge to fidget, and soon he was rewarded with the faint sounds of activity from somewhere up ahead. As he continued to listen, and his ears became attuned to the particular sounds, he heard faint but boisterous voices raised in what sounded like friendly banter, travelers anticipating rest and food after completing the first leg toward the southern border.

Hanshee heard all that Raymond did and no doubt more. He now turned to his companion.

"They have recently made camp," he said. "They are not yet about their real task."

Raymond again noted the detached way that Hanshee spoke, but now understood what simmered beneath the calm of his words. He looked to Hanshee with the unvoiced question of their next move. Hanshee was quick with a plan.

Using his head to signal Raymond to follow, Hanshee led his horse into the brush beside the road and tied him to a sturdy tree. Raymond followed suit. Then Hanshee faced Raymond squarely and spoke.

"Don your harness and quiver," he said. "String your bow."

The words struck Raymond like a blow to the head.

His mouth began moving, struggling through an instant dryness to speak words that the turmoil of his mind had not yet formed. Though well aware of the mission on which they now rode, somehow Raymond had never considered any endgame but Hanshee stepping in and saving the Menowin family. Now, by his words, Hanshee had as much as committed Ray to a life and death struggle against regulars of the military of Rayine!

Raymond again sought Hanshee's face, but the warrior had turned to outfit himself as soon as he had spoken. Ray felt he had no alternative but to do as he was told and he turned to his saddle. Clumsily, with leaden arms and wooden fingers, he reached for his weapons harness. He slipped it on, his mind still in a daze, and he wondered how the sword had gotten into its sheath even after he himself had just sheathed it.

The cool breezes of recently fallen night felt icy upon his skin due to the perspiration that seemed to flow in torrents from his pores. He fumbled for his bow, glancing back over his shoulder at Hanshee while searching his pouch for the bowstring. It seemed to take forever to find. Once found, it seemed too delicate for his stricken fingers to manipulate. The bowstring slipped from his grasp as he tried to attach it to the bow, and a panicked Raymond found himself on his knees searching the ground and the foliage in the evening darkness. His eyes were betraying him and his hands could not tell the bowstring from the grasses and stems they encountered. Without consciously making it so, his search was becoming a mad thrashing about in the grass, twigs, and dead leaves of the forest floor.

Hanshee reached down and picked up the dropped bowstring, patiently holding it in front of Raymond's face until he took note of it and stood upright, a sheepish look on his face. Hanshee continued to watch, his calm gaze somehow seeming to steady Raymond's hands. Now focusing on his task, Raymond strung the bow. Exhaling deeply, he reached for the quiver and arrows, all of which were gifts from King Moton IX of Cantor.

Now outfitted, Raymond again sought Hanshee's face. Locking his eyes with Hanshee's, Raymond spoke in a whisper almost too quiet.

"I'm not ready for this…" he began.

Hanshee had known this was coming. He was prepared.

"Way-mon," Hanshee said in a voice patient yet firm, "do you not recall the carnage we left behind us; the death and defilement of the innocent? I watched you then as I do now. Do you not remember the fire that roared within you upon your witness? Will you now leave Delno and his wife…his sons and daughters… to such a fate?"

Hanshee's words were not many, but they rang truc in Raymond's mind. Once images of the savaged bodies of the farmers they had stumbled upon again danced before him, Raymond's demeanor had changed. The fear that had first gripped him receded, replaced by a steadiness and a growing sense of purpose.

Raymond again sought Hanshee with questioning eyes, but now he sought reassurance instead of release.

"Do you think I'm ready?" Raymond asked.

"Remember your first lessons with the bow, beside the stream in the southern mountains and in the courtyard outside our quarters in the Royal House. Your arrows will find their marks. If you *know* that what we now do must be done, then you will be ready."

Hanshee held Raymond's eyes an instant longer until Ray nodded his head to signal his readiness. Then he turned and silently moved off through the brush with Raymond close behind.

Going over these events again in his mind seemed to steady Raymond as he and Hanshee crouched in the brush above the Menowin campsite.

It appeared that the soldiers of Rayine had chosen a more open killing field for this night's work. They had led the

Menowin family off the road to a campsite regularly used by travelers of the Merchant Way. A wide path led from the road about three-hundred feet up an easy incline to a well-worn campsite on the far side of a high rock formation. Being worried about bandits, Delno found the spot both comfortable and secluded and was happy to make camp here. The soldiers said that they would camp at the foot of the trail near the road so that none could wander up and disturb the family. Delno being Delno, he offered the men a sample of his wife's amazing stew, but the leader of the soldiers waved him off with a laugh, saying his men were not used to such rich eating.

Hanshee and Raymond had first snuck into the woods adjacent to the soldier's camp. It had indeed been their boisterous voices that had alerted Hanshee to the camp. The men sat around a fire sharpening their weapons and passing around skins of ale and wine. Out of earshot of the Menowin clan, they quietly but openly spoke of the coming slaughter, the comely women, and the three heavily laden wagons.

Raymond counted eleven soldiers; a few more than had accompanied the farmers the day before. *Word must have spread of the fun and profit to be had raping and butchering pilgrims,* he cynically thought.

Hanshee took note of the camp and made his own calculations before leading Raymond deeper into the woods. When he felt it safe Hanshee paused to speak.

"They have more drinking to do before the bloodlust is fully upon them. Still, we must move quickly."

Having now moved to the woods just above the Menowin wagons, Hanshee gave Raymond instructions.

The Menowin men, Delno, his eldest son Danior, and Galid, husband to his daughter Lakshmi, had been about clearing the campsite and seeing to the care of the animals. The women, Delno's wife Valda, Lakshmi, youngest daughter Flora, and Tilda, wife of Danior, had been preparing the meal and beds.

Now the evening meal was finished and all pitched in to secure the campsite and their belongings for the night; all except the youngest son, Vano, who was playing with some figures his brother had carved for him when not busy handling a team of horses. Knowing how the lad had bonded with Raymond, Hanshee instructed him to gain the boys attention without alarming him.

As dubious a plan as this sounded, Raymond found it easily done.

He had but to crawl on his belly through the brush until he was about twenty feet from Vano. He then rolled a pinecone into the clearing to catch the boy's attention. Vano looked up from his figures at the pinecone as it rolled near his feet. Instinctively he looked toward the woods from which it surely had come and there saw Raymond smiling and waving.

Raymond expected the boy to run screaming to his parents, but Vano was overjoyed to see his friend again. Before the lad could call out, Raymond put his index finger to his lips and Vano fell quiet under the apparent universal sign for silence. Now Raymond called him over and the lad crawled on hands and knees to where Raymond lay partially concealed at the edge of the clearing.

"Raymond!" Vano whispered excitedly as he rose up onto his knees and threw himself into a big hug for his friend. "I thought we left you behind, but you found us!"

Raymond returned the boy's embrace but, aware of the moment, quickly separated. Now holding Vano at arm's length, he locked eyes with him and tried to speak in a calm but solemn tone.

"It is good to see you again too, Vano, but right now it is important that you listen carefully to what I say. I need you to find your father and whisper in his ear that my master and I need to see him immediately. Walk carefully so that no one can see your excitement. You must not let anyone else know that we are here. Do you understand?"

Vano gave Raymond a puzzled look.

"Why can't everyone know?"

"I will share that with you very soon," replied Raymond, "but for now no one else but your father can know. Now, can you do this just as I asked for my master and me?"

The boy briefly considered what Raymond asked of him and nodded his head.

"Good! Now you must be quick... careful but quick," Raymond said as he gently pushed Vano toward the sounds of his family.

As the boy walked away, he glanced back over his shoulder. The sight of Raymond's smiling face again brought a smile to his own as he rounded the wagon in search of Delno.

As soon as Vano was out of sight Raymond was wondering if they had done the right thing by trusting a young boy with such an important task. Within moments his concerns were laid to rest as Vano reappeared with his father in tow.

Delno rounded the wagon with a look of puzzlement and concern as he peered into the shadows of the clearings edge. Vano continued eagerly forward, tugging at his father as he pointed to the place where he said he had spoken to Raymond.

Raymond waited until they were close before revealing himself, again with his finger to his lips to stifle Delno's natural exuberance. Upon seeing Raymond, Delno's face broke into a huge smile. Then he noticed the signal and approached his friend quietly, but still grinning from ear to ear. Raymond rose to his feet and embraced Delno, then stepped aside so Delno could embrace Hanshee, who had been waiting further back in the shadows. With pleasantries now completed, Raymond got right down to business.

"My friend, you and your family are in grave danger," Raymond said.

Caught by surprise by this greeting, Delno looked quizzically at Raymond's expression; a mixture of concern and alarm. Delno then looked to Hanshee and back to Raymond, and he then knew that whatever had to be discussed was not to be taken lightly. Instinctively putting an arm of protection around the shoulders of his son, he replied.

"What danger do you speak of? What do you mean?"

Raymond took a deep breath and launched into an explanation of what Hanshee had noticed back at the bridge and what the two of them had found just off the trail. He watched Delno's face grow ashen as he described the slaughter of the farm family whose wagons had been escorted before theirs. When he finished, Delno gripped Raymond's arm and pulled his young son in tighter to his side.

"What shall we do?" was Delno's plea to the wind, and Raymond now found himself in the role that Hanshee often took for himself; putting another's fears to rest and preparing them for what lay ahead.

"Fear not, Delno. My master has a plan.

CHAPTER 7

The soldiers of Rayine took their time as they made their way up the shallow incline toward the Menowin camp. There was no rush and nothing to be concerned about. They knew the family was right where they had been left and would be just as docile as a pet hog right before slaughter.

Each man carried his weapon of choice, mainly short swords and fighting axes, either sheathed or in hand. Each also carried a lighted torch. They would need the torches to adequately search for valuables… and to better see those pretty girls, the daughters just as beautiful as their mother.

Flush with the warmth of much ale and wine, they moved forward in anticipation of claiming the ample rewards promised them from another day of deception.

As they continued around the gently curving trail, a few in the front noticed an unexpected glow from up ahead. Rounding the huge rock formation to their right, the soldiers were met with the sight of a bonfire situated in the center of the trail, just as it began to widened into the clearing. The heat and light that the fire threw off brought the men to a temporary halt as they pondered the reason the Menowin family had built such a thing.

As the soldiers continued to stare and mutter among themselves, a figure stepped into the light on the fires opposite side.

Delno stopped well back from the heat of the blaze, but was bathed completely in its wildly flickering light.

"Your men are late, Captain" Delno shouted. "My wife's stew was so delicious that there's not so much as a spoonful left."

Drawn by the voice, the man chosen to play 'captain' now noticed Delno standing on the other side of the blaze and laughed out loud at his greeting.

"No worry, man," he shouted back with a snicker. I'm sure you have something in your wagons to satisfy my men."

Upon hearing this some of the men laughed aloud. Others set their jaws, ready to get on with the nights business.

"And what could that be, Captain?" replied Delno, raising the sword he held to waist high' ensuring the firelight would flicker on its length.

As he stood there, terrified, Delno was joined on either side by his son, Danior, and his son-in-law, Galid, a sword now visible in each man's hand.

"They've armed themselves!" someone from the pack of soldiers cried out and an ominous silence, punctuated only by the crackling of the burning wood, settled over those on both sides of the fire.

"Damn this...!"

The words came from a soldier standing just behind the captain, and he pulled his blade noisily from its scabbard as he strode purposefully past his leader to sweep these merchants aside.

As the soldier moved forward, circling to the right of the bonfire, he was caught in mid stride by the arrow that struck the right side of his skull with a loud crack, the force of the impact sending his body careening sideways into the flames. Already as good as dead when he fell across the burning wood, he nonetheless screamed in anguish and thrashed uncontrollably until his body finally lay still, no longer reacting to the hellish heat.

It was a gruesome spectacle.

While his comrades stood in stunned, wide-eyed silence at what had just happened, another arrow struck the 'captain' in the right side of his neck. He dropped to his knees and then onto his back, where he rolled back and forth in the firelight, grasping and clutched at the death now protruding from both sides of his neck.

"Up against the rock!"

A leader emerged from among the remaining soldiers and as a group they threw themselves against the base of the rock formation on their right, trusting it to hide them from the deadly archer who fired down on them from above.

Fffffith!

An arrow struck one of the soldiers in the leg, lodging in his knee even as he held his position at the base of the rock formation.

"Aaaaaghh!"

His cries alerted his comrades as he pointed towards the forest on the far side of the trail. "In the woods!" he cried as he grasped his leg and braced himself against the rock wall. "It came from the woods!"

Instantly an as yet untouched soldier sprinted across the wide trail toward the woods, only to be struck from behind and above by the arrow which drove his running body into the dirt before he could reach the trees.

Now panic tore through the group as the men hugged the base of the rock formation while locking their eyes on the darkness of the forest beyond the firelight. There were shouts and cries of alarm, and a few of the men even began to climb the rocks, assuming this to be the only way to dislodge the deadly archer who kept them pinned down from above.

Raymond's first arrow had not followed his aim, but the men had been packed so tightly together at the base of the rocks that it nonetheless found a target in the soldier's knee.

Hanshee had picked out his place in the woods, about thirty feet off of the trail and adjacent to the kill zone that he had improvised with the bonfire. He had instructed Raymond to remove his arrows from their quiver and place them in a line before him, out of his line of sight but within easy reach.

Although first concerned with being so close to the killers, Hanshee assured him the intense blaze of the fire would cause them to lose their night vision. If any were to reach the forest, they would be easy prey for an arrow or a sword stroke. This had not set Raymond's fears to rest. Seeing this, Hanshee also assured him that, from his perch atop the rocks, he would see that none reached the tree line.

Now, having been calmed by his first arrow finding a mark, Raymond took his time and placed his second shot into the back of the lead climber. The man was about twelve feet up the twenty-foot rock face and grunted with the impact of the arrow in his low back. He struggled to maintain his grip on rocks that were already difficult to climb and finally fell backward onto the trail below, sending the remaining soldiers into an even greater sense of panic.

Raymond let loose another arrow and another of the climbers was struck from the rock face. As he reached for another arrow, he heard a whistle followed by a 'thunk', and Ray lifted his eyes in time to watch another soldier, who had tried for the woods, collapse on the trail. With the arrow still protruding from his back, the soldier managed to rise and struggled anew toward the supposed safety of the shadowed woods.

Fffffithunk!

He would not rise again.

Now Raymond took aim at the last climber. The soldier had almost reached the top of the formation and stood a good chance of taking Hanshee by surprise should he be distracted. Raymond let fly and watched as the arrow caught the man high up between the shoulder blades. He fell backwards, his body turning in the air so that he struck the trail head first. The angle of his head told any who was watching that his neck was broken.

There were now three remaining soldiers who as yet bore no wounds from this engagement. As one they pushed off from the wall and tore off down the trail toward their encampment. Raymond expected to see at least one fall from Hanshee's bow, but the three of them quickly disappeared beyond the far side of the rock formation. The soldier who still carried Raymond's arrow in his leg was not so lucky.

Watching his fellows push off from the wall and sprint down the trail, the wounded soldier tried his best to follow. After two steps he found himself face down in the dirt of the trail. Awkwardly he pushed himself back to a standing position and again attempted to limp to safety, but it was too late. The Menowin men had rounded the bonfire and were upon him.

Seeing the last of their would-be attackers' stumble and fall, Delno called to his sons and took out after him. When the man again gained his feet, he had time for one more step before Delno ran up from behind and slashed his good leg. The soldier again went down and lay sprawled face down on the ground… until he felt the first blade tear into his back. Instinctively he rolled away from the assault onto his back and, in this position, bore witness as the three men gathered around him, fighting to slash and stab any part of him that they could reach.

Raymond had stepped from the shadows of the forest and watched from a distance as the Menowin men finished the soldier he had wounded. Now he looked down the trail and wondered what had become of the three that had escaped in that direction. More than that, he wondered why Hanshee had not put an arrow into one of them from above.

Raymond tilted his head back and looked to the top of the rocks. Though the wall was still bathed in the glow of the bonfire, the top was immersed in shadow. If Hanshee was still there, he would remain unseen.

Then Raymond heard the distant clashing of metal – not rhythmic like a blacksmith at work, but in quick bursts of what were probably extremely fast parries and attacks, followed only by the sound of the crackling flames.

Not knowing what to make of this, Raymond notched an arrow and started to make his way carefully down the trail, the same way the soldiers had escaped. He knew what he hoped to find, but this world had yet to give him anything near what he expected. So it was that he was relieved when, halfway down, he ran into Hanshee trailing the last of the soldiers as he walked him toward the camp.

Away from the brightness of the bonfire, Raymond could barely make out his friend and had to wait until they rounded the rocks before he could examine Hanshee for any wounds. Hanshee did the same to him and both smiled when they realized what the other was doing.

The Menowin men had by now pulled the soldiers body from the fire and stood together examining the carnage that had been wrought largely by Hanshee and Raymond in defense of their families. Hanshee and Raymond also took account of all that lay about them before Hanshee turned to Raymond and spoke words that only they could understand.

As Hanshee turned and walked toward the rocks to retrieve his bow and quiver, Raymond addressed Delno Menowin.

"My master asks that you tie this one securely," he said pointing to the man that Hanshee had pushed to the ground in front of them. "He will be left here. Then you should see to your families. This place is no longer fit for a camp. We will leave tonight."

The three-quarter moon had just passed its zenith when the three wagons and two horsemen again found themselves southbound on the Merchant Way. They had no plan or desire to push hard in the middle of the night. Their goal was only to put some space between themselves and the slaughter they left in their wake.

Raymond had only just gotten his shaking under control.

This had begun not long after the killing was done; shaking, sweating, hyperventilation, first noticed as he canvassed the bodies, checking to see if all were dead and if any arrows were recoverable. He had kept his distance from the Menowin family, not wanting anyone to notice his reaction to what had been done – what had needed to be done – this night.

For their part, the Menowin men were as proud as if they had slain every soldier of Rayine themselves!

The women and children had been hiding in the wagons, the teams of horses already in place as per Hanshee's instructions. They were out of sight under some blankets and were told to stay hidden until one of the men came personally to get them. When they were finally brought forth, all were allowed to see, from a distance, the results of the carnage they had only heard until then.

Now, as the wagons rolled steadily south, Raymond overheard snippets of conversations as the men retold the events just past to their women, sometimes seeming to place themselves in the thick of the battle.

Raymond didn't mind. He now understood that the events of this night, the clash of men hacking and killing each other with edged weapons, were a part of this culture and not a rarity. It seemed the only way men fought in this place and most, especially those who traveled, knew that the day could come when they had to heft a knife or a sword and defend themselves, their families, and their livelihoods, from trespassers, bandits, killers or whoever.

This type of combat was almost unthinkable in the world Raymond came from.

When told of what had happened to the farmers who had gone first, and what the soldiers of Rayine no doubt had planned for his family, Delno had been aghast. His first impulse was to hitch up his teams, turn his wagons, and charge down the trail, running through the soldier's campsite, over some soldiers in the process, and continuing south as fast as his wagons could carry them. It was a sound plan of escape, the element of surprise making it likely to succeed.

Hanshee, through Raymond, had persuaded Delno to reconsider.

Delno's plan could indeed succeed in saving his family, Hanshee had pointed out, but what of the other families waiting in line for escort to the southern border? How many families would fall prey to these renegade soldiers from Rayine? What of the farmers that had been found just up the road? Did they not deserve justice? How could their souls find rest if these soldiers were left to have their way with other travelers unlucky enough to fall under their watch? Who would avenge them?

Hanshee's words had been persuasive and Raymond strove to repeat them as he had heard them; as a plea to stand and strike for justice and righteousness, against evil.

The odds had not favored them and yet in the end these merchants, with help, had found it within themselves to stand their ground. Raymond was more than content to let them be heroes in the eyes of their families. They had aided in putting an end to evil.

They *were* heroes.

The same should apply to him but, for some reason, Raymond did not feel like a hero. Heroes didn't throw up... twice.

Hanshee was the *true* hero. Raymond had simply joined with Hanshee in doing what had to be done.

The renegade soldiers had already tasted blood, slaked their lust, and enriched themselves at the expense of the weak. None had stood in their way then and, not being held accountable, they would continue to prey upon any they could. They were not going to be lectured into giving up their ways, returning their gains, and doing penance. There was only one way their evil could be brought to an end. Following Hanshee's lead, Raymond had merely done what he could in support of his friend.

Didn't that make him a hero too?

Raymond thought back to the other time he had done what had to be done. It was after awakening from the sleep induced by the medicinal potions of Hanshee in order to heal his body from a grave wound. While still staggering from the effects of those potent potions, he had arisen from his sickbed to kill the last of the assassins who, at the time, had the upper hand on his friend. It was the first time he had taken a human life and he had been able to live with it only by pushing the episode from his mind since its occurrence just over three weeks ago.

Nobody knows what a week is in this place, Raymond thought. *So, it was what... about a moon ago?* But, in that time, he had yet to fully own up to his actions.

He could argue that he had been distracted.

Escaping their fourth assassination attempt, then fleeing the Royal House by way of the impassable Eastern Cliffs of Stronghold valley. Evading the Citadel pursuit, a pursuit meant either to capture and protect them, or finish the job at which the assassins failed. Making their way along the Cantor Road to its capital, Gunjunson. Confronting The Robes and accepting the aid of King Moton IX himself in escaping those imposing walls undetected. And now, after a few days of relative peace in the nation of Rayine, he and Hanshee had again been thrust into a life-or-death struggle alongside their new friends, the Menowin clan.

'Distracted' doesn't begin to cover it, Raymond thought, with a wry smile and a shake of his head.

CHAPTER 8

After the events of the last night, it was decided that a long rest was both required and deserved. Just before dawn the Menowin clan and their companions, Hanshee and Raymond, made camp along the Merchant Way about four leagues south of their previous campsite and the carnage it held.

With his mind still in turmoil from the battle beside the rock, Raymond could only find a fitful sleep. He awoke late in the morning to find that he wasn't the only one whose thoughts had yet to settle into a semblance of calm.

The aroma of fresh baked bread permeated the campsite, and this made Ray sit up and breathe deeply. Looking over to his left he noted that Hanshee's bedroll was deserted, its owner somewhere out of sight. He was not surprised. Between the two of them Hanshee was always the first to arise. The shock would have come had he seen Hanshee stretched out on his blanket, 'dead to the world' asleep.

Casting his gaze toward the campfire, Raymond saw Valda and one of her daughters – Flora by her small stature – separating the small loaves of bread from the pan and placing them in a basket woven of grasses no doubt found in the more temperate climates near Olmire, Valda's homeland, that bordered the Great Inland Sea far to the south.

A sight and smell to make one thankful to arise, Raymond thought as he fought his way to an upright position and immediately headed into the brush to relieve his bladder.

In the brush he came upon Hanshee, his back propped against a tree as he used his knife to work a long, slender piece of wood into as straight a form as could be made. Raymond continued watching as Hanshee, satisfied with his effort, placed the stick with several others to his left before reaching to his right and picking up another candidate to go under his knife.

"Fashioning arrows?" Raymond guessed.

Without looking up, Hanshee gave a single nod of his head and continued shaving off the excess wood a little at a time.

Raymond took pride in guessing correctly.

Almost all the shafts of the arrows fired last night had been ruined; if not by the thrashing of their victims, then by the effort need to cut them free of the corpses. Arrow shafts could be found in any hardwood forest, but good arrow heads were only produced by a smithy. As no blacksmith rode with them, and they had no idea when they would again be in a settlement, Hanshee had told Raymond to retrieve every arrowhead that he could. It had been a gruesome task and Raymond had been overjoyed the few times an arrow pulled free or pushed through easily, with the head still attached. He shuddered anew at the memory of cutting so many arrowheads loose as he stepped past Hanshee, moving further into the brush to pee.

When Raymond came back, he found Hanshee on his feet and still holding his knife and an arrow shaft. But now he looked beyond the brush that stood between him and the campsite with a look of curiosity and concern. Raymond craned his neck toward the campsite too, and thought he saw something on the other side of the three wagons that had been lined up just off of the road. Deliberately he started off in that direction, pulling up short when he saw Delno smiling and greeting three men on horseback who appeared to have been headed north on the Merchant Way.

Almost always jovial, Delno waved and smiled as he waited for the trio to pull their mounts up before him, but his smile faded at the words spoken by the soldier – it was clear now that the three were soldiers – who sat astride the center horse.

Under the stern look of the leader, Delno appeared to be explaining something. He frowned up at the man as he gestured with his hands to his wagons and members of his family standing close by. He was being very emphatic about something and under continued questioning Delno turned and cast his eyes around the campsite again. Spotting Raymond, he smiled and beckoned him forward with a wave of his hand. Hanshee had emerged from the brush and he joined Raymond in moving toward the Menowin patriarch. As they drew nearer Raymond could now hear some of what was being said and whispered hurriedly into Hanshee's ear.

"The man in the center appears to be the captain from three days ago" Raymond said and Hanshee nodded. "He just asked Delno how he singlehandedly slew a renegade contingent of Rayine regulars."

"Already he has spoken too much" Hanshee said just as they stepped up behind Delno.

"See captain," Delno started in even before greeting his companions, "these are the men who protected my family. Together they slew almost every man. I say almost because Hanshee," Delno pointed to Hanshee, "insisted that one be kept alive."

The captain turned a critical eye toward Hanshee and Raymond, looking first one and then the other up and down. Now fixing a hard stare at Hanshee, the captain again spoke to Delno.

"Do you expect me to believe that a company of renegade soldiers offered to guide you to the southern border, but really planned to kill you and your family and take your valuables, and the three of you…"

"Five of us, Captain," Delno interrupted. "My oldest son and my daughters husband stood with me… but Hanshee and Raymond did most of the slaying. You should have seen them! It was an awesome spectacle to behold!"

Delno said this last with eyes wide and a smile creeping back onto his face.

As the captain continued to look incredulously at the three, the remainder of his command rounded the bend from the south. Ray counted thirty-three mounted soldiers in all, with three additional horses used as pack animals.

Now that the captain had his full command to back him, it seemed he spoke a bit more plainly.

"I can tell by your accent that you are not of Rayine or Cantor, and I can tell by the dark complexion of 'Hanshee' that he too is a foreigner."

Again, Delno cut the captain off.

"I am a merchant returning with my family from a trip to Gunjunson. We go every third year for the counting. We offer the very best of food and entertainment" Delno stated proudly.

Raymond took the opportunity created by Delno to enter the conversation, lest the jovial merchant talk them all into a beheading.

"My master, Hanshee" he said as he gestured toward Hanshee, "is a holy man…a wandering priest from lands west of the Blue Towers. I am his acolyte, Raymond, sworn to serve him by debt of honor."

"Then maybe Hanshee can explain why you are on the Merchant Way, south of the barricade, without an escort?" the captain spat.

"My master does not speak the Merchant tongue" Raymond quickly responded.

"Then *you* tell me, acolyte" the captain fairly bellowed, "did you and your master act as the merchant said, killing a number of men who were in the garb of soldiers of the Nation of Rayine?

As he spoke, the captain gave a signal with his hand and his command moved to spread out on both sides of him, their horses forming a semi-circle around the three travelers.

Raymond knew his next words would serve to incriminate himself, Hanshee, Delno, and Delno's family, but he saw no way out of this situation.

"Captain, they left us no choice…"

At another signal from the captain, the assembled soldiers, those who were archers, notched arrows in bows already strung and sat at the ready, waiting for the third signal that would mean the death of the three men who stood before them.

Hanshee reached out and grabbed Raymond's forearm, steadying Ray as he himself assumed a stance of quiet calm, his head held high before the show of force that surrounded them.

When the captain saw that there would be no attempt to fight, he barked orders to his second.

"Bind the priest and his acolyte" he said. "Search the wagons and confiscate all weapons. If the women can handle the teams, bind the other men as well. The barracks are not much further. We will take them all back and sort this thing out properly."

"M' lord Captain," Raymond found himself speaking up. "This good man and his family merely offered my master and I their hospitality on the road. Any killing that was done… that had to be done… was done by us." Raymond gestured to include Hanshee and himself. "There is no need to bind this family. Please allow Delno and his sons to guide their wagons. I am sure they will follow willingly." Raymond looked to Delno as he spoke and the merchant nodded his head vigorously in agreement.

"Very well," the captain said as one of his men stepped forward with a length of rope. "Bind only these two." Turning back to Raymond the captain continued.

"Are those your horses tied behind that wagon?" He asked, pointing toward the two horses given Hanshee and Raymond by King Moton.

"They are, Captain," Raymond replied. "Given to my master and I by King Moton IX of Cantor."

"Ha!" The captain exclaimed, amid a chorus of laughter from his men. "And I guess he also gave you the bow and arrows with which you admittedly killed soldiers of the Nation of Rayine," he sneered.

Raymond was speechless, struck dumb by the irony of the captain's words.

****

True to his word, Hendric pushed his command hard over the remaining distance to the Rayine capital of Wroughtmire. Even so, it was not until late afternoon of the fourth day after the return of Lucius that the group halted near the crossroads of the Wroughtmire Road and the Merchant Way.

As camp was struck, Hendric took time to take stock of those who followed him.

His small company had numbered eight men when they had departed the southern gate of Stronghold valley. Those were the men who had tracked the Harbinger to old Chezza's stables and found the half-eaten body of the stable master near the foot of the stairs leading up to his doorstep. Seven of those same eight were present when the chest of gold coins had been found, Fevor having been sent ahead to trail the Harbinger.

Hendric recalled how the gold had affected them - the myriad emotions that danced across their faces - until he had made it crystal clear that the penalty for abandoning their duty for treasure was certain death. The instant support of Lucius and Jared had served to quell the spirit of rebellion growing in some of the others – Maleek and Felton especially – and eventually all had taken the vow to hide the chest and return as one only after their mission was complete. When all had been explained, Fevor also took a knee and swore fealty to his captain, his duty, and the will of his companions.

Since that moment, just eighteen days past, there had been changes to the command. Sergel and Blige had been waiting for the company as they approached the road leading to Strongholds Gate. Their story was that Galin had given them a choice; face his punishment or wait at the crossroads for Captain Hendric and join in the pursuit of two 'escapees'.

This story had instantly placed Hendric on his guard.

While harbored at the Citadel, there had been four unsuccessful attempts on the life of the Harbinger. Though the reasons were not entirely clear, it was obvious someone did not welcome this 'warrior-priest of old' and what he represented. This, Hendric was sure, was the reason the Harbinger and his acolyte had decided to take their leave of the Kings hospitality. This was also why Hendric had worried so about the makeup of his command.

From the beginning Hendric had carried the suspicion that some among them could have been placed there to insure the death, and not the return, of the Harbinger. With the addition of two more *unfamiliar* men to his command, Hendric's suspicions had only been heightened. Still, he could not send them away and risk insult to High Commander Galin, so Hendric remained saddled with the unanticipated additions.

But he had lost men, too.

Of the eleven men, counting himself, who left Strongholds Gate, eight now remained.

Maybe it was fortuitous that Maleek and Felton, the two most eager to make a claim for the gold and who Hendric had first thought most likely to be assassins, met their end on the Cantor side of The Ravine. Having been sent across the rope bridge to the other side, they were to lay in wait while the bulk of the command entered the gorge and drove the harbinger into their arms.

They were supposed to capture and detain the harbinger and his acolyte. The evidence that Hendric had himself inspected told the true story.

The body of Maleek was found among a rock formation that bordered the ravine. It had been the perfect location from which to view the head of the trail emerging from the ravine while remaining concealed. His bow lay on the ground before him, as did an unused arrow from his quiver.

Felton's remains were found in the brush on the other side of the clearing. He had been in the process of defecating when he was struck down, but his bow and quiver were located against a large boulder opposite the location of Maleek. This had been his position in their plan to catch the Harbinger in a cross fire, and where he most likely would have died had he not felt the call to relieve his bowels.

Tomar had been sent with them, but it could not be shown that he was part of their plan. He had been discovered down trail from the ambush sight and carrying such wounds that Lucius had actually offered to kill him so as not to slow the pursuit party down. Though Hendric forbid that action at the time, Lucius was later tasked with hunting down Tomar for desertion and returned to camp with proof of his death.

Since fate had dealt with the assassins, Hendric felt he led a more cohesive group of seven who were of a mind to find their quarry and return them to His Majesty at the Citadel. The oath that they took, along with the trials of their journey so far, had forced them to place things in their proper perspective. Tomar's rash action had changed that, forcing the death of one of their own and again bringing the distraction of treasure to the surface of their thoughts.

Since the morning after Lucius returned with Tomar's head, their pace had been a grueling all-day grind along the well-traveled Merchant Way. There were only brief stops to rest the horses, with little thought given to the comfort of the men. Hendric felt they needed such a pace to clear their minds of the fate of Tomar and the distraction brought on by new thoughts of the chest of gold.

He had been correct.

Hendric had called a halt to the day's travels with several hours of sun left in the sky, and the men showed palpable signs of relief. As veteran soldiers and trackers, the pace that Hendric had set was not unfamiliar. Most had endured worst. Still, it was a relief to know that, having reached the outskirts of their destination, they could take a long night's rest.

The priest Petri was the lone exception.

Though his studies in preparation for the priesthood were intellectually strenuous, the young priest had led a physically pampered life, even prior to his arrival at The Temple. Nothing he had ever done had prepared him for the challenges he now faced. Even the time spent with the elite of the Second Expeditionary Force in the Southern Ursal Mountains had been as an extended vacation in comparison. Travel had been at a leisurely pace and he had ridden in a wagon, not astride a horse. Once camped, his only duties were familiar ones in support of Jusaan, his mentor and one of The Council of Nine.

Now riding with this pursuit force, at the request of Jusaan and with the blessing of High Priest Mayhew, Petri's stamina had been taxed even when the pace had been stalled due to the injuries to Tomar. The pace of the last four days had been hell in a saddle for the young priest.

Petri never knew one could become so sore from physical activity. It seemed he felt it over every inch of his body. His arms and shoulders ached the worst, or so he thought until some movement called attention to the pain in his legs and thighs. This was due to his constant attempts to hover over his saddle. Sitting the saddle for hours on end in little more than priestly robes had formed painful abrasions on his buttocks. The abrasions had quickly worsened and now were nigh unto fully formed blisters.

Petri's every movement now broadcast his discomfort and Hendric watched with a practiced eye as the young priest strained to properly place his bedroll down before collapsing onto it in total exhaustion.

"Jared," Hendric called out quietly as he approached the sergeant of the Southgate Guard. "Once you get settled, see to the priest. He moves as if death hovers over him, and I'd wager there are blisters somewhere on that arse that will need attention."

"Yes, captain," Jared replied with a chuckle. He had noticed long ago Petri's lack of comfort in the saddle and had been attempting to teach the young priest how to care for his mount and himself since the pursuit had begun. He could only imagine what damage the last five days had done to the only member of their party who was not a soldier.

The following morning was crisp clear and sunny, the perfect herald of early spring. Hendric arose to see that Lucius had already gathered wood and stirred the glowing embers back into a fire. Presently he was slicing dried bacon to go along with the hardtack biscuits that were already baking at the edge of the new blaze.

Soon all were up and about.

After everyone had partaken of the morning meal, Hendric laid out his plan for the coming day.

"Gather round men," Hendric began. "It's time we earned the confidence our King has shown in us."

Since he had spoken from the center of the camp, no one really need move to hear him, and once he saw that he had all their attention, he began.

"Lucius brought to us our last word that the prisoners had managed to evade us at Gunjunson by taking a barge downriver in the dead of night. We've busted our arse' to get here, but be assured that they arrived many days before us. In truth, we don't know if they are still in the city or have moved on. We have little time to waste so we will split into three groups. Two will search the city while the third continues south along the Merchant Way."

This last pronouncement managed to galvanize the attention of the scattered command who looked first to their captain and then to one another. After another moment of questioning looks, the tracker Ishmed spoke up.

"Captain, I don't know 'bout these others, but Fevor and me, we follow sign over open land. Don't make no difference if it be highland or lowland; forest, desert or swamp. If it leaves a sign, we can track it. But I don't know what good we'd be in a city, and we wouldn't know these prisoners if they was to come sangin' 'n dancin' into camp right now."

"I've given that some thought," said Hendric. "You and your brother will take one of the pack animals and go south. You'll scout the land and what lays ahead should we need to proceed in that direction. Lucius will go with you. He has seen the men we seek and would recognize them at a glance. Also, he knows the tongue and can inquire about them to any you meet."

Turning to Lucius, Hendric continued.

"If any you meet can put you on their sign, at least one of the trackers must remain with it while one of you comes back for the rest of us."

Lucius nodded his understanding.

"The rest will be going into Wroughtmire," Hendric continued to the group. "Sergel...you and Blige will come with me. We will begin in the city proper. I know the looks of the two and can make myself understood here. Jared and Petri will begin at the docks. Being of the priesthood, Petri is well versed in the languages of the plains and was among the first to lay eyes on the escapees when they were first captured. Isn't that right Petri?"

This was the first time since the journey had begun that Hendric had called on Petri in such a public way. It startled the young priest, who stammered and stuttered his response before recalling the gist of the question thrown his way.

"Huh?... I ... well, I uh... ahem... Yes Captain... I was present when the uh, prisoners... were first presented to Lord Galin. Oh, and I do speak the native language of Rayine though, as the Rayine are in all things the loyal vassals of Cantor, the Cantorese language should suffice in this situation."

When he finished speaking, Petri looked around the camp to find all eyes still fixed upon him. Instantly he dropped his head, unable to meet the eyes of the soldiers who now stared so openly

Hendric saw this and gave a slight smile. None but he and Jared had spoken at any length to the priest since they left Stronghold. For rough men like Blige, Sergel, and the brothers Ishmed and Fevor, such precise language, spoken with such proper diction, was both unexpected and out of place here.

"Alright then" Hendric said, bringing all attention back to him. "We'll break camp and be on our way. We'll meet back here after sundown to see where we stand and plan our next course, agreed? Well, off with you!"

CHAPTER 9

The Rayine infantrymen standing guard behind the barricade watched as the procession slowly wound north toward them on the Merchant Way. While still an arrows' flight away, the captain veered off of the road, leading his command westward toward the barracks of the soldiers who, by order of the King, were stationed here to escort travelers along the important trade route.

The barricade guards saw that three wagons were returning with the escort.

This was an unusual sight for this time of year, especially considering The Counting had just ended, and heavier southbound traffic was to be expected. From this distance they could not discern the identities of the travelers, though some said that the wagons looked familiar. From this distance, none of the barricade guards could see that two of the travelers sat bound in their saddles, their horses moving forward under the lead of fellow soldiers in the military of Rayine.

Spring was always a busy time of year. The warehouses of Maestell and Durr were bursting with the goods that the nations of the north had become accustomed to and had no other way of receiving. The much more temperate climate of the southern region meant that crops there, be they from the land or the sea, could be harvested literally year-round. Only the more seasonal climate of the plains and mountain nations, quite severe in comparison to that along the Great Inland Sea, kept the goods and merchants at bay until ice and snow were no longer thought to be a threat to commerce. Every third year The Counting of Cantor served as the signal that trading season was upon them and everyone expected that northbound traffic on the Merchant Way would soon be increasing considerably.

As the captain approached the compound, he noted that more men had arrived from the capital and the western garrisons. This pleased him. The few men he had under his command up till now were wearing thin with the constant duty of guiding mostly pilgrims of Rayine to the south, away from the devastation that even the eastern farmlands were becoming. These new troops meant that his men could get a well-earned rest.

But even with the new arrivals, the captains' rest had to be postponed. His first order of business had to be getting to the bottom of what he had witnessed on the trail the evening past.

The friendly merchant, Menowin, had been very cooperative in leading them to the place where they had camped the night before. It fit the description given; it was indeed a scene of carnage. Beside the remnants of a large bonfire at the trail head, and a smaller fire nearer the road, he had counted ten dead men; all ten of a soldiers age and all wearing the uniform of Rayine. This Menowin fellow was very free with what had occurred there and it appeared that the scene matched the story he had told earlier in the day.

The captain had left two of his most trusted men there to investigate the occurrence, see to the gathering of usable equipment and to the disposal of the bodies. He then allowed this 'Raymond' fellow, an acolyte to the wandering priest, 'Hanshee', to show him to a second clearing somewhat off the road behind a glade of young trees and half a league closer to the barricade.

This scene was also as this Raymond fellow had earlier described it. A farm family massacred. All stripped of their clothing to some degree, the younger women completely naked. Tracks of two wagons were clear in the earth, but only one wagon remained. Most of what was thought to be its contents had been strewn about with hardly a care given.

Again, the captain left two trusted men to survey the scene, recoup any equipment, and report to him directly. As dusk had been approaching, his command had camped nearby and now returned to their barracks late on the following morning.

"Sergeant," the captain spoke to a capable looking soldier riding to his left. "Get those two," he motioned towards Hanshee and Raymond, still bound and sitting their horses that were led by two mounted soldiers, "secured in 'the cage'. Have the merchant and his family camp in the field south of the barracks, past the latrines, and place them under guard. With their women, children, and wagons, I doubt they pose a threat of violence or escape, but it may be wise to protect them once word gets out as to what was found last evening."

"Send a message to the barricade," the captain continued, "that none will be escorted on the Merchant Way this day. Commission a burial detail and a wagon to be sent to the massacre sights. And upon their return, tell my lieutenants to find me no matter where I might be!"

He knew this last order was unnecessary. His men had been made aware that, as of the finding of the first campsite, nothing was to take priority over the situation surrounding this priest and his acolyte… and possibly the merchant family.

What the captain didn't say was that *dealing* with those they arrested may entail allowing them to go on about their business. Both campsites appeared to support the outlandish story that they had given him upon their first meeting, including the presence of the survivor, bound and gagged, but left alive at the site of the bonfire slaughter. If the men he left to investigate came to the conclusion that the captain suspected they would…well…then he knew he would have problems much bigger than a wandering priest and a minstrel family.

Turing in his saddle, the captain now addressed the soldier riding to his right and leading a horse with the survivor still bound and gagged sitting astride.

"I will need one hour to wash away the dust of the road. By then I will expect you to have this one prepared for my questioning. I've a feeling we have much to discuss."

The 'Cage' was made up of four walls and a roof, all constructed of heavy iron bars. It was eight feet wide by twelve feet deep, with a narrow door on the back end. Six inches separated each bar. Small containers could be passed through, but even a small child would find it impossible to slide between them. Snow, rain, sun, wind; all manner of discomfort passed easily through the bars. The only protection was a tarp that was kept handy to spread over the roof, at the discretion of the jailer. It was a simple and effective prison for all who found themselves condemned to its confines.

What made the Cage unique is that the entire structure was built onto the oversized bed of a heavy cart. The floor was an iron frame covered with planks of hickory cut two inches thick and laid in two layers sealed together with iron bolts. The cart required oversized axels to handle the weight of the cage and any prisoners inside. The wheels were reinforced, and to move the entire contraption for any distance required a team of at least four horses; six for difficult terrain.

Raymond had spent the last hour examining every joint of his new prison, much as he had the hour before…and the hour before that. Exasperated, he looked over to Hanshee who was sitting calmly at the center of one of the two wooden planks that ran the length of the cage. Somehow, he knew that Hanshee had examined the cage almost as thoroughly as he had without ever leaving his seat.

"Damn…" Raymond said under his breath as he grasped the bars with both hands and tested, for the umpteenth time, the strength of the structure. Though he rocked his body back and forth, straining the muscles in his arms and back, the cage remained completely unmoved. It was as if carved from bedrock.

"Damn!" Raymond said again, this time louder and with anger and disgust at their situation. He fell into a seated position beside Hanshee, first staring straight ahead, then turning his face toward his companion and almost willing a reaction from him.

None was forthcoming.

Raymond finally turned his head away from Hanshee with a shake and a mirthless chuckle.

"How can you remain so calm." he said, "We're caged like animals with no idea what they have planned for us."

"Calm is our greatest possession," was Hanshee's stoic reply.

Raymond was having none of it.

"You just sit there like we have nothing to worry about. You haven't even tested the strength of the bars. If you made an effort, maybe you wouldn't feel so damn calm."

"I've watched you test them," was Hanshee's reply.

Raymond could only stare at his partner, shaking his head in exasperation before launching himself from his seat and again attacking the iron bars – with the same result as before. A pair of soldiers walked by, both staring in curiosity at the robed figure throwing himself against the unyielding iron. Raymond paused in his efforts to return their stares. As they passed, he shook himself against the cage once more before again collapsing beside Hanshee.

"I don't like being behind bars…and I don't like being on display," he said.

It was now late afternoon. Neither Raymond nor Hanshee had eaten anything for two days. The soldiers had come upon them while the Menowin women were preparing breakfast the day before, and the two of them had been tied to their saddles before anyone had thought to at least get a loaf of fresh baked bread. They had been given water on the ride in, but nothing since having been placed in the cage. Their last meal had consisted of a few bites around mid-day of the day they snuck past the barricade, and both were now feeling the pangs of hunger.

Raymond was gearing up to complain about his rumbling stomach when he noticed a commotion coming from the eastern perimeter of the camp. Hanshee took notice too and both turned to watch the small company of men just arriving.

Both Raymond and Hanshee recognized them as the men the captain had left behind to investigate the two campsites. The burial detail rode in the wagon behind them. They were sitting in the wagon bed, among scavenged weapons, tools and uniforms that had belonged to the soldiers who, if the story could be believed, had fallen at the hands of the priest and his acolyte.

The entire party cast their eyes toward the cage as they passed, straining to see what it was about these two that they could lay low ten soldiers from among the ranks of Rayines' finest. The stares continued as the soldiers headed directly to the building that served as the captains' quarters. Once there, those on horses dismounted and bade the others to take the scavenged uniforms and equipment to the armory. They then knocked on, and were quickly ushered through, the captain's door, leaving Raymond wondering in frustration.

The men in the wagon continued to stare into the cage as they passed by on their way to the armory, further fueling Raymond's anxiety. Add to this the number of soldiers and civilians who had followed the cart out of curiosity, and now joined with everyone else in viewing the spectacle of the two robed prisoners, and his discomfort continued to grow.

Knowing he was powerless to stop them, Raymond finally took a seat beside Hanshee and tried to emulate his calm. Still, he found himself periodically casting brief glances at the small crowd of onlookers.

Then something caught his eye.

****

Seenio and Nola arrived at the ports of Wroughtmire mid-afternoon of their third day on the river. It was a relief. The cramped quarters on the barge, really only a corner on the first level, would have been barely tolerable for a single traveler. Having to share the space with his daughter had only added to their discomfort.

The patriarch of the Masscus clan, leader of the Guild of Assassins, barer of the legendary moniker 'The Beast', still harbored issues with Nola's dual roles as his daughter and a proven Reaper of the Guild. When questions arose in his mind, he would fall back on his position and his duty. He reminded himself that the life they now lived is the life his daughter had chosen and trained for since her earliest days. Had she not proven herself many times over, most recently in the Milkmaids Rest when, alone, she faced three stout men and laid them low?

A smile came to Seenio's face as he contemplated his daughter. Truly he had sired a warrior, a worthy addition to the Guild. The fact that this guildmember was a woman was a complication but, in the Guild of Assassins, Seenio ruled. It was his word that had allowed her to pursue her passion. He would be less than a father… less than a leader… if he treated her as anything other than what she is… a Reaper, and now a comrade-in-arms.

'You ride with a fellow of the Guild', Seenio told himself. *'A born assassin, studied in every art that is needed to uphold the legacy of the title she has sought and now holds. To treat her as anything less would be to dishonor her and the Guild.'*

This had been his frame of mind when he made the decision to bring her along on the hunt. It had not faltered until he saw her reaction to a simple lack of privacy at the hot springs. That incident had place doubts in his mind. The Milkmaids Rest had erased those doubts.

The bargemen were deft hands. Before Seenio was fully aware, the barge was tied on to a dock and a ramp was being pulled into place. Now everyone waited as Seenio and Nola gathered their belongings, saddled their horses, and without a word guided them up the ramp and onto the crowded pier. A silent sigh of relief went up from the bargemen as the pair disappeared into the crowd. When making the arrangements, Wiley had conveyed to all the danger involved in dealing with such as these two. The bargemen had been on pins and needles for the entire time they were on the river.

Seenio guided his horse through the throngs that had descended upon the docks in search of both unique fare and bargain prices. Now and then he glanced behind him to be sure that Nola had not become separated. Each time he looked she was right behind him, head high, taking in the many sights and sounds, and odors, that made a port different from anything she had ever experienced. Since Nola appeared unfazed by this new environment, The Beast now focused on his reason for being here.

Seenio's eyes were sharp as he scanned the crowd for the telltale signs of a specific type; the predator.

In almost every setting where crowds regularly gathered, there were those present whose talents and inclinations were geared toward taking advantage of any that they deemed unprepared. Their livelihood depended on their ability to scan the throng and pick out those who were strangers, inexperienced, or seemed out of place. Seenio knew that these would be the first to notice the two that he sought and so he scanned the crowd to seek them out.

Continuing through the crowd, he came upon what he sought in the form of a lone man leaning against a shabby wooden stall. Various items were on display there, but the fellow made almost no effort to entice those passing by to purchase any of his wares. Instead, he kept a keen eye on the crowd that ambled past him. Now and then a young boy or girl would break from the crowd and approach. Words would be exchanged and he would either nod his approval or scowl and send them away. Seenio paused and watched this *handler* for some time before he determined he was one to be approached. As he was about to move in the handler's direction, something else caught Seenio's eye.

Two men were working their way down a line of stalls toward where Seenio now stood, stopping at each to survey the goods before speaking briefly to the proprietor. Both were young men but that is where any similarity ended. One was of medium height with short cropped hair and a stocky build. He wore a nondescript gray tunic under a leather chest piece. The hilt of a sword could be seen above his left shoulder and he followed behind the other fellow, eyes sharp, but speaking not a word.

It was the talkative one who truly stood out.

He was half a head taller than his companion and clad in a dirty full-length robe that nevertheless seemed out of place in this throng, unless draped from the shoulders of the wealthy or the nobly born.

Or a priest.

The man moved from stall to stall, making a show of examining the merchandise before approaching the owner. He never made a purchase and by the looks on the faces of the stall owners, his true interest lay somewhere else besides the goods on display.

What cinched it for Seenio was the leather cord that hung around his neck. It supported a small dagger, likely decorative, good for nothing more than cleaning one's nails or picking one's teeth. Others may have looked upon this with a passing curiosity, but Seenio recognized it for what it was; the decorative blade that adorned the neck of every priest of The One Spirit in the nation of Pith.

Sensing what the priests' presence here could mean, Seenio pushed forward.

"Hail the morning," Seenio spoke in the Pithian tongue as he stepped in front of the stranger. The man could only stop and fix a startled stare as this fellow, who now blocked his path with a weathered smile and a knowing look in his eyes, continued. "Do you dwell in the power of The One?"

Jared now pushed forward to confront this bold stranger, but was caught by surprise when Petri placed a hand in his chest, preventing him from moving past him. Having heard the precise wording of the strangers greeting, Petri's expression now changed from one of startled surprise to cautious familiarity.

It was commonplace for believers to accost one another by asking if one dwelled in the *bosom* of The One. Sometimes *bounty, goodness, or blessings* was substituted. To be asked if one dwelled in the *power* of The One was to imply a shared familiarity with the Temple. It was a greeting common only among fellow priests, who did not feel the need to present a façade of humility when among their peers.

But this fellow, by his appearance, did not present as a priest of The One Spirit.

Broad in the shoulders and more heavily sculpted than most, he appeared to be a man accustomed to heavy and consistent physical activity; a lifestyle foreign to any priest that Petri had ever known. Yet his knowing look ignited a host of questions in Petri's mind. After another moment, Petri took the bait.

"I find your choice of greetings to be interesting but, lest I speak out of place, to whom am I now addressing myself?"

"I am called Seenio," The Beast said with a small bow of his head.

"Well, Seenio, do you present yourself as a priest of The One Spirit?"

"Oh, no," Seenio chuckled at the thought of himself as a priest. "Though I do have a certain familiarity with the Temple of The One Spirit, I stand before you as nothing more than I am; a humble servant."

Monotheism was not uncommon among the nations and peoples of the middle plains. To Petri's knowledge only the southern nations, those bordering the Great Inland Sea, recognized a pantheon of gods. Still, to reference The Temple of The One Spirit was to plant your standard squarely in the heart of Stronghold and the Nation of Pith.

"Well, Seenio, I *am* a priest of The One Spirit," Petri spoke the words with pride, "from the Temple Proper, in the Citadel of Stronghold." He drew himself up to his full height as he made this pronouncement, adopting the posture and manner of an authority figure conversing with a supplicant. "Where are you from? In what way did you serve your Temple?"

The hook was set.

"I was raised in the foothills of Strongholds Crown," Seenio began, "a farmer and a herder of the flocks, as are all of my tribe…"

"I am aware of your people; 'the wanderers'," Petri interjected. "Your forefathers claimed a special relationship with The Temple through the High Priest Cassius.

Seenio smiled broadly and again bowed his head toward the young priest, gently inflating his pride and ego.

"As a young boy I became proficient as a hunter and protector of the flocks. Later my father lent me out to a local temple in the valley, where I was taught swordsmanship by soldiers positioned with the local township. As my stature and proficiency with the sword grew, I was tasked with accompanying the priest on trips beyond the township, to provide comfort, and protection from bandits and the like. When my local priest reached an age and disposition that discouraged travel, my services were no longer needed. I became a mercenary for nobles and merchants; those within Stronghold and beyond its walls...

Seenio said this last with bowed head, as if ashamed to be a simple sword for hire. Then he quickly raised his head and added, "...but I have always been happiest offering my services to a Temple."

"Is this the work that brings you to Wroughtmire?" Petri asked.

My partner and I," Seenio motioned toward Nola, who stood apart and held the reins of the horses, "were in the employ of a wealthy merchant who we accompanied to Gunjunson for The Counting. He was wealthy, but ancient, and unfortunately did not survive the excitement. Upon his passing, his sons released us. "We are now journeying to the southern nations in hopes of finding employment among the many merchants that will soon be traveling north along the Merchant Way."

Petri took in all of what Seenio shared and appeared to be intrigued. He paused, considering something for a brief moment, then stirred from his pondering and spoke.

"It is good to know that the Temple has earned the devotion of one such as yourself. These byways can be treacherous." He gave a slight shiver as he finished speaking, picturing Tomar's disembodied head as it sat atop the canvas sack.

"If I may," Seenio said, sensing an opportunity. "If you are also journeying south, perhaps we can accompany you. No disrespect to your man…" Seenio nodded toward Jared as he said this, "but, in times such as these, a single sword is rarely sufficient."

"I am no bodyguard for a priest," Jared quickly said, probably with more disdain than was meant.

"Oh? Then allow us to travel with the two of you. Four swords present more of a challenge than two…or one," Seenio corrected himself as he considered that Petri bore no arms.

Petri opened his mouth to cry poverty, but it was as if Seenio could read his mind.

"Though we would answer to your grace, we would accept no coin. We travel along the same path, and your learned company would be a welcome respite for the two of us. If the time comes that our paths are no longer the same, then we will thank you and go our way."

Petri now considered what it would mean to have his own personal bodyguards in a camp full of hardened soldiers. Seeing Tomar's disembodied head reminded him that his companions were capable of anything. What burden would there be in adding two more swords to their party at no cost?

"It so happens that, for now, we are heading south," Petri said. "That can change. But you should be warned that Jared here is not the only sword that travels with me. Come back with us to our camp tonight. There you can meet the others and we will see if both our paths will continue to the south.

Petri did not notice Jared standing slightly behind him, staring at the back of his head with wide eyes and a slack jaw.

CHAPTER 10

Lucius and his party, the brothers Ishmed and Fevor, made their way south along the Merchant Way, taking their time and speaking a few words to anyone they came upon. Not many on the road were headed south and those who were seemed reluctant to engage with three heavily armed and unsavory looking fellows.

Around mid-morning they came upon a traveler who had camped about twenty feet off of the eastern side of the road. By the position of his wagon, he seemed to have been heading north. He eyed the three southbound travelers with suspicion when they veered off of the road and approached him.

"Good morning to you," Lucius spoke in Cantorese as he walked his horse up to what he assumed was the edge of the encampment.

"I have nothing here worth taking," the man volunteered.

Lucius could see him clearly now and saw that he was a man well past his prime. He sat on an upturned log a little distance from his fire and immediately resumed puffing on a hand carved pipe. Lucius noticed a fighting axe lying on the ground near his right hand, but the man made no motion toward it. As he continued to size up the man, Lucius noted what he now recognized as a wooden leg lying on the ground in front of him. Another glance at the wagon and the two mules that had been unhitched, and Lucius replied.

"We know better than to challenge an old soldier," Lucius said jovially.

The old man now focused his eyes on Lucius as he removed his pipe and blew a billowing cloud of smoke toward the open sky.

"Did you campaign for Rayine?" Lucius asked.

"That I did," the old man replied, "and did my time for those heathens in Cantor. They look down their noses at all other infantry, but I kept step with 'em…showed 'em a few things too."

"I would wager you did," replied Lucius, again taking time to look around the campsite. "How long have you been camped here?"

"A few days," the old man seemed to be warming up to him. "Will be here a few more; got a lame mule. Nothing a little rest won't cure. I'll be movin' on when she's ready. T'was delivering supplies to the barricade down the way."

"There be a barricade?" Lucius asked with new interest.

"South… about seven leagues," the old soldier replied. "They're stopping pilgrims and merchants and anybody going south. Had some trouble with highwaymen so His Majesty is supplying armed escorts to the southern border. T'was them I was delivering supplies for."

Lucius nodded his head in silent contemplation of this new development, then addressed the old soldier once more.

"Your camp is sparse. Do you need anything?"

"Didn't plan for more than two – three days. Ya got any biscuits?

Lucius smiled as he turned toward the pack mule. Opening a sack, he fished around for a moment before producing a small bundle containing a dozen hardtack biscuits.

"Here you are soldier. It isn't from the Kings bakers, but it should keep you for another day or two."

"Many thanks," the old soldier said, smiling for the first time. He waved his pipe in farewell as Lucius mounted up and guided his horse back toward the Merchant Way.

"Did you see?" Lucius asked his companions as he turned his horse south. "That is why you keep a good word for everyone."

With a known destination ahead, the trio made no other stops. Instead, they pushed their mounts to make it to the barricade the old soldier had spoken of. It turned out to be a bit farther than the soldier said and they arrived late in the afternoon, their horses showing the signs of having covered roughly nine leagues in less than half a day.

As they expected there were various wagons lined up behind a barricade that covered the northern end of a bridge that extended about seventy-five feet over a small river. The owners of these wagons were in a particularly foul mood and, when asked, loudly complained that no wagons had been ushered across the bridge this day. Lucius spent some time commiserating with first one then another, all the while secretly inspecting their wagons and the persons who accompanied them.

It was almost sundown when the trio decided to ride the short distance to the military encampment. They had been told of a tavern there and local taverns were always the best place to learn about the surrounding places and its people. If any here had word of this wandering priest, this *Panther*, and his acolyte, it would most likely be bandied about in a tavern.

The three had long ago dismounted and were slowly walking their spent animals toward the road that led to the military encampment, when they were forced to pull up and make way for a small procession. As they watched, they were passed by four soldiers on horseback riding two abreast, followed by a wagonload of dirty men who sat among what appeared to be a pile of digging implements, weapons of war, and discarded uniforms. This by itself was only a minor curiosity. What made it more curious was the small crowd of both military and civilians that followed in its wake.

Apparently, word of some event had gotten out and the crowd now followed behind, yelling questions to those on horseback as well as those in the wagon. The leaders of the procession sat upright in their saddles and looked straight ahead, unconcerned with those that followed in their wake. Those in the wagon tried to imitate their leaders, but their constant glances to the rear hinted at their eagerness to tell of where they had been and what they had seen.

Lucius and his companions took the opportunity to fall in among the crowd that was following the wagon and so entered the military compound without anyone taking any particular notice of them.

They followed the wagon as it passed through the heavy front gate and into an open square surrounded by barracks, stables, a blacksmith shop, an armory, and what looked like officer's quarters. On the very end was a building that seemed to stand apart from the rest. By the banner it flew Lucius guessed it to be the commander's quarters. It was there that the horsemen led the procession.

In the center of the compound, the parade ground, there stood an awkward looking cart that was best described as a prison on wheels. As the procession passed, many looked toward it. Even the stoic leaders were seen to turn their heads to examine those inside.

Busy looking over the compound, Lucius did not cast a glance at the prison until he was almost upon it. When he did, he was stopped in his tracks, causing Ishmed and Fevor to pull up short, too. Those coming up behind ran into the rear ends of the three horses and cursed their handlers as the foot traffic was forced to flow around them.

Though unfamiliar with the language, Ishmed and Fevor had a good idea of the words that accompanied the looks that were coming their way. They responded with surly glances of their own, muttering curses under their breath in the language of the tribes of the eastern Ursal Mountains, their mothers' people.

Lucius was well versed in the language of Cantor and had some familiarity with that of the nation of Rayine. Despite that, he could not hear them. Lucius could hear nothing but the pounding in his head as, between the moving heads of the people surging past him, he spied *the Panther* and his acolyte secure behind heavy bars with no way to escape.

****

"Way-mon..." Hanshee spoke his name as if making conversation and received no response. When he spoke again, though still conversational, his voice was infused with authority.

"Way-mon!"

Raymond whipped his head around, the many staring faces in the throng temporarily banished from his thoughts.

"Sit down, Way-mon."

"But Hanshee..." Ray began, "...there's..."

"Sit down, Way-mon!

The authority in Hanshee's voice again won out and Raymond found himself seated beside the young warrior, the crowd of onlookers now behind him as he turned to face him. But Raymond had seen something...something that needed to be shared, and so he searched out Hanshee's eyes and began once again.

"Hanshee, there's..."

"Did he see you?" Hanshee injected, holding Raymond's eyes with his own so he could not turn back to the crowd.

"What..." Raymond was taken completely by surprise.

Hanshee tried again.

"Does he know that you saw him?"

"You saw him too?" Raymond asked, still somewhat confused at Hanshee's apparent knowledge.

"He is the soldier whose archers stopped us on the eastern slopes of the mountains called Ursal," Hanshee responded. "He was also with those who pursued us to the ravine."

"What's he doing here?" Ray asked, still trying to make sense out of what he had seen.

"They still pursue us. Our lives, or our deaths, are important to the Pith."

"So, you think they want us dead." It was a statement

"Perhaps some among them do." Hanshee responded. "Others may wish our return. It matters not. Should we escape this prison, our way is south."

****

After being stunned by the sight of his quarry, Lucius first settled his flustered mind before leading Ishmed and Fevor forward with the rest of the crowd. They came to a stop well behind the wagons they followed, but the wagons no longer held any interest for Lucius. The trio was still surrounded by men, women and soldiers fueled by rumors, with conversations raging all around them. It was in the midst of this that Lucius huddled his cohorts together and shared what he had just seen.

Both brothers reacted with alarm, turning their bodies and stretching their necks to get a good look at the cage and its occupants.

"No, no..." Lucius grabbed them by the front of their shirts and pulled them back into a huddle.

"But they be right before us!" Fevor spat.

"We've chased 'em this far," Ishmed protested. "I'd like an up-close look at 'em."

Lucius looked each man in the eye, swinging his head back and forth between them until he was sure he had the attention of both.

"What the hell are you thinking?" He began "They are prisoners in a Rayine military camp. We don't know what they've done or why they are held. We shouldn't be here ourselves! If we just walk right up to the bars and gawk at them, we could be mistaken for their friends, or their accomplices. Once their guards question us, they would know we are of Pith. We are in Rayine! Men here hate none so much as the Pith! What do you think would happen if they found three soldiers from Pith in their midst? Where do you think we would be then?"

Lucius' words had the ring of brutal truth and so quieted the two trackers into momentary submission, allowing Lucius to continue.

"What we will do is carefully make our way back through the gate...before those in the cage lay eyes on us. They'd not know you two from a mountain goat, but they would surely recognize me. We'll find that tavern; raise a glass in celebration...and for our nerves..." Lucius smiled at the brothers, "...and think through how we will handle this situation."

CHAPTER 11

Having only the docks to canvas, Jared and Petri were the first to arrive back at the campsite with Seenio and Nola in tow. It was dusk and Jared busied himself with gathering wood and rebuilding the fire. Petri showed the two strangers to a spot near where he bedded the night before. After rummaging through their bags for a bite to eat, they all settled down and Petri began asking questions about Seenio and his experiences with the temple.

Nola sat in quiet amazement as her father wove truth and lies into stories so convincing as to delight the fledgling priest with life in the foothills and in the great valley of Stronghold, where the lesser priests toiled. But Seenio knew that his cache of stories and lies would only last so long and, by his guile, soon had the priest waxing about his own life growing up in the Temple Proper behind the high stone walls of the Citadel. Jared sat close by, tending his equipment and listening in whenever something piqued his interest.

This is how they were found when Hendric, Sergel and Blige arrived back at the camp.

Sergel was the first in, still gushing about the city of Wroughtmire, the capital of Rayine. Having grown up in the countryside and joining the military at sixteen, he had no experience with life in a big city. While Hendric had been busy canvassing the people and establishments most likely to know something about their quarry, Sergel was taking in the sights, gawking at displays of wealth and decadence, sampling the local foods and flirting with the ladies. Blige had been right beside him and together they had been more of a hindrance than a help to Hendric.

Now Sergel strode up to the fire, rubbing his hands against the chill of late winter/early spring. He thought that Blige was right behind him and so was talking nonstop until he glanced toward Petri and saw that more than the priest and Jared were in the camp.

"What the…" Sergel paused as he focused upon the two strangers. He quickly looked around for anyone else, then looked behind him for Blige or Hendric, before again turning toward the priest and asking, "who the hell are these two?"

Sergel bellowed his question loud enough to bring Blige running into the camp.

Blige pulled up beside Sergel looking around the fire and seeing no one. Then he took in his fellow soldier and followed his eyes toward the four figures sitting at the edge of the firelight.

Not wanting to be associated with what he knew was coming, Jared stood and took a lazy stretch. Then he sauntered a few feet away from Petri and his two guests, turning back to take in the expected drama.

This is how Hendric found them when he finally entered the camp; Sergel and Blige standing beside the fire and staring daggers at the three still seated about twenty feet away. Petri was staring straight back at the two with a defiant light shining in his eyes; a new look for him.

Hendric took a moment to survey the scene, and then barked at the young priest.

"Petri, who are these people?"

Upon hearing his captains voice, Petri rose to his feet in greeting. Seenio and Nola followed suit.

"Captain, I'm so glad *you're* here," Petri cast a scowling glance toward Sergel before continuing.

"Allow me to present Seenio Masscus. He is as late employed as a mercenary…uh," Petri shifted his eyes to Seenio in apology, then back to Hendric "…guarding a rich merchant at The Counting in Gunjunson. While there, he suffered the misfortune of having his benefactor die and so is available for new employment."

There was a pause after Petri finished his introduction.

"Bwaaaa, ha,ha,ha,haaaa…!" Sergel fairly exploded in laughter! "You mean…ha,ha…you mean he went and got his master killed…ha,ha,ha…and now he wants to work for us! Bwaaaa, ha,ha,haaa…!"

"He'll work for me!" Petri spat, even as Blige joined in with a belly laugh of his own.

Hendric waited until Sergel and Blige had quieted to a condescending giggle before again speaking.

"And who is that beside Seenio," he asked.

"This is Nola" Petri spoke up. She works with Seenio…uh…they work together…"

Sergel and Blige roared anew!

"Ha,ha,ha,ha…, Blige…ha,ha,ha… he was working beside a woman…ha,ha,ha…no wonder his master was croaked! Bwaaaaaaa,ha,ha,ha,ha,ha…!

Even Hendric had to suppress a giggle at the scene before him, as did Seenio himself. But the fire in Petri's eyes only flared brighter.

"He has a relationship with the Temple," Petri fairly screamed, "and he'll work for me without charge!"

Upon hearing this, the camp went silent. Then Blige spoke up.

"He works with a woman," Blige said, "but he cozies up to a priest."

Now the laughter was out of control and even Jared, still standing off to the side, struggled not to collapse onto the ground in mirth! Petri looked from one face to another, fuming, and completely frustrated with these damn…soldiers!

When the laughter began to die down Sergel again spoke up, this time directly to Seenio.

"I'll tell you what you can do," Sergel said, a huge smile creasing his face. "You work for the priest there, and I'll allow your woman to work for me, eh?" He nudged Blige, who giggled as if on command.

"And how would I work for such as you?" Nola said, as she stepped fully into the light.

"Oh, I'd find something for you to do," Sergel said, as he took in the beauty of her face. "Why, you could start tonight… keeping me warm beneath my bedroll."

Again, Blige giggled.

"My warmth is reserved for my blade," Nola said, surprising all but her father. "If you would partake of me, you must first secure *its* permission."

With this, Nola reached behind her right shoulder and slowly drew the slender blade from the sheath strapped to her back.

Sergel's eyes now grew wide with surprise and anticipation at the obvious challenge leveled at him. Blige egged him on with another round of lecherous giggling. Jared looked on in fascination, and Petri stood frozen in stunned silence.

Hendric looked from face to face, calculating when the situation was about to get out of hand; poised to step in and quash it should that time come. But, when his gaze rested on Seenio's countenance, something changed. Despite all the laughter, insults, and open disrespect directed his way, this Seenio fellow had a smile on his face as broad as Sergel's. And he was making no attempt to rein in his partner.

Maybe it was the frustration of the days search, the lack of interest or help from Sergel and Blige, or a need for some form of entertainment. For some reason he could not put to words, Hendric made a conscious decision to let this situation play out.

When Nola cleared her blade, Sergel expected to hear his captain speak up and put an end to what he surely thought was foolishness. But the moment passed with Hendric remaining silent. Taking this as consent, Sergel moved away from the fire and slowly drew his own sword. It shown in the firelight, longer, broader and heavier than the blade that graced the woman's hand, and Sergel's eyes searched her face to take in her dread when she realized what she was up against.

But he saw no awakening dread on her face; only the faint beginnings of... a smile.

Puzzled, Sergel looked to the face of her partner.

Seenio's face carried the happiest of grins and he appeared ready to find a comfortable seat from which to enjoy the festivities. Sergel again shifted his gaze to the woman, Nola, and saw that her budding smile had now reached full bloom.

Confusion now clouded Sergel's thoughts.

Could these two think that this woman...no...they couldn't believe that a woman...this woman...stood a chance against a man such as me?

Nola saw the confusion in Sergel's eyes and took this time to move away from the fire. Knowing that Sergel's eyes were again upon her, she allowed her hips to swing as she had observed with the serving girls at the Milkmaids Rest. She smiled as she saw that her movements had the expected effect on Sergel. As he continued to watch, Nola established herself and struck a fighting stance, her sword at middle guard.

Nola had much experience competing against bigger, stronger men who thought themselves superior to her. It could be said that she specialized in situations such as this. Her eyes pierced Sergel's as she released the slightest giggle from her lips; a giggle directed at the man standing before her; a giggle meant to belittle him... and goad him on.

Rushing forward, Sergel meant to quickly overcome the girl by swatting the slender sword from her grip and…

Dipping the point of her sword below his sweep, Nola raised it again as his blade passed, parrying his stoke to her right while at the same time moving diagonally forward and to her left. When in position, she dipped her blade under his arm, then quickly raised it and brought her sword arm across her body, opening a cut along Sergel's right ribcage, underneath his outstretched arm, as his momentum carried him by.

Nola's movement occurred in the blink of an eye, the speed and fluidity bringing gasps of astonishment from those assembled. Sergel seemed unaware of just what had happened until he felt a stinging mid-way up his right side. Searching his body with his left hand, he soon felt the dampness under his tunic. Pulling his hand free, he stared down on his bloodstained fingers.

Sneering in disgust, he quickly turned again to face Nola, who he found surveying him as a sculptor would a block of granite; wondering where the next cut should be applied.

Whereas before he had meant to disarm her and drag her kicking and screaming to his bedroll, now Sergel intended to draw a little blood before he took his pleasure. A shallow slice along an arm or a thigh shouldn't ruin her for his needs.

As if she could read his mind, Nola flowed into a high guard position, crouching slightly on her back leg, the ball of her left foot barely in contact with the ground, her left thigh tantalizingly exposed.

Sergel couldn't resist.

Going into a half crouch and feinting in high, Sergel dropped his blade at the last minute in an attempt to draw blood from Nola's unguarded thigh. But as he approached, Nola dropped her sword to middle guard and spun away on her right leg, where all of her weight had been placed. As Sergel struck toward her now moving left thigh, Nola again parried his thrust. She then allowed her blade to drift up the length of his, avoid his guard, and slice into his hand.

Sergel lunged backward to avoid the thrust to his torso that should have been Nola's next move, the cut to his hand disarming him of his sword which now lay in the dirt before her.

Now they faced each other from a distance of about fifteen feet, Sergel having retreated even more to ensure he was out of the immediate reach of Nola's sword. Clutching his right hand in his left, and with his right elbow glued to his side, he alternated scowling toward the woman and looking longingly at his sword lying at her feet.

Nola followed Sergel's eyes to his sword and, still smiling, stepped over it to place her body between him and his weapon. Then she flourished her own blade, the firelight reflecting on its polished surface to briefly create the illusion of a wheel of fire, before she stilled it and casually dropped it behind her. Then she stepped forward again, everything about her a taunt to Sergel as she stood before him unarmed.

Puzzled, Sergel took a step toward her and Nola dropped her arms to her side and threw back her shoulders, thrusting her chest in the soldier's direction. Sergel, not so quick now to rush in, took two more cautious steps toward her. Nola ran her tongue over her lips and pursed them at the now hesitant soldier. Upon seeing this, Sergel stepped closer, and raised his arms as if to embrace her. Nola never moved, but her smile became brighter.

Confusion covering his face, yet determined to salvage his pride, Sergel moved ever closer, his hands reaching for a prize that showed no desire but to be claimed.

Just as his hands were about to grasp her shoulders, Nola shifted slightly, leaning her torso back until just out of reach of Sergel's outstretched hands. So close to claiming his prize, Sergel leaned further in and lightly touched the shoulders that Nola, arms still hanging by her sides, made no attempt to defend. Just before he could take a firm grip, Nola dropped under his outstretched arms and lunged forward, dipping her chin toward her chest and driving the crown of her head into the center of Sergel's face.

Sergel staggered backward a few paces before falling to the ground, clutching his bleeding and broken nose in his bleeding right hand while pressing his right upper arm tight to his body in an attempt to staunch the blood leaking from his right side.

After watching him fall, Nola stepped back, stooped to retrieve her sword, then stood tall as she approached the prone figure of Sergel. There she stood, towering over him with her blade once again in hand.

"My blade wants to know," she spoke to Sergel, but loud enough for everyone to hear, "if you still have an eye for my beauty, or a need to feel my warmth?"

Sergel looked up at the young beauty standing above him, causally holding a razor-sharp blade… and he was speechless.

This did not satisfy Nola.

For the first time tonight, Nola's expression twisted into anger as she lowered the tip of her sword until it was inches from Sergel's face…

"If your eyes still see a woman fit only to fulfill your needs, perhaps I can fix that by removing…"

"That is enough!"

It was the voice of Seenio Masscus, and it froze Nola in mid thrust.

"That is, with your permission Captain?" Seenio said, shifting his gaze toward Hendric.

The question snapped Hendric out of the spectator role he had assumed during the combat. Now he stared at Seenio from across the fire as Nola stepped away from Sergel, brandished a cloth, and first wiped Sergel's blood from her forehead, then from her blade. Blige very cautiously stepped around her to help his comrade up and see to his wounds, Jared and Petri looked on in silent awe, and Seenio and Hendric continued to hold their stare. Finally, Hendric gave a strange smile and nodded his head towards Seenio.

"Quite enough," he said to Seenio, before turning to go prepare his bedroll. After a few steps Hendric turned back toward Seenio, making sure to catch his eye. "You and I will talk in the morning," he said before moving off in search of his rest.

****

Lucius, Ishmed and Fevor had been drinking in the small tavern for the better part of two hours as Lucius turned the current situation over again and again in his mind.

Lucius took pride in being good at everything he did, a trait he learned from his father. When they set out to find the warrior-priest - the Panther - he knew it would be difficult, but he knew he would succeed. Galin demanded no less.

Though attached to this small band under the command of Captain Hendric, Lucius worked for Galin. Lucius *always* worked for Galin.

Galin had raised Lucius after his own father had disappeared, and so became a father figure to him. Galin, at the request of his mother, had taken him as a boy to be his messenger and ward. He had recognized certain talents Lucius possessed, talents taught to him by his birth father, and allowed the boy to hone them through training. When Lucius was of age, Galin brought him into the military at the lowest rank and demanded twice as much from him before he would consider a promotion of any kind. Still Lucius had earned his way to the rank of sergeant in the Second Expeditionary Force fairly quickly. He could have risen much higher, but Galin valued his special skills to a great degree and figured Lucius would be most valuable without the added responsibility, and visibility, of command.

Galin brought Lucius in as his personal assistant at the rank of sergeant. But, though merely a sergeant, it was understood that Lucius answered to none below the Council of Seven and in truth only to Galin.

Galin had made sure to attach him to the pursuit, and Lucius knew what Galin expected of him.

No one else outside of the Temple knew of the arrangement between the Lord High Priest Mayhew and Lord Commander Galin. The current plan had been executed with layers of operatives available to both ensure success and serve as scapegoats. The first layer, Maleek, Felton, and Tomar, had botched their chance. Still fortune had smiled when the Panther had killed two of the three. Of course, fortune was not completely benevolent and Lucius had to end Tomar's life. This had always been the plan, as Tomar could have indirectly pointed back to Galin.

He never saw it coming.

It was why Lucius was here.

Layers of operatives.

Lucius recognized Sergel and Blige as another layer. Since the mishap at the ravine, he had planned, without their knowledge, to put them in the right position, at the right time, to try their hand at ending the Panther. If they succeeded, Lucius would instantly kill them in retaliation for their slaying the Harbinger of the Fourth Prophecy. If, like so many others, they were to fail, then it would fall to Lucius to carry out the assassination.

No matter the cost.

Now Lucius found himself in the den of his enemy, a Rayine military camp near the foothills of the western Ursal Mountains, with two trackers from the frontier who knew nothing of what was really going on, and with the Panther delivered right into his reach.

Five hundred feet away.

Locked in an unbreakable iron cage.

No means of escape.

Lucius didn't know how they came to be there or how long they would remain. What he did know was that an opportunity now sat before him that he had never thought possible. His quarry had no way to run and no way to strike back. Lucius had simply to walk up to the cage, kill the panther, and walk away.

It was as simple as that.

But of course, it was never as simple as that.

The Rayine were the only nation that hated the Pith more than the nation of Cantor. This was partly because they felt the Pith, the last people to rise to power in this region, accomplished their ascendance on the backs of the Rayine.

The Rayine saw the beginning of their decline as a true power among the plains nations as having begun when the Pith were forced to migrated from the Blue Towers far to the west, east along the Southern Plateau, and north into Stronghold. Of course, the Shifting of the Earth that accompanied the last great battle of Stronghold, what the Pith refer to as 'The Miracle at Stronghold', is what changed the landscape of the plains and most probably brought about the expansion of the Great Desert. This expansion proved to be a slow death to the richest farmlands on the plains, destroying the basis of the economy of Rayine.

The Rayine blamed the Pith for this too because…why not?

Another basis for the Rayine hatred of the Pith was the embarrassing defeat the Rayine military suffered at the hands of the tribes of the Ursal Mountains, trained and aligned with the armies of Pith. History recorded it as a slaughter, and only the timely intervention of Cantor saved the Rayine from falling completely to the heathens and their allies from Pith. Since that time the Rayine have existed under the thumb of Cantor, an indignity born of need as, should Cantor withdraw their support, the Rayine would be in a fight for their existence with those half naked savages to their east.

So now, Lucius sat in the stronghold of his most hated enemy, with two brothers descended from those 'half naked savages' that the Rayine also hated and feared, and with a golden opportunity to serve his Commander and reinforce Galin's undying gratitude and respect. That opportunity was sitting in the middle of a walled encampment of Rayine military, at least fifty strong and growing by the day.

Lucius knew he was going to try.

He had too.

"Fevor," Lucius turned to the youngest of the brothers. "I'm sending you back for the others…tonight. Don't kill your horse, but get there as fast as you can. Tell them what we've found down here and lead them back.

Fever, having discovered Rayine wine, and consumed enough to call into question his ability to ride, simply looked at Lucius with bloodshot eyes and nodded his head.

"Ishmed and I will stay here and remain watchful until you return. If the prisoners are moved, we will follow and leave sign for you. But you must hurry. We do not know if the Rayine are planning to execute them."

Fevor again nodded his head in agreement, but didn't move.

When Lucius showed the first signs of losing his patience, Ishmed spoke up.

"I'll make the ride Lucius," he said. "My horse is faster and Fevor ain't in no shape to go. Look at 'em."

Before Lucius could object, Ishmed pushed himself up from the table.

"I'll get there before dawn. We should be back at the suns peak."

Lucius watched as Ishmed made his way out of the small tavern. The horses were tied up a short distance away and it should not be long before the elder brother would be sitting a saddle and guiding his mount north on the Merchant Way.

All's the better, thought Lucius. Now he could get down to his real work.

CHAPTER 12

Lucius had been waiting in the darkness between the two barracks for almost an hour; enough time for him to observe the positioning and timing of the guards as they made their rotations atop the wall walks of the military enclosure.

The fort had been built to provide a base from which the military of Rayine could patrol the portion of the Merchant Way stretching from the Wroughtmire Road to its southern border. This section of road was nestled at the base of the western slopes of the Ursal Mountains which had historically provided perfect terrain for launching attacks on the rich merchants that used the road, and for evading any resulting pursuit. Staffed by a skeleton force during the winter months, postings here began a steady increase with the spring thaw until their peak in late summer. Carrying a full complement of soldiers until well after the fall harvest, the detail was again paired back to its minimum before the first snow.

A little more time and Lucius felt he would be comfortable having marked each of the guards and their positioning at any given time. While he waited, Lucius went over in his mind all that had occurred since Ishmed started north to retrieve the others.

Fevor had already had an abundance of strong wine, still Lucius had another urn brought over. With his encouragement,

Fevor drank almost every drop in celebration of their good fortune of finally finding the escapees. When Hendric and the others arrived, it should only be a matter of presenting to the soldiers that they had been on the trail of these wanted men for many days and were ready to take possession and return them to face their punishment. After that their only concern would be how they would spend their gold!

This was the tale Lucius spun for the young tracker, and they enjoyed many a toast to the riches they were now poised to claim. Caught up in joy at the prospect of gaining his portion of the riches, Fevor drank with gusto, never noticing that Lucius led every toast with a cup that was near empty. When the urn too was finally empty, the pair staggered out of the tavern to find a campsite and get some rest.

They walked under a nearly full moon as Lucius led Fevor deep into the adjoining woods to find a suitable place to sleep, but Fevor's condition made it difficult. Several times Lucius had to steady Fevor over obstacles, sometimes lifting him to his feet after he had stumbled and fallen. Eventually Lucius found a good spot and he helped Fevor lay his bedroll and bid him to lie down and rest while he gathered wood for a night fire.

When Lucius returned a short time later with wood, Fevor was sound asleep.

Lucius was careful as he slowly rolled Fevor off of his bedding and onto the forest floor, watching the young tracker who, although moving slightly due to being disturbed, still appeared deep in sleep. Lucius briefly wondered how long Fevor could be trusted to sleep, then decided he could not take the chance. Glancing once more at Fevor, Lucius quietly walked over to his saddle and returned with his hand axe.

Fevor barely twitched when Lucius brought the axe down on his exposed throat. The sharp heavy blade severed muscles, windpipe and blood vessels before lodging in the vertebrae of his neck. Lucius had to brace his hand against Fevor's face to gain the leverage to work it free. After cleaning his axe, Lucius remade Fevor's bedroll and tied it back on his saddle. As if an afterthought, he searched Fevor's corpse and found a small pouch containing a few silver coins. Lucius added these to his own purse and made sure to drop the now empty purse close enough to Fevor's body to be easily found. Then he found a young pine branch and swept the area of any prints of horse or man. Satisfied with his work, he headed back to the fort.

Lucius had approached the fort from its western side, opposite the main gate. Choosing his place carefully, he unfurled a length of rope and a leather covered grapple which he used to scale the walls where he believed the barracks to be.

Once on the inside Lucius stayed to the shadows, picking his way until he had an unfettered view of the cage still resting in the parade yard. From this spot, he could just make out the bundled figures sleeping in its confines, and the lone guard who sat the wagon seat as if expecting to take the reins of horses that had yet to be led out and harnessed. With his shoulders bundled in a heavy cloak, the guard leaned over the pot of hot coals between his feet to further ward off the chill of the night.

Having confirmed that the wagon remained where he had seen it in the daylight, and that a single soldier was on guard there, Lucius left his hiding place to locate the nearest latrine. Afterward he crept back to the shadows to watch the rotation of the guards.

****

Lucius' reminiscence was cut short as he noticed the stirring of the guard who sat upon the wagon.

Watching closely, he saw the soldier stand and stretch before stiffly descending to the hard packed earth on which the prison wagon sat. By the time the soldier had made it to the ground and stretched again, Lucius was in position and ready. He noticed how the soldier walked as he moved away from the wagon; stiff from the cold, but also with a noticeable limp that favored his left leg. He walked with his head down as if still half asleep, looking more at the ground than ahead of him, and trusting his nose to lead him to the latrines.

Entering the shadows, the guard moved carefully in the darkness between the two barracks until he reached his destination. He thought to reach for the bit of leather used to pull open the door, but found that his arm wouldn't move. As his knees buckled and his body collapsed, he was caught by Lucius, who first pulled the slim blade from the back of his skull before dragging him further into the shadows.

When the guard reemerged from between the barracks, nothing about him had changed. He still hung his head and half limped-half shuffled toward the prison wagon, the heavy cloak still pulled tightly about his shoulders. Lucius knew that the three guards atop the wall walk were too far away to judge him a different man. As long as he kept this ruse, he could move about freely.

That was his plan; simply walk up to the Panther and his acolyte, stab him with the quill attached to the end of a foot long hollow rod, and squeeze the bladder at the other end. The poison would do its work quickly and the warrior priest would probably never awaken. Although it wasn't ordered, he would do the same to the acolyte. He judged he had more than enough poison for both. After the killing, he would take the guards seat atop the wagon and wait. When a suitable amount of time had passed, two to three hours, he would again shuffle off to the latrine, but his time he wouldn't return. Instead, he would shed the uniform and go back over the wall.

When he reached the wagon, Lucius moved along the cage, presumably to check the prisoners; in actuality, to identify the Panther.

But as he approached, something appeared amiss.

His inspection found only one bundle of blankets, covering what was surely not big enough to be more than one man. Thankfully the blankets lay close to the heavy bars and it was an easy thing to reach through and pull them back from the end he took to be the prisoner's head. To his surprise, a bearded, long haired, fair skinned man looked up at him with equal parts surprise and annoyance.

Lucius stood there with his mouth agape, tearing his eyes away to search the interior of the cage and coming back again to the only man confined there. Once he realized nothing was expected of him, the strange man snatched the blanket back over his head and settled back in to try to find sleep on the hard cold planks of the cage.

Lucius now stood before the cage, trapped in a situation he had not prepared for. The Panther and his acolyte were gone! And here he stood, in the middle of the parade ground of the camp of his enemy, disguised as one of them and with the tools of assassination on his person. Coolly, Lucius left the side of the unknown prisoner and climbed into the seat of the wagon. Pulling the cloak tighter around his shoulders, he leaned in and allowed the heat from the coals between his feet to rise up to his outstretched hands.

Nothing has changed, he thought. *Another hour, maybe two, and I'll again visit that latrine.*

****

It had been only minutes after Hanshee and Raymond watched Lucius and his two companions leave, that a company of cavalry arrived and dispersed the reminder of the crowd. Once this was accomplished the sergeant in charge approached the cage with a key dangling from his hand.

"Which of you speaks Cantorese," he said as he looked from one to the other.

"I translate for my master," Raymond said, slipping again into the role of acolyte to the 'wandering priest' Hanshee.

"Tell your master the captain is waiting to speak to you," he said as he moved his horse up next to the door and unlocked it. Raymond spoke to Hanshee in his native tongue even as he stepped forward with his arms extended and his wrists pressed together.

"There'll be no need for that," the sergeant said as he replaced the key on a loop at his waist.

Raymond turned to look at Hanshee with an expression of curious satisfaction before bowing his head to get through the door and jumping down from the cage. Hanshee soon followed and the two were ushered by the sergeant toward the captain's quarters. At the door the sergeant gave a quick knock, then entered without waiting for permission.

The trio found themselves in a medium sized room that covered the width of the building, but not the depth. In it was a table large enough to have eleven chairs around it, all of which were empty. The table and chairs were the only furniture in the room, but there was another portal; a door situated at the back of the room. It remained closed.

Raymond was expecting to be told to take a seat, but the offer was never extended and he and Hanshee, along with the sergeant, stood in silence for what seemed an unusually long time. An actuality, it was only two or three minutes before there was another knock on the door and another soldier entered. This soldier was escorting Delno Menowin.

Delno's face lit up when he saw Hanshee and Raymond again. Raymond smiled in response and gave a slight nod in Delno's direction, but no words were spoken until the door at the far side of the room swung open and the captain, who had captured them four leagues south of the barricade, entered. The captain was followed by two junior officers and another sergeant who had in tow the renegade soldier that Hanshee had left bound, but alive, at the scene of the battle beside the rocks. Raymond noticed that the renegade remained bound.

Once everyone was in the room and both doors were closed, the captain spoke.

"My lieutenants," he motioned to the first two men to follow him in, "have made a thorough search of both massacre sites, including examining all the bodies. It seems the farmers were all killed with edged weapons, similar to those carries by our soldiers and retrieved from the second massacre site. In contrast, seven of the ten bodies left at the second site were slain by arrows. These seven were found close to the remains of the bonfire. There were two more bodies found close to a small campsite nearer the road. They were killed by an edged weapon, but not one as large or heavy as our short swords and hand axes. A tenth body, found between the two fires, bore the marks of short swords, and an arrow wound to the knee."

The captain finished speaking and turned to his lieutenants.

"Did I recite your findings correctly?" he asked.

"Yes, my Captain."

"Yes, M'lord Captain"

"Good," the captain replied before again turning to the three lined up in front of him.

"I tell you this because their findings are exactly as you two," he motioned to Delno and Raymond, "told me it would be."

The captain looked again from one to the other and back.

"I should still take your heads," he calmly stated.

Raymond saw the blood drain from Delno's face as they looked at one another. He was sure the same could be said about him only his darker complexion would make it harder to see. Hanshee remained stoic, guessing that some threat had been made but unwilling to respond to what he didn't understand.

The captain continued.

"While my lieutenants were investigating the scenes of both massacres, I was having a conversation with this …soldier…" he spat the word, "that was left behind."

As he spoke the captain turned and stepped in a leisurely fashion toward the soldier in question, whose bearded face contorted in ever increasing fear as the captain moved closer. When he stood before the soldier, the captain whipped around, turning his back to him, and continued.

"It took some…coaxing, but he was persuaded to tell the entire story, even to where in the woods south of this camp they have hidden the stolen goods, wagons, and animals."

The captain smiled in satisfaction as he related this information, before once again leveling a hard stare at his three prisoners.

"I should still hang you," he said, "for the admitted peacetime killing of soldiers of the Rayine military, regardless of their crimes."

By this time Delno was dripping sweat, his breathing ragged and heavy. Still, he cleared his throat in preparation of launching a defense of himself and the men who had saved his family. The captains raised hand stopped him before he could start.

"There is one more piece of information I have that weighs on your fates, the captain said, turning on his heel and going back through the door from which he had entered. He returned almost instantly with two pouches in his hand; one of leather and one of heavy canvas. Hanshee and Raymond recognized the pouches as theirs and looked to the captain as he laid them on the table. Opening the canvas pouch, the captain pulled forth two scrolls and placed them side by side on the table. He then stared daggers into Raymond before making his demand.

"Tell me how you came into possession of these?"

A long silence filled the room as Raymond searched his mind for what to say; the correct way to handle this potentially touchy situation. He looked to Delno who had never laid eyes on the scrolls before; his panic almost an odor leaking off of him. He turned to Hanshee who he knew was unable to respond in the captain's tongue. But Hanshee seemed to know what was needed. He reached out his hand and placed it on Raymond's forearm, his grip conveying confidence and strength. Raymond looked to Hanshee's grip on his arm, then to Hanshee's face; the set of his jaw and the light in his eyes. He watched as Hanshee gave a slow nod and, as one, they turned their faces and their eyes toward the captain.

"Captain, your question tells me that you recognize what those are, and their meaning." Raymond found himself saying. "If you truly don't, then I will speak it now so that none here will be in doubt."

Ray felt emboldened as he stepped up to the table and picked up a scroll. Without untying it he held it aloft, displaying the royal seal for all in the room to see.

"This is the seal of King Moton IX, Ruler of Cantor, he who sits upon the Granite Throne in his capital of Gunjunson." He continued to hold the scroll aloft as he moved it before the face of every man present, even the prisoner.

"If you have opened these scrolls, you know that they mention my master and I by name... and guarantee our unobstructed passage under any flag that claims itself an ally of Cantor. If you had stood in the Kings Chambers, witnessed his carriage and heard his words, as have we," Raymond motioned to Hanshee and himself, "you would know that it is our safety and not our deaths that should be of the utmost importance to you."

Raymond met the captain's hard gaze the entire time that he spoke and now braced himself for the arrogant rage he fully expected to pour down upon them. Thus, he was truly surprised when the captain burst into laughter.

By the looks around the room, Ray wasn't the only one surprised. The two lieutenants wore puzzled expressions,

expressions mirrored on the faces of the sergeants and even the prisoner. After a moment, the captain regained his composure and addressed the room.

"After hearing heroic stories of battle, where two 'wandering priests' rallied a merchant family to stand their ground and defend themselves against hardened soldiers bent on thievery, rape and murder; stories of bonfires that raged as if from the pits of hell, and death that flew from the dark, striking down all who would lay siege to the wholesome and good…heh, heh… after hearing this story…and then finding these scrolls of passage from King Moton himself… I wondered if the silent priest and his soft-spoken acolyte could possibly be the men at the center of such a storm."

The captain again took the time to enjoy a laugh and this time his soldiers tentatively joined in.

"Warrior priests such as your master and yourself should never walk too softly," the captain now said between chuckles, "lest someone else appear and claim credit for your feats of daring."

Now it dawned on Raymond.

The captain had doubted that he and Hanshee could be the heroes at the center of the tales spun by the merchant, much less be worthy of personal letters of transit from King Moton himself. The captain had needed proof to assure him that a decision to release them was merited. By his boldness in the face of possible death, Raymond had just provided it.

****

That night Hanshee and Raymond stood in a pasture south of the Rayine Fort and bid the Menowin clan goodbye. Delno and his family were sad to part with the priest and his acolyte, who had become such good friends in such a short period, and who stepped in to save them when they were so close to death.

Upon their return to camp the Menowin family looked forward to continuing their journey south with their new friends as traveling companions and guests. It was at Hanshee's insistence that Ray explained their current situation. After being told of the numerous assassination attempts, their eventual escape, and of spying one of their pursuers at the Rayine camp, the Menowin more than understood the necessity of their leaving immediately and riding alone.

There were plenty of hugs, plenty of tears, and plenty of food, as Delno's wife, Valda, had insisted on making a special meal to celebrate their release from the custody of the Rayine.

And she made sure there was enough to pack a bundle for each of them to carry when they finally waved goodbye.

CHAPTER 13

Ishmed arrived at the campsite a few hours before dawn. His horse was exhausted, as was he, but the importance of his ride had been impressed upon him by Lucius and he had pushed himself and his mount as hard as he dared.

The fire had long since burned down to coals and embers when Ishmed staggered into the clearing and dropped down beside it. He felt the much-needed warmth on his face and hands begin to radiate into other parts of his body, and thought he would just sit here for a while and recuperate while deciding on the best way to alert the camp. The sound of movement over his right shoulder told him that his approach had awakened someone, removing the decision from his hands.

Hendric yawned and stretched from his sitting position atop his bedding. Always a light sleeper, he had heard the hoof beats of a horse as it drew close. He wasn't surprised to see Ishmed enter the camp. It would have been foolish for a stranger to ride so close then simply walk into an unfamiliar camp. The fact that he was alone heightened Hendric's curiosity, leading him to leave his bed and join Ishmed beside the remains of the fire.

"Report," said Hendric as he stood above the young tracker/scout of the southeast Ursal Mountains.

"We've found them," Ishmed said.

Hendric stood in stunned silence, his mind taking in what he was just told and waiting to see if Ishmed had more to add.

"Wha…what did he just say?"

It was Jared who spoke up from the other side of the clearing. He too slept light.

Hendric watched as other blankets around the clearing began to move and one by one, the members of the pursuit that he led came awake yawning, stretching, and blinking as they took in the dim figures that surrounded the pile of burning embers in the center of the clearing.

Hendric reached for the pile of firewood and, taking hold of a long branch, stirred the coals until a small flame erupted. He added more wood to the fire until he had a blaze strong enough to make Ishmed back up a few feet, then he spoke so that all could hear.

"Ishmed has returned, and brings word that the escapees have been found."

This pronouncement set the camp to buzzing and caused Hendric to raise his voice to be heard.

"Quiet down! Let Ishmed speak so we know how things stand."

Turning to Ishmed, Hendric continued.

"Spill it, man. Where were they found?"

Ishmed, who was taking a drink from his water skin while Hendric was addressing the camp, wiped his mouth and looked up at his captain.

"The Rayine have 'em," he said. "They sit in'a iron cage in the middle of the Rayine fort, 'bout nine leagues to the south."

This revelation took everyone by surprise and they all stared at Ishmed as if doubting what he had said.

"The Rayine have them?" Hendric found himself repeating the news as a question, his words ripe with all the implications. "For what cause do the Rayine hold them?"

"There was no time for questions, captain, nor anyone we could ask. There were rumors of missing soldiers of Rayine, some thought them killed, but those stories were heard from passersby. I can't say if they involved the escapees."

"Well," Hendric said, "if they be prisoners of the Rayine, they'll lead us on no further chases. But not knowing the reason for their capture means guessing at their fate. They could be imprisoned, set free, or hung before we get there." He looked around at the motley collection of soldiers, mercenaries, and clerics that he now led.

"Gather your bedrolls." Hendric said. "I want to be half the way to this fort when the sun rises.

Come sunrise the group had put four leagues between themselves and their previous camp. Ishmed had the lead, sitting astride the horse once used by Tomar. Though still exhausted, his experience as a tracker and scout meant that he was accustomed to long, arduous rides. A fresh horse meant that he did not have to walk his tired mare the entire distance back. She was being led by a rope attached to the two pack mules and guided by Jared who brought up the rear. Between Ishmed and Jared were Hendric, Blige, Sergel, Petri, Seenio, and Nola, in that order.

That was how the journey had started out.

Now Hendric looked back over his shoulder and into the face of Petri, followed closely by his 'personal guard' of Seenio and Nola. Searching beyond them, Hendric saw that Blige and Sergel had fallen back to ride beside Jared and the three of them were beginning to lag some distance behind the rest.

"Keep the pace," Hendric barked at Ishmed as he pulled his horse from behind Ishmed and loped back toward the three stragglers.

Sergel and Blige rode on either side of Jared, both men leaning from their saddles toward the man sandwiched between them. Someone was doing a lot of talking but, as Hendric pulled closer, the two sat up straight in their saddles and kept a still tongue. Hendric brought his horse in beside them and matched their pace.

Now they rode together in silence, the three soldiers looking straight ahead, making a point of avoiding the gaze of their captain. Finally, Sergel could take it no longer and chanced a glance to his left.

Hendric's smiling face greeted him.

"Reliving your epic battle before last nights' fire?" Hendric teased.

"Huuagh," Sergel grunted in disdain while Blige and Jared snickered and giggled.

Sergel cut his eyes toward his companions, who made a show of trying to contain their mirth. Another period of riding in silence passed before Sergel could take no more.

"Damn it," he spat, "I was trying not to injure her!"

"*She* said the same about *you*," Hendric shot back, his smile growing even wider as Jared and Blige again erupted in quiet laughter. Sergel wheeled on them.

"You don't think I could best a girl?" he challenged.

"Not that one," said Jared, and now he and Blige burst into open laughter.

Sergel set his jaw and stared daggers at his companions, then looked ahead to see Seenio and Nola looking back their way. Mumbling curses under his breath, Sergel held his head down and attempted to ride on in silence.

But he couldn't.

"So now we have two more riding pursuit with us." Sergel said quietly to the air. "And now we must split the gold between two more."

That got a reaction from Blige and Jared, and not one of laughter.

Jared looked past Sergel to catch the eye of Hendric.

"Is it true, Captain?" he asked in half-whisper. "Does anyone who saunters into our camp get to share in the gold?"

"I've not said such," Hendric snapped at Jared while staring at Sergel. "They know nothing of the gold."

"But how long will it be before they find out?" Jared pressed. What will you tell us then?"

"Are you to tell them?" Hendric asked in annoyance.

"Mayhap Petri already has." It was Blige's contribution to the conversation. Both Sergel and Jared turned to consider him, while Hendric considered the words he had just heard.

Hendric didn't think that Petri would divulge any information about the gold to two strangers he had just met, despite their supposed connection to the Temple. Still, the words had been spoken, seeds had been planted, and doubt had been sewn.

Hendric left the three soldiers and trotted his horse toward Petri and his new friends.

"Petri," Hendric hailed as he pulled up alongside the young priest. "You ride at the convenience of His Majesty Ammon IV and under my command. What right have you to commission additional swords to join us? What did you offer in return for their service?"

"Captain," Seenio began, "We…"

"I question a member of my command, sir!" Hendric cut him off. "I will thank you to hold your tongue until such time as I grant you leave to speak!"

"As you say, Captain," Seenio said with a nod and a smile, holding his tongue as Hendric waited for Petri's response.

Petri was taken aback by the tone of Hendric's questioning, especially this early in the morning. Had he still labored under Jusaan, this demeanor would be expected, but Hendric had shown himself to be a different sort; as open to a jest as the next soldier and, in any case, having few words for Petri.

"M'lord Captain," Petri began, "I believe that the events of last night cast a cloud of confusion over our…arrangement." He motioned toward Seenio who had spurred his horse forward so he could ride on Petri's right.

"Well, perhaps you can take this time to bring an end my confusion," Hendric replied.

"M'lord Captain," Petri continued, "I did not mean to imply that you were confused, I simply…"

Hendric's upheld hand put an end to Petri's ramblings.

Now Hendric looked past Petri to Seenio who, though riding on Petri's opposite side, and being the topic of discussion, sported a look of complete disinterest as he pretended to survey the tops of the trees that bordered the Merchant Way. Nola was thoroughly entertained as she watched the three men interact in front of her.

"Seenio? Is that your name, 'Seenio'?" Hendric spoke up.

Seenio continued to chart the flight of the birds for a moment longer before turning a smiling face to Hendric and replying.

"Yes, it is, Captain," he said, "and my partner is called 'Nola'."

"Your partner," Hendric asked, "not your woman?"

"Never my woman," Insisted Seenio

Hendric pursed his lips before continuing.

"Well, Seenio, perhaps you can tell me what arrangements you have made with one under my command that finds you now riding in my company?"

"I am a countryman, of sorts, Captain," Seenio began. "My people claim the highlands beneath the Crown of Stronghold, land set aside for us many centuries ago by the great High Priest Cassius.

"Your people are farmers, and herders," Hendric injected, "renown for the quality of the wool your sheep produce."

"This is true," said Seenio, "but we are also hunters and, long ago, warriors. And due to the benevolence of the then High

Priest, we enjoy what we consider to be a unique relationship with the Temple."

"In what way?" queried Hendric.

"We renounced deference of the gods we once knew for the proven goodness of The One Spirit. For centuries we have considered the priests of the Temple to be our partners in survival. We sent, and send, our young to be taught in the many temples of Stronghold valley. After completing their educations, many chose to stay, and served in several different capacities. Some have even risen to the priesthood."

"When I saw Priest Petri on the docks of Wroughtmire, I immediately noticed his medallion; the dangling blade that marked him as a priest of The One Spirit. Of course, I approached him to pay my respects and in conversation learned that we were both traveling south along the Merchant Way. Nola and I are traveling to the nations of the Great Inland Sea, where we hope to continue providing our swords to merchants traveling north. We simply offered to ride with his eminence and provide for his security until our paths no longer run together."

"I see," said Hendric. "And what were you promised for your services?"

"If a price were agreed upon," said Seenio pointedly, "it would be between Priest Petri and ourselves. However, it is as he told all last night; there is no charge for our services to him. It is our statement of devotion to the Temple, as well as a matter of practicality, to accompany the priest where so many bandits and highwaymen are rumored to roam."

Hendric leveled a steady gaze at Seenio and received one in return. Then he looked to Petri, who smiled and nodded his agreement to every word Seenio had spoken. Lastly, he turned and looked to Nola, who had been listening intently to all that was said between the three.

"It is rare to find a woman who handles herself so well," Hendric said with a slight bow of his head. "How did you come to learn the sword?"

"In my land, my father is a great leader and war chief," Nola explained in a husky feminine voice. "Though I be a woman, he saw that my training was both thorough and relentless." She spoke with the fire of her pride ablaze in her eyes.

Hendric nodded his head in appreciation before turning to look further behind them.

"Break from your damned gossip and bring your mounts up into formation!" he yelled back to the trio of stragglers.

Hendric's band arrived at the barricade late in the morning.

The line of wagons waiting to cross the bridge was bustling now. With no movement the day before, everyone was excited to learn that a full complement of troops was available to take the next group to the southern border. All of the twenty-plus wagons in line were to be ready to depart by the noon hour.

Ishmed led the band southwest along the river toward the Rayine fortification. Hendric rode beside him, scanning ahead for any soldiers they may encounter along the way. Since Hendric had demanded that Petri conceal his medallion, none of them were showing clothing or trinkets that would mark them as Pithian. Still Hendric felt uneasy to be so deep within the land of a rival nation and so close to a garrison. After it was discovered that Seenio possessed a talent for language, speaking fluent Cantorese and Rayine without an accent, it was decided that he would assume the role of leader if they were questioned by the local authorities. Thus, he rode beside Ishmed and Hendric.

They came upon the tavern, situated as it was within an arrows flight of the gates of the fort, and Lucius was there waiting for them. He was sitting on a stump on the eastern side of the building, a perfect spot to watch for their approach. Slumped over like he was, he resembled an inconspicuous drunk still recovering from the night before. Upon seeing the approach of his companions, he slowly arose from his seat, stretched, and sauntered toward the rear of the tavern as if looking for a place to relieve himself.

Hendric noticed this and spoke low, but in a voice that all could hear.

"We are travelers, weary from the road," he reminded them. "Refresh yourselves," he nodded toward the tavern, "but keep apart from all others. Ishmed…come with me."

Hendric turned his horse toward the rear of the tavern with Ishmed close behind him. Lucius waited there and held the horse's bridle as Hendric dismounted.

"Ishmed tells us the Rayine hold the escapees," Hendric said as he dismounted, glancing toward Ishmed as he said *escapees.* "Can you take me to them?"

"They've been released, Captain," Lucius said.

Hendric's eyes went wide.

"When? What happened? Are they near still? The questions came pouring out of him at the unexpected news.

"I can't say when, Captain. Ishmed, Fevor and I spied them in an iron cage in the fort's center well after the sun peaked yesterday. We then came back to the tavern to plan. It was after sundown when I sent Ishmed to bring you here. Fevor and I were to keep an eye on them until you arrived."

"Where's Fevor," Ishmed asked.

"I don't know," Lucius said, his voice now filled with confusion. "He was drinking a good bit last evening…you saw that…and when I woke this morning, he was gone. I went to check on the prisoners and they were gone too."

"Damn, damn, DAMN!" Hendric barked in frustration, but quickly regained his composure. "We need to know if they are still in the camp or moving on to the south."

"And we gotta find Fevor, Captain," Ishmed said, clearly irritated that the captain didn't mention his brother.

"Of course, Ishmed," Hendric said. "But we must move quickly. Lucius, you've boasted of your skills. We must know what happened to the escapees. The rest of us will scour the area for Fevor. If he drank as much as you say, he may have just fallen over a log and passed out."

Turning to Ishmed, Hendric continued.

"Ishmed, you've ridden twenty leagues on two horses in two days without sleep. You should rest while we search."

"I'll be searchin' for Fevor, Captain," Ishmed flatly stated.

"Fine," Hendric said before turning again to Lucius. "The moment you learn of their fate, you find me, understand?"

"Yes, Captain."

Of those tasked to look for Fevor, only Hendric and Petri spoke Cantorese, the second language of Rayine. Seenio and Nola were an exception, but they knew nothing of Fevor and, regardless, would not leave Petri's side. Accordingly, they split into two groups; Petri and his newfound guard, and Hendric with everyone else except Ishmed, who preferred to search alone. Hendric's orders to those following him were to look with their eyes only. If words need be spoken, he would speak them. It was understood that Petri's group would follow his lead.

After several hours of searching the two groups met back at the tavern with no one having a clue to Fevor's whereabouts. Not long afterward Lucius arrived with news.

"The escapees were released as heroes," Lucius said to unbelieving ears. "They engaged bandits disguised as Rayine soldiers, saving the lives of many travelers."

"That's a lie," Blige blurted out. "Escaped prisoners don't do such things." He looked around the group for support and was puzzled to see only Blige nodding in agreement. Jared looked confused, but no one else was incredulous. Hendric held Lucius' eyes while Petri looked at his boots. The two that rode with Petri, Seenio and Nola, simply exchanged knowing looks.

Before anyone else could protest, Hendric spoke up.

"Then they are still southbound," he said with surety, "and maybe a full day ahead of us."

"Wait," Blige said. "You don't believe…"

"Do you have better information? Hendric turned on him with a fury. "If so, Speak It!"

Eyes wide with surprise, Blige wilted back into silence.

Hendric now addressed the rest of the group.

"Does anyone here have better information than we've just heard from Lucius?" His eyes roamed from face to face. "Well?"

When no one spoke up Hendric allowed himself a measure of calm.

"Good," he said. "All we need do now is mount up and move our arse's south."

"Where is Ishmed," Petri asked of no one in particular.

Hendric again swiveled his head and cursed under his breath. He was so excited by the news, and in such a rush to catch up to the Harbinger, he had forgotten about the search for Fevor. But even as he took a second look around, he saw Ishmed make his way out of the woods behind the tavern.

Ishmed cut a truly haggard figure with what appeared to be sorrow heaped upon exhaustion. He made his way up to the group with his head hanging and his feet scraping along the ground. When he reached them, he stood there, looking through drooping lids at the eyes that surrounded him…asking of him the unspoken question.

"I found 'em," Ishmed finally said in a hoarse whisper that everyone heard. "They robbed and killed 'em," Ishmed continued. "He didn't have much…but they robbed 'em…and damn near cut off his head!"

Hendric rushed forward and wrapped his arms around the tracker who appeared to be on the edge of hysteria. He held on for what seemed like a while until Ishmed showed signs of regaining his composure. Then, holding him at arm's length, the captain looked him in the eyes.

"Ishmed," Hendric said, "we feel for you and your brother, but we must be in pursuit of the two escapees. We must continue on the road south."

"Well, you go then!" Ishmed said, tearing himself free of Hendric's grasp and on the verge of sobbing uncontrollably. "You just go... but I'll not be comin' 'til I see Fevor into the ground!"

Hendric was stunned. He knew he would need his one remaining tracker, but they had no time for song and ceremony. Why, if he were in the field with regulars, he would...

"Captain?" It was Jared who spoke up. "We have five or six shovels among us. It shouldn't take that long..."

Hendric looked around and saw heads nodding in agreement.

The captain sighed.

"It will be as you wish, Ishmed," Hendric said. "We will stand beside you ... we will see Fevor to his rest in the earth..."

Turning back to Jared he whispered, "Be quick."

CHAPTER 14

Raymond and Hanshee rode through the night and all the next day, determined to put as much distance as possible between themselves and the Rayine fort, the last known location of the pursuit they now knew was almost upon them. The traveling was easy as the Merchant Way carried nowhere near the traffic it would have in the full bloom of spring. In the spring time, there would be many times more wagons, most heading north to reestablish trade between the plains' nations and those of the Great Inland Sea; trade that had been very beneficial to both cultures.

Because they left the night before, they had gotten out ahead of the twenty plus wagons and their escort scheduled to leave the barricade that morning. They had the Merchant Way to themselves for as far as they could see in either direction. Their focus now was to cover as much ground as possible without exhausting the horses. Without Kellen to guide them, they found it difficult to gage what was a good pace for their mounts.

The day was overcast and windy. The bare branches of the winter trees were visibly bending before the strong gusts. Raymond found himself hoping it wouldn't turn into rain. They had been fortunate on the journey from the stables south of Stronghold to Cantor. Brief snow flurries had been the only precipitation. Ray didn't imagine riding in a cold rain would be any more bearable than walking in one.

As they made their way down the road, Ray's mind drifted to thoughts of their ever-changing journey...not simply a journey, but an escape...since leaving the Citadel. Had he not lived it, it would be impossible to believe.

He and Hanshee remained on the run from a company of Pithian soldiers whose motives neither of them knew. Their pursuer's wanted either to kill them, or simply return them to the protection of King Ammon IV and the walls of the Citadel... where others waited who no doubt wanted to kill them.

Fortune had favored them during their escape and they had met several good people.

The young boy, Kellen, guided them to Cantor while teaching them the rudiments of horsemanship, eventually paying dearly for his association with them.

The master of the stable where they stopped on the way to Gunjunson was willing to exchange their horses despite the shady explanation offered by Raymond as the reason.

There was Jedidiah, or 'Old Jed' as he preferred; the kindly proprietor of the Golden Lantern, who for a fair price had offered a comfortable room, a warm fire, cool watered wine, and the second-best stew Raymond had ever tasted, all with a friendly smile.

There was Guyzull, captain of the Kings personal guard, whose company escorted them to a meeting with the King himself; Moton IX of Cantor. And the King, who offered the comfort and safety of his walled castle and a life for Kellen after he recovers from his injuries, and who outfitted them with the weapons, clothes and horses that had seen them this far. Good King Moton also arranged passage on a river barge to help them escape those who had trailed them the distance from Stronghold.

And when they finally made the Merchant Way, the Menowin family had provided the *best* stew he had ever tasted, along with song and dance and laughter and camaraderie; all of which were a balm to his spirit after the pain and death and fighting and killing Raymond had seen to that point. As he looked back, he was thankful for the role he played in defending them, and thankful that they had all parted in good health and in the favor of one another.

Thinking back over their escape, Raymond realized all that had befallen them since his awakening from his life-threatening wounds. Or had he awakened from death, as Hanshee had said? Or was that Hanshee, the 'joker', having fun with him? Sometimes it was hard for Raymond to tell. But he had kept count, and all that he recalled had actually happened over the twenty-one days that had passed since he awakened from his healing sleep.

Twenty-one days ago.

The day Raymond Covington first took a man's life.

It had been eating at the corners of his mind for all of this time, but he had been unable to face it head on. He knew that now was not the time either. Though still being pursued, this was a time of relative calm. He needed this to remain a time of calm. The way his life had been playing out, he had no doubt the calm would be short lived. There would be another time to come to terms with himself and the things he had been forced to do in this land.

It had been a quiet ride. but both the horses and their riders were now exhausted and the sun was about an hour from setting. They needed to find a place to spend the night. Raymond was glad the rain had held off. Maybe they would continue to have good fortune. He felt they were due.

They had covered a lot of ground in a night and a day. They had moved with the urgency of knowing their pursuers were almost upon them. Maybe if they had not tarried so with Delno and the Menowin clan, their pursuit would have never gotten so close. Maybe they would have lost their trail, given up, and returned to Stronghold.

Ray knew this was wishful thinking.

The way these men had doggedly pursued them; had quickly found them at the most out of the way tavern in Gunjunson, had even trailed them down the Manchess River after he and Hanshee had booked passage on a cargo barge in the middle of the night. It seemed their pursuit was supernatural and could not be shaken.

As if the pursuit was somehow meant to be.

If meant to be, maybe it was meant to succeed?

Raymond looked to Hanshee, his partner for more than two seasons.

Over seven months if anyone used months in this world, he thought.

Raymond had never imagined someone like Hanshee could exist. Hanshee had gotten him...gotten *them*...out of every situation that had arisen. No matter what the obstacle or how long the odds against them, Hanshee had always prevailed. He had been able to out think, out anticipate, and out fight every force sent against them. How could he not believe he and Hanshee couldn't out distance and out last this pursuit? How could he ever lose hope with Hanshee at his side?

They had left the road now and found a spot that was flat, somewhat secluded and fairly clean. It had probably been used as a campsite in the past, though not lately. While Hanshee tended the horses, Raymond set about further clearing the sight and building a fire. With so little traffic on the road, Hanshee had OK'd it. The fire would be used to warm their stew and their bodies as they slept.

It surprised Raymond how easily he fell into the old routine he and Hanshee had established in the river valley east of the Ursal Mountains so long ago. It felt kind of ...natural.

When the fire was strong, Raymond went about gathering the wood to keep it going for most of the night. Afterward, they enjoyed a meal of warm stew and day-old bread made by Valda Menowin and her lovely daughters. Their bedrolls rarely looked as inviting as they did this night and, despite the weight that their shoulders carried, sleep came easily.

Just before he dozed off, Raymond's thoughts drifted to the journey still ahead of them. Since he took up with Hanshee, their destination had ever been Hanshee's homeland. To get there they would have to find a way past the barren expanse of the Great Desert and the breathtaking heights of the Blue Towers. These titanic obstacles lay far to the west, a direction that fate had prohibited them from taking.

How long would they be forced to travel south? What new obstacles would confront them? Would they be up to the task?

Raymond didn't want to disturb Hanshee, but he felt the need to reach out, to ask him how they could possibly complete this journey to the western slopes of the Blue Towers. Then he remembered one of the many lessons Hanshee had taught him along the way to where they now lay, and he spoke to himself in the words of his friend; *'no matter the obstacles lying before us…we will endure'*

****

Nola had learned much since joining her father on this quest.

Not about swordplay, knife fighting or the artful ways of killing; in these areas she was more than competent. But, as she observed Seenio, she was learning lessons in social interactions that were not a part of her training with the Guild. Lessons in subtlety, persuasion, patience, self-control and the social feints sometimes required to steer a situation, and people, in the direction that favored you and your objectives.

Nola had been correct in describing her training as "thorough and relentless". In matters of exercising her craft as a member of the Assassins Guild, she was a Reaper through and through. Prior to her being sent to observe her brothers in their mission to kill the warrior-priest, she had taken a handful of assignments of her own within the confines of Stronghold.

Assignments such as these were initiated by agents of the Guild who had been dispersed throughout Stronghold Valley, living among the Pith, and always with ears to the ground and fingers on the pulse of their community. When opportunities were uncovered, in the form of someone in truly desperate straits and with enough coin to pay for services, a message would be sent to the foothills of Strongholds Crown, to the elders of the Masscus clan. They would study on the particulars of the message and render a decision as to whether to involve the Guild. Acceptance would lead to a subtle contact by an anonymous party. If negotiations were fruitful, a portion of the payment was given up front. When all was judged to be in order, a Reaper was dispatched and the negotiated agreement fulfilled.

The action taken could be quite simple; theft of another's property that was coveted by the client, or of something that someone had taken from them. It could be as subtle as the planting of incriminating information or evidence to damage a reputation, facilitate an arrest, or motivate a third party to unwittingly act in their interest. It could be arson of the client's own property or that of a rival, or sabotage of a rival's business or its resources. More straightforward endeavors of a physical sort, harassment, intimidation, beatings and kidnappings, had at times all been sanctioned and performed by the guild of assassins.

And, of course, assassinations.

Everything, from the initial contact to the completion of the task, was done in complete secrecy. The client did not know the identity of the Guilds agent who began the process. The agent was not known to the Reaper to whom the task was given, and the Reaper was given only the information needed to complete the task, seldom knowing the identity of the client unless this knowledge was integral to the assignment. And unless leaving a witness was part of the plan, the assignment was carried out without witnesses or any evidence left behind to even hint at the existence of an Assassins Guild.

There was often evidence…planted to incriminate someone else if needed. But the existence of an Assassins Guild was widely accepted to be myth, legend, or fable; the subject of stories told late at night around a dying fire, or at bedtime before tucking the children in.

Nola had cut her teeth on such missions. They required a wide array of skills that guaranteed the assignment was carried out and no finger could be pointed to anyone involved. In these missions of stealth, thievery and even brutality, she had excelled. Having been birthed into, and raised in, the culture of the guild, and having surpassed all of her male peers in her training, she was expected to.

But these missions remained the only times Nola had been away from her home. And requiring secrecy, she had never interacted socially with anyone not of her clan, her tribe, or the Guild. This is why she watched carefully as Seenio skillfully navigated the many new people that they came into contact with.

Sometimes Seenio concealed himself in a cloak of mystery and danger, as with Suleski the blacksmith. Sometimes he feigned ignorance and naiveté as with Wiley. With Petri, it was adoration and subservience, an appeal to his pride and his position. And with Hendric…she wasn't quite sure about Seenio's approach to the captain. Competence was a part of it. Unflappability was another. But there was something under the surface too; subtle teases and challenges that seemed designed not to undermine Hendric's authority, but to keep him intrigued.

Though she was learning, Nola was also proud to have been a help to her father.

He had shown himself to be completely confident and at ease around other men, but his experiences with women led him to always assume a role of authority and domination. This was his problem when questioning the tavern girls at the Milkmaids Rest.

Somehow, Nola had known instinctively how to approach the girl, and her information proved vital to their mission. Was it because *she* was a woman? It could be that simple, but after spending their initial time at the tavern observing how the customers interacted with the 'wenches', Nola had developed a burning curiosity about the lives of the women who worked there, the roles they assumed, how they were treated, and how they navigated the demands of Wiley and a wide assortment of lecherous and aggressive men. Nola had never experienced anything like it, and was just as anxious to question the girl about it as to ferret out information about the warrior priest who had killed two of her brothers.

In her village, Nola was known as the eldest child of Seenio Masscus, patriarch of Clan Masscus, leader of the tribe of Strongholds Crown. Only to the chosen was he known as leader of the Guild of Assassins; a prodigy in all things brutal, anointed at an early age as The Beast. This meant that, within the clan, Nola was ever 'the daughter of the Beast'. She never suffered the advances, or even the wandering eyes, of the men of her village not closely related to her. By decree of The Beast, she was treated as the prized student that she was during training. After attaining her first kill, she was treated as a Reaper of the Guild.

To see the men fawning as they did over the tavern girls was both surprising and intriguing to Nola.

She knew, from her many years of being the only woman training for the Guild, that she would always be underestimated and sometimes completely dismissed, by men who did not yet know her. Continually insulted by their attitudes, she learned early on how to use their belief in their natural superiority against them, and she took great pride in punishing them for it. None underestimated her twice.

But Nola had seen something different at the Milkmaids Rest. Far from being insulted by the disrespectful and dismissive treatment of the men, the girls seemed to subtly encourage it. They bent the men to their will, and emptied their purses, by accentuating what the men perceived as their weakness; their femininity.

Nola had tried it herself on the guards at the Milkmaids Rest, and on Sergel. She had allowed her hips to swing as she walked, and saw with her own eyes how this simple movement had served to distract and disarm them. And with Sergel, even after she had shown herself to be far from helpless, having twice drawn his blood, still he dropped his guard when he thought her to be offering herself to him. She had found it both fascinating and insulting, and had decided to remove his eye as a lesson, until stopped by the voice of her father.

And even now, after demonstrating her martial prowess, she still caught the men she rode with casting glances her way when they thought her unaware. When caught in the act they would quickly look off into the distance, or down at their boots, or in some way pretend to be preoccupied with a simple task like checking a knot or pulling a tick from their horse. Her first thought had been to challenge them about their wandering eyes but, after a moment's consideration, she began to treat it…and all the experiences that were new to her…as learning moments.

Apparently, the men she rode with thought her attractive.

Nola had never dwelled on things so trivial. Her training was too demanding and had held her complete focus. She spent no time with the other girls her age. Pretty hair, eyes, and clothes were never a concern. She always aspired to be the exact opposite of what she saw in them. She wanted to be like her father and, because he indulged her, even her mother had refrained from introducing her to aspects of femininity that she obviously had no interest in.

Now, for the first time, she thought she might possibly be attractive. The behavior of her current comrades, strangers until a few nights ago, strongly suggested as much. And lest she forget, the four highwaymen who had discovered her naked at the hot spring were certainly impressed, if only for a short while.

The more thought she gave to it, the more she felt that this aspect of being a woman was worthy to be considered, and maybe explored, when she had the time.

At present, she was a Reaper on a mission sanctioned by the Lord High Priest himself. That it was also a quest to avenge the death of her brothers was secondary. The fact that they had brought their deaths upon themselves with their selfish and immature behavior was inconsequential. Once they found this warrior-priest and dealt with him as the High Priest had instructed, she imagined she would have time to explore this new world of womanhood that seemed to be occupying a little too much of her attention of late.

CHAPTER 15

If Raymond were to guess, he would put the season at early-Spring, the month, probably late March-early April.

Young leaves were already fleshing out the bare branches that had surrounded them since the beginning of their journey. The still cool nights often gave way to genuine warmth during days that were now lasting slightly longer. Were they not being pursued, it would have been a wonderful time to travel the uncongested Merchant Way.

Raymond estimated they had crossed the southern border of Rayine about three weeks earlier, by his frame of reference. Beyond the bustle of the border town of Bayiel, and the fort that had been established there, were the now unclaimed lands of the southern plains.

Not always unclaimed, a portion of these lands once belonged to Rayine. Two disastrous military campaigns, and the toll that the western drought had taken on its farmlands, had convinced the kingdom that expending its resources here had become a waste. After fortifying its new southern border, Rayine left the dying towns and homesteads, spread out along the southern expanse of the Merchant Way, to fend for themselves; a decision that had led to difficult times in this land.

The Great Desert had expanded much faster in the south, wiping out much of the fertile farmland that had contributed to a thriving Rayine in the past. The expansion had begun after the seismic occurrence that breached the walls of Stronghold valley and allowed the Pith to escape the combined armies of Cantor, Rayine and Byrne some eight-hundred years ago.

Along with providing a divine intervention for the Pith, it had shifted the courses of many rivers, causing some to now flow beneath the surface of the plains. Since that long ago time the desert, originally confined to lands immediately beneath the southeastern slopes of the Blue Towers, had increased many times in size. Although a concern to all the plains nations, it represented a direct and growing threat to the economy and wellbeing of Rayine.

The small towns just south of the Rayine border still had some fertile land to their west, but the farther south the town, the more the desert had encroached, until some parts of the Merchant Way were said to snake through its easternmost boundaries.

To the far south, the desert was held at bay by water running close to the surface of the land. Rather than provide for fertile ground, this water had settled and created a vast area of swampland, harboring all that made swamps inhospitable to man; stagnant fetid waters, hordes of bloodsucking insects, poisonous snakes, and bogs that had been known to completely swallow a wagon in a matter of hours; a man in much less time. The people of Rayine considered it the peak of hellish irony that so much water could be located next to an ever-expanding desert, with both being completely useless to them.

It was many centuries after the seismic occurrence, referred to by the Pith as the Miracle at Stronghold, that the nation of Rayine relinquished its claim to the lands beyond the border town of Bayiel. Soon after, the deserted towns and settlements fell into lawlessness.

Soldiers of Rayine were forbidden to cross the border into the southern plains in uniform, and only with express permission were they to go unadorned. Each knew that, should he disobey orders and something unfortunate were to befall him, no party would be dispatched for a search. If unable to make his way back, he would be counted as missing or dead and his family notified of his fate.

At first the chaos of the southern plains was a detriment to commerce. Trade along the Merchant Way was just beginning to blossom and much was gained on both sides from the exchange of goods and cultures, not to mention the immense profits merchants from both the north and the south were reaping. When those newly cut off from Rayine decided that their best and most reliable means of survival was to form bands of highwaymen and prey upon the merchants, it threatened to destabilize the economies of the plain's nations. Even the rich nations that bordered the Great Inland Sea felt distress caused by the ever-increasing attacks on their commercial ties with their northern partners.

Fortunately, the solution was found within the problem.

The wily merchants began hiring the most savage of the bands as protection against the rest. This not only provided respectable employment and a steady seasonal income to many of the abandoned men of the southern plains, but also helped to thin the ranks of those who were still intent on pillaging the merchant caravans. Many now in the employ of the merchants knew the ways, hideouts, and even the identities of those still making a living through thievery. These escorts more than earned their wages as deterrents to attacks on the caravans and, when attacks occurred, by brutally crushing those who sought to come between them and their new livelihoods. In the winter months, when trading diminished, some left the plains to hire out as mercenaries in established nations. They developed sterling reputations as fighting men, both in the lands to the north and the south. The year-round coin earned from their sword arms helped families and communities reestablish themselves.

There were many settlements along the Merchant Way that resembled ghost towns, with skeletal buildings that harbored nothing but beggars, foragers, and various wildlife. But one could also find settlements that had rebuilt themselves around the steady traffic that plied the Merchant Way from the early spring to late fall.

Taverns and inns catered to all from the most prudent and introverted, to the most permissive and indulgent. Dry good shops, blacksmiths, carpenters, butchers, even tailors and those who dabbled in the healing arts, could be found along the southern portion of the Merchant Way. These stops, spaced out as they were, went far in making the long journey between north and south more hospitable for those who regularly trod its length. Some establishments attained such status as to become destinations, and not just stopovers, for the merchants.

Raymond and Hanshee had seen all of this on their journey south and may have stopped to savor what hospitality was available if not for the weight of the pursuit ever constant on their minds. For this reason, they trod carefully among both the settlements and the ruins, most times leaving the road to circumvent the lights and sounds of people whenever they deemed it prudent.

When they did stop, it invariably involved care for the horses. Some grain and much water were needed to keep them as fit and healthy as possible. There was very little surface water in the southern plains and when rain was scarce, as it usually was, almost all water came from wells. There was also the occasional need for a smithy to secure a loose shoe to a hoof.

Seldom would they spend a night in a town. They felt more comfortable camping off the road, just outside the settlements, and keeping to a minimum those who could claim to have witnessed their passing. Ever aware of the tenacity already shown by the Pithian soldiers, they had no doubt they were still pursued. The fewer people that laid eyes on them, the better.

After traveling roughly two-hundred leagues beyond the southern border of Rayine, Raymond and Hanshee were fast approaching a crossroads. The Merchant Way had veered to the east and again brought them into contact with the foothills of the Ursal Mountains, this time the southwestern slopes. This was all according to Hanshee's plan.

Hanshee had taken great care in memorizing as much of the charts as he could during the extensive questioning by King Ammon IV. His plan had been to use the information to chart a course back to his homeland by retracing the path the Pith had taken when leaving the western plains beyond the Blue Towers.

He knew he could not return to his homeland by the same path that he used leaving it, the high cliffs and caves through which the Elders had guided him on his way east. It had always been his plan to make his way to the southeastern foothills of the Towers. From there he had faith that he could find the passage that the Pith had taken through the mountain range. The charts of King Ammon had only served to reinforce his faith in this plan.

Since their days in the Citadel, Raymond and Hanshee had learned much. Now they knew that to try to retrace the steps of the Pith was next to impossible. They would have to navigate maybe weeks of swampland, with dangerous bogs, before challenging the widest expanse of the Great Desert. These two obstacles were not present when the Pith made their journey over one-thousand years earlier. To attempt to traverse these two punishing landscapes would be a fool's errand, certain to end in their deaths.

Continuing to push south was the only option they had, but to journey deeper into unfamiliar lands carried its own risks.

The Menowin Clan were the only people they had met from the lands that bordered the Great Inland Sea. It would be foolish to believe all the people of the region were as open and friendly. Every stop since ascending the Ursal Mountains had taught them that the brutality of the lands west of the Blue Towers seemed to be never ending.

They were now well south of the last settlement and, per the charts he had memorized, Hanshee knew that a decision had to be made soon. To the west lay the death of the bogs and the desert sands; to the southeast lay the road to the southern nations.

Neither was a good choice, thought Hanshee, *but better to take their chances in the nations than in Mothers most barren embrace.*

Presently, they were camped atop a sparsely wooded knoll east of the main road. Hanshee had spotted it as they traveled and knew that, though it would take a little longer to reach, it would offer a good view to the north, west and south.

As dusk approached, Hanshee stood further up the hillside atop a rocky outcrop, searching the southern expanse of the Merchant Way through the quickly receding light. Raymond was below, gathering materials for a fire. On a whim, Hanshee turned his eyes back the way they had come. Instantly his senses were on the alert.

"Way-mon," he spoke in a low voice that nevertheless carried the distance to where Ray knelt, just about to strike a flint with the edge of his knife. Raymond froze his hand and looked up toward his friend.

"There will be no fire this night," Hanshee said, still looking off to the north.

Puzzled, Raymond tried to follow Hanshee's eyes, but all he could see was the surrounding bush. Then he noticed Hanshee gesturing him to climb up beside him. After climbing up beside Hanshee, Raymond knew why this spot had been chosen. Even through the dim light of dusk the knoll gave an excellent view of the flat landscape surrounding them in three directions. At Hanshee's bidding, Ray turned his eyes to the north and felt the breath rush out of his chest.

Off in the distance was a feint pinpoint of flickering light.

As they watched, and darkness continued to descend, the flame became brighter, leaving no doubt as to what it was.

"How far away do you think it is," Raymond asked.

"If it is a large fire, maybe a half a day," said Hanshee, equating time with distance.

"That close?" The concern was thick in Raymond's question. "Hanshee, we need to ride through the night."

It was a gut reaction to the shock of seeing the fire; a thought grasped upon and thrown out almost in desperation. Raymond was surprised when Hanshee agreed.

Together they descended the rocks, swept their camp of any sign, and again saddled their weary horses.

****

Captain Hendric watched as the flickering light from the fire danced on the faces of his command. Since taking to the Merchant Way, they had lost two more members; Tomar and Fevor. On the other hand, they had gained the aid of the mercenaries Seenio and Nola, bringing their number back to nine and, if Nola's display was any indication, increasing their fighting strength.

Ishmed had taken the death of his brother very hard and pined for the slow painful death of whoever was behind Fevor's robbery and murder. It had taken all of Hendric's authority and persuasion to convince the tracker to continue in his duty for king and country.

With the comings and goings around the Rayine barricade, and the growing number of soldiers arriving almost daily, it was nigh impossible to determine who could have killed Fevor, even if they had not been Pithian soldiers on a mission in the land of their enemy. Reluctantly Ishmed had agreed to continue and, as a form of catharsis, threw himself into tracking the fugitive escapees.

The band had left the barricade early the following morning, before the caravans could be formed up for the Rayine soldiers to lead to the southern border. Still, this was no advantage. The constant forays along the road to the border and back, along with the lack of rain, made for a well-worn surface and a vast jumble of sign.

It had been difficult even for Ishmed to pick out the freshest hoof prints, but he threw himself into it until he could identify a dozen individual mounts from little more than a glance. This was of no value between the barricade and the southern border, but once they had passed the border town of Bayiel, the number of tracks was significantly reduced. Now several dozen sets of tracks was reduced to five or six that were recognizable. As they traveled beyond different settlements, and riders apparently reached their destinations, a single pair of tracks began to dominated the way south.

"It's gotta be them, Captain," Ishmed had said to Hendric, his eyes still taking in the minute details of the sign so as not to lose it again. "They's pushin' south pretty hard, like they's tryin' ta outpace somethin'…maybe get clear of a robbery an' a murder," he finished.

Hendric stared hard at Ishmed, but the scout/tracker never lifted his head from the sign.

"Well," Hendric finally said, "if you're sure, then we can pick up our pace and begin to run them to ground. How far ahead do you think they are?"

"They started out about two days ahead of us, but they was movin' faster than us between the fort and the border. They have at least three days on us now…closer to four."

"Damn!" exclaimed Hendric, as he looked around at his mounted command. "Hopefully their horses are just as worn as ours. Regardless, we must push hard."

That had been many days ago. Since then, Ishmed had never lifted his nose from the trail and the small band had held up well. Hendric was actually proud of them.

Some of their progress was due to Ishmed's nose for the trail. But Hendric thought that some of it was due to their newest members, Seenio and Nola, the two mercenaries now bonded with the young priest Petri. Hendric was sure that Sergel and Blige felt pressure to at least ride better than the lone woman who was now a part of the pursuit. With Sergel acknowledged as the better of the two with a sword, it was accepted that neither of them could out-fight her. Since Nola had voiced no complaints, nor shown any tendency to tire, the two soldiers could do naught but gird their loins and keep the pace, no matter how frantic it became.

As Hendric considered it, the addition of the mercenaries had been a benefit to the pursuit. As well as providing two more skilled and experienced swords in a land filled with potential enemies, Seenio's language skills had proven invaluable back at the barricade. In no time at all he had the barracks captain agreeing to allow them access to the southern road without escort.

Not that they needed one.

Though he could only guess at their nationality, the barracks captain saw that they were mostly experienced swordsmen, the slim one being the lone exception. Even the woman wore her blade as if it were a part of her and not just for display. If anything, the captain eyed them as if he expected to encounter them further down the road when they invariably tried to rob a caravan of merchants.

Seenio had stepped forward, speaking to the captain in the merchant's tongue without accent, and presenting himself in such a way as to at least minimize the captain's natural distrust. He had also promised that they would check in with the captain of the fort in Bayiel, to assure both captains that they had indeed passed quickly through the part of the Merchant Way for which Rayine provided protection.

Seenio had also provided a change of pace around the evening fire.

The fellow was surprisingly knowledgeable about a great many topics concerning different lands and customs, and his conversation was both enlightening and entertaining. Even Sergel and Blige had warmed up to him…as much as they could be expected too.

They still kept their distance from Nola.

Jared had struck up many a conversation with both Seenio and Nola, mostly about their work as mercenaries. Compared to his experiences in the Infantry of Pith, their stories seemed filled with wonder and adventure. And Petri was overjoyed to find a duo of their abilities that, even in this wilderness, offered him the respect due a priest of The One Spirit.

The only one who still appeared to harbor questions about the two was Lucius.

Lucius had been caught off guard when he had been introduced to Seenio and Nola as at least temporary members of their company. He maintained a cool demeanor with both, even after many days of riding together.

Having seen firsthand how easily Lucius moved among strangers, gaining their trust and ferreting out information, Hendric found this reserve around Seenio and Nola to be a little disturbing. He would watch as Lucius threw long sideways glances at Seenio when he thought no one would notice. Always with curiosity, sometimes with suspicion, he took in as much as he could about the pair without any real interaction between them.

Did Lucius know something, or was he trying to figure something out?

Whatever it was, Hendric was of a mind to let it lie for now. The band was making good time and could stumble upon their quarry any day. Any discord, real or imagined, needn't be addressed immediately.

Whatever it is going through Lucius' head will probably work itself out in time with no help from me, Hendric thought.

Lucius was indeed taken aback when first introduced to Seenio and Nola. There was something about Seenio that instantly set off an uneasy feeling in his head; like an itch that couldn't be scratched. And like most itches, it was very difficult to ignore.

Lucius tried to keep his wondering to himself, fearing that the other members of the company might somehow pick up on his misgivings about the new additions. After a few days this was no longer a concern. He noticed how the others seemed to be drawn to the two – even Sergel and Blige had gotten over their initial irritation and distrust - and no one seemed sharp enough to question, or even notice, that Lucius stayed apart.

But not everyone was oblivious. Lucius was sure that Hendric had noticed his hesitation in befriending the duo. But he was confident he had a good feel for his captain.

Lucius knew that Hendric was a 'King and Country' type through and through. His uppermost concern was the successful completion of their task, as it should be. But Lucius had watched as the captain sometimes wavered under the weight of his mission; was sometimes hesitant to give orders and take a firm hand; how he sometimes needed an extra push in order to do what Lucius could clearly see had to be done. At these times Lucius had offered both council and assistance but he could see that, even in accepting the offered assistance, Hendric could not help but wonder if Lucius undermined his own authority.

He needn't worry, thought Lucius. *This sergeant had no designs on command of this bunch, unless it was the only way to complete his mission.* He saw Hendric as a reasonably steady hand and was content to do his work in the shadow of the captain's command.

Hendric felt that the best way to complete the mission was to keep the men at relative ease, and so did not address any issue that did not cast a noticeable cloud over the morale or readiness of his group. Lucius was satisfied with this and knew he had nothing to fear from Hendric's curiosity, as long as things continued to run smoothly.

But there was still that damned itching in his brain every time he considered this Seenio fellow. Lucius found himself wondering if he knew him from an earlier time; if their paths had ever crossed, either in his duties as a soldier or simply at a tavern in some forgotten settlement. Though he had been searching his memories and finding nothing, Lucius could not shake the feeling that he had seen Seenio before…maybe even shared the same space with him.

If he could only remember!

At one point Lucius had hoped that the female companion, Nola, would point him in the right direction, but she produced no such feeling in his mind. He had heard about the night near Wroughtmire, when she and Seenio had first been brought to their camp. Sergel still wore the bandages, and the embarrassment, from that encounter. Any woman as beautiful and deadly as Nola would certainly have earned a place among his memories if he had met, or even seen, one such as her before. Lucius was sure this was their first meeting.

Seenio was different.

Lucius knew he was condemned to have this dilemma running round and round in his head until it either worked itself out, or he had to split his own skull to scratch the infernal itch.

There was one other who noticed Lucius' reluctance to engage with Seenio.

Seenio himself.

He had made note of Lucius' cool greeting. Some fighting men were that way, not so eager to establish a bond with a stranger. He had noted the sergeant, though slight in stature, commanded a good deal of respect among the others, including the captain. And he had also noticed, while still at the fort, that

Sergeant Lucius had a way of fading into the background; calling very little attention to himself while taking in everything around him.

A few days of riding with Lucius and Seenio too had an itch. But, unlike the sergeant, Seenio *knew* he had seen Lucius before. Over the past several days Seenio had spent much of his time in the saddle trying to remember where, and of what value the knowledge might be to him now. He wondered if Lucius' reluctance to interact was because *he* knew where they had crossed paths.

But Seenio was never one to become consumed by wonderings. If the fellow knew him, or knew of him, then let him come forward with his knowledge. It could be that Lucius was having as much trouble placing him as he was having with Lucius. In time the answers would reveal themselves…they always did. Until that time, he would appreciate the comfort, safety, and anonymity that now surrounded him.

Joining up with Petri, and through him this band in pursuit of the warrior-priest, was a stroke of great fortune. He had but to stay in their good graces and they would lead him straight to that which he most desired.

And when the time arrived, would he wait for the assassin he knew must lurk in their midst to strike the killing blow, accomplishing the mission the High Priest Mayhew had set for him, without exposing himself? Or would he feel the need to seize the moment, thereby addressing the wishes of the High Priest, and the revenge burning in a father's heart?

This was a question Seenio knew would not be answered until the time came.

CHAPTER 16

"They stopped here alright, Captain."

Ishmed had just descended from the knoll back down to the road and was reporting to Hendric. The tracker had noticed the sign veering off to the east and into the brush surrounding the foothills of the southern Ursals. He had bid the others to wait here while he followed the sign.

"Up on that knoll is a good place to camp and watch the road," Ishmed continued. "They was there, but they didn't stay long. They covered their sign as best they could before they left. I'm guessing they climbed a little higher up into the rocks and seen our fire last night. Then they covered their sign and moved on."

"We're that close?" Hendric asked.

"Less than a day behind 'em, I'd say," was Ishmed's reply. "And with them riding all day then pushing their horses through the night, they can't be moving too fast. If we push hard, we might be on 'em by nightfall."

Hendric took in what his tracker said as he looked back at his command. He knew that their fire last night had been a bit much, but his pride in his men had led to leniency, which had tipped off his quarry to their nearness. Nevertheless, they had enjoyed a good night's rest and had again taken to the trail before sunrise. They had been riding for only a few hours when Ishmed held up here.

Turning back to Ishmed Hendric said, "Mount up tracker." Then he turned in his saddle to face his command.

"They're close," he said excitedly. "Ishmed says we could have them by nightfall if we push hard. What say you?"

"We're fresh, Captain." It was Jared who first spoke up. "Let's be about it!"

"Aye, let's ride!" It was Blige who now spoke and Sergel joined in with a whoop. Soon everyone was whooping and hollering, and building on the excitement that accompanied the good news.

"Alright, men," Hendric said. "Not so fast now. Steady and strong, and we'll ride them to ground by day's end!"

Another round of hollers rolled across the hills as they started their horses at a trot down the Merchant Way.

****

Sometime during the night Raymond's horse picked up a limp.

Hardly noticeable at first, by dawn the limp was slightly more pronounced and by midday it was affecting their progress. Unable to keep pace with Hanshee, Raymond called a halt and dismounted to check his mount.

"What I would give for Kellen now," he said under his breath as he looked first at one hoof then another. He found a small rock that had somehow wedged itself between the shoe and the hoof of a back leg, but this was not the leg the horse was favoring. Unable to diagnose the problem, unable to even understand, Raymond looked up at Hanshee in frustration.

"This horse can't continue with me riding him, Hanshee. This foreleg looks swollen and I can't see a reason why, much less know what to do about it."

Hanshee looked down at Raymond whose exasperation was written plainly on his face, then raised his eyes to take in the surrounding terrain.

They were on a stretch of road both flat and straight for several leagues. It no longer followed the base of the mountains which appeared to be reseeding behind a scrub forest to the east. The same stunted vegetation was to the west of the road, but not nearly as dense. Hanshee knew that the swamp lay in that direction, and the desert beyond that. Up ahead, about half a league distant, was a slight rise beyond which it was impossible for him to see from here. Taking all of this in, Hanshee made a decision.

"We have ridden for a day and a night. We will rest the horses here for a while," Hanshee said as he dismounted. Nodding toward Raymond's horse, he said, "He may recover without your added weight."

It was all they could do but, although Raymond was hopeful, he knew that Hanshee understood no more about horses than he did. After moving them into what little shade they could find, they gave the horses a hand full of grain and water from the large bags tied to their saddles. They were limited in what they could carry in their water bags and so were very careful not to waste any of the liquid so scarce and precious to the southern plains.

Raymond always felt that the little they offered their mounts was never enough. Today they compensated by allowing the horses a long overdue rest, not stirring again until late in the afternoon. When they again returned to the road, Raymond judged maybe an hour and a half of daylight remained.

The many hours of rest had proved beneficial to Raymond's horse, but he still limped when Raymond took the saddle. Seeing this, the pair decided to walk the horses for a while. Though now on foot, and guiding their mounts, they still tried to make good time. Hanshee started at a jog, looking back frequently to make sure Raymond and his horse could match his stride. Once satisfied that they could keep up, he settled into a steady pace that continued until they reached the crest of the rise he had seen earlier. From here he had a good view of what awaited them up ahead.

Raymond had been monitoring his horse as they moved along, and so did not take notice of the road ahead until he drew up alongside Hanshee. Once there he let his eyes take in the most southern stretch of the Merchant Way.

From where they stood Raymond could see that the road ran almost arrow straight for another league, maybe a little more, then seemed to come to an end at a low wall of vegetation set against an immense sky of blue accented with distant white clouds. Not sure what he was looking at, Raymond glanced at Hanshee to judge his reaction to the sight that lay before them.

"It is the end of the Merchant Way," Hanshee said as if reading Raymond's mind. The King's charts say this road ends at the Southern Plateau. From there we must take the road east to reach the southern nations, for we cannot go west."

"My horse won't go much further," Raymond replied. "Before we start for the southern nations, we've got to get him a proper rest or I might as well walk the rest of the way. We've got to find some fresh water too. My bag is almost empty and..."

Raymond paused in mid-sentence as he noticed Hanshee's attention was no longer on the road ahead, or even on him. Alarmed, Raymond turned to see what it was behind them that had captured his friend's attention.

The road to the north was almost as straight as it was to the south, and appeared to fade away to nothing in the distance. Raymond again cast a curious glance at Hanshee, whose eyes were glued to something Raymond couldn't see. Since Hanshee's gaze never wavered, Raymond again turned to the north to try to see what was, up to now, invisible to him. He saw nothing but a straight earthen track dividing a scrub forest and extending so far that...

What is that? Raymond thought, not sure if he was actually seeing anything. Continuing to strain his eyes to the north,

Raymond again thought there was something there but couldn't put his finger on what it was. Hanshee continued to look on in silence.

"Hanshee," Raymond spoke up, "what are we looking at?"

"Dust," was Hanshee's reply, "rising from the Merchant Way."

Now Raymond fixed his eyes far off into the distance and could just make out a wisp of…something… at the very limits of his vision. Maintaining eye contact, he noted the wisp never disappeared, but seemed to change subtly in size and shape.

"They still come," Hanshee said.

"How close do you think they are," Raymond asked, his calm words relaying nothing of the lurching in the center of his chest.

"Too close" said Hanshee as he looked to the west to gage the height of the sun. "Come. If we hurry, we can stay ahead of them until night has fallen."

With that, Hanshee turned and led his horse down the road toward the distant plateau. Hanshee gradually gained speed until the horse was trotting beside him. Raymond was right on his heels, his injured horse able to keep the pace without the added weight of a rider.

Fueled by adrenalin, Raymond never even considered slowing down as Hanshee led them ever closer to the low wall of vegetation that marked the edge of the plateau. He simply kept his eyes on Hanshee's back, maintaining a trust born from experience that Hanshee would make the right choices at the right time. All he had to do was keep pace.

Daylight was noticeably fading when they reached what used to be a crossroads. The Merchant Way widened as it met the road leading east/southeast to the southern nations. There was some evidence that a road may have once led off to the west also, but it was now nothing more than a small clearing; an overnight campsite for those finishing their journey on one road and not yet ready to take on the other.

As they came to a stop, Raymond was covered in sweat, his legs shaky and his breath labored.

But he had made it.

Looking back, he thought he had never run so fast for so long in his life. Still fighting to catch his breath, he turned to Hanshee who, ever focused on their survival, was busy surveying this new terrain. Hanshee too was covered in sweat, but his breathing was deep and steady, not labored like Raymond's.

Raymond followed Hanshee's gaze as his partner took in the road that moved off to the east. The southern foothills of the Ursal Mountains could be seen in the distance and it was known that the road ran along their base as it turned in a more southerly direction. The road itself appeared to become more rock and gravel further to the east, blending with the sand and dirt of the Merchant Way closer to where the two roads met.

Hanshee led his horse to the edge of the plateau. Raymond, his breathing now under control, followed.

Together they looked over a vast expanse of vegetation spreading out before them. It was a tropical rainforest, lying so far below them that the tops of the tallest trees were still several hundred feet below the lip of the plateau. The lush green foliage, stunning even in the fading evening light, seemed to glisten with moisture.

Standing where he was, Raymond could feel the warm humid breeze rising up the plateau walls from the forest floor. The breeze brought moisture up from both the forest and the distant sea; moisture that condensed into clouds that were constrained by the prevailing northwest winds to traveling no further north than the rim of the plateau. These clouds seemed to hover over the forest, continuing to gather until their density demanded they release their life-giving liquid onto the lush greenery below. Evaporation insured that the cycle was repeated; day after day, year after year.

Both Raymond and Hanshee marveled at the sight that lay before them, equal to their midmorning view of the Ninum Valley as seen from the high cliffs that served as Strongholds eastern wall.

Although they were overwhelmed with the view, Hanshee never lost his focus on insuring their survival. He saw that the low wall of vegetation they had seen from the distance was actually a mass of vines and creepers that had been growing from the valley floor for thousands of years. Abhorring the dry conditions atop the plateau, and with no additional plateau wall to cling to, they grew only a few feet above the rim before cascading back down toward their roots. Hanshee kicked at a vine here and there, and even bent a knee to grasp and shake a few. Then he rose and again looked east, down the road to the southern nations, and north, toward their oncoming pursuit. Finally, he turned to Raymond.

"This is what we must do…"

****

"One of they's horses is gone lame."

Ishmed made the pronouncement without fanfare, but it was obvious that he was excited by what he discovered.

"Are you sure?" Hendric asked.

Ishmed prepared to launch into an explanation of changes in the gait pattern, length of stride, and depth of the hoof print, but caught himself. In the past, those unskilled in tracking would just stare down dumbly from their horses until he finished, then ride off.

"Yes, Captain, I'm sure," Ishmed replied as he mounted up.

Hendric looked back at his command and saw that Ishmed's words had put back some of the fire they had lost after almost a full day's ride.

"I'd wager they're not going far nor fast now," he said to all. "We should have them before the sun sets!"

Hendric led his men forward at a trot and the ten horses and two pack animals began to kick up a cloud of dust as they made haste down the Merchant Way. But it wasn't too long before Ishmed raised his fist and brought the company to a halt once more. Vaulting from his saddle, he again stooped to examine the road before them.

"They's on foot," he said, this time the excitement clearly evident in his voice. As he stood up, he sought the captain's eye. "They's leadin' the horses."

Again, the party started down the road, Ishmed scanning the ground in front of them while the others cast their eyes from side to side, hoping to catch sight of the fugitives hiding among the scrub oaks that littered the landscape this far south.

After crossing a slight rise in the road, the tracks spaced out a bit indicating that, though leading the horses, the men were now running, Ishmed kept it to himself. The way he saw it, running while leading a horse was a sure sign of desperation. He half expected to come upon two exhausted figures standing beside the road, waving them down to give themselves up. This sight never materialized and it was almost twilight when the party reached the crossroads of the Merchant Way and the road to the southern nations.

With the light almost gone and their quarry nowhere to be seen, there was some grumbling about having missed their opportunity. Ishmed again dismounted to scan the ground in the waning light. What sign he could make out led him onto the eastern road. While he continued to follow sign, others of the group dismounted. Some walked over to the edge of the plateau to gage its height and take in what they could see of the forest below in the waning light. Soon Ishmed returned with a report of two horses moving east toward the southern nations.

"No foot sign, Captain," the scout said. "Just two horses, the same two, movin' off to the east. The road gets rocky farther down apiece and, between that and the dark, I lost the tracks. But they's definitely movin' east."

Hendric cast his eyes around in frustration, taking in the gathering darkness, the shadowy terrain, and the looks of disappointment still visible on the faces of the pursuit.

"There's no use trying to trail them in the dark," he said. "We'll camp here for the night and continue on in the morning. They can't be far ahead."

Hendric again scanned their position, looking down both roads before making a decision.

"We'll move back up the road," he ordered, as he began walking his horse north on the Merchant Way, "unless you want a cold camp tonight. They won't see our fire if we stay behind the bend.

"And it'll keep these dimwits from wandering over the rim of the plateau in the middle of the night," Sergel laughed, delighted with his own sense of humor.

No one joined in.

****

Hanshee and Raymond were using the ancient structures of vines and rocky holds to work their way down the face of the plateau wall. They were less than a quarter of the way to the forest floor when they heard the horses of the pursuit come to a stop above them.

Hanshee's plan was simple.

At his direction, Raymond had taken his bow, quiver, and bedroll, from his saddle and strapped them on alongside the weapon harness and pouch that he already wore. Then he watched as Hanshee mounted his horse and took the reins from

Raymond. Leading Raymond's horse behind him, he trotted his horse east, down the road that led to the southern nations.

Raymond watched until Hanshee was out of sight.

As worry began to descend upon him, Raymond alternated his gaze from the road leading off to the southeast, to the road leading north to the Merchant Way, and back again. After a while, he caught sight of Hanshee working his way through the brush that bordered the northern boundary of the road. He didn't cross the road to Raymond until he was almost opposite him.

As Raymond watched, Hanshee shed his boots, which were easier for riding horseback, and launched them over the edge of the plateau. Then he replaced them with his sandals, quickly lacing them up his calf and tying them off just beneath his knees. He already had his full complement of weapons, his water bag, and his bedroll slung to his body.

"Our boots have already made sign here," he said in explanation to the quizzical look Raymond gave him.

Now Hanshee straightened up and turned toward the edge of the plateau. Looking once more over his shoulder up the Merchant Way, he spoke to Raymond.

"Now we climb down."

As he spoke, Hanshee stooped and took a firm grip on a root as big around as his wrist. He shook it to test its strength, then stepped over it and found a foothold. With his back now to the rainforest spread out far below them, he began working his way down the plateau wall.

Raymond hesitated for just a moment. Then he swallowed his fear and followed his friend over the edge.

The descent was slow, but surprisingly easy.

The vines had grown into the rock wall and around each other for centuries as they made the climb up to the rim of the plateau. They were thick and sturdy and the men had no problem finding secure handholds and footholds as they probed their way ever farther down the wall. Raymond only had to remember not to look down; trusting that Hanshee would alert him to any obstacle or difficulty before he reached it.

They were still well above the highest trees when they felt the vibration, then caught the feint sound, of hoof beats approaching. Realizing what was above them, Raymond heard Hanshee cease all motion. He followed suit. The evening shadows were even darker along the plateau wall and without any motion or sound to call attention to them, Hanshee was sure they would remain unseen by anyone looking for them from above.

He was correct.

The pair was too far away to make out words, but they continued to mark the sounds of voices and the shod hooves of horses dancing above them for several minutes. After a while, a single voice burst forth with rough laughter, and then the hoof beats grew faint as the horses seemed to retreat from their position near the rim of the plateau.

Raymond held his position and his silence until Hanshee tapped his foot and again began his stealthy descent toward the forest floor far below. Cautiously, with as little noise as he could make, Raymond followed the sounds of his friend. They climbed this way for close to an hour, descending farther and farther into the pitch blackness, before finally reaching the floor of the rainforest.

Raymond and Hanshee spent their first night in the rainforest where they first touched foot to firm ground at the base of the wall. Huddled in the unyielding darkness, they took in the varied sounds and fragrances that told them they were in a place that neither had ever been before. It wasn't long before the insects found them, ensuring that their welcome to the jungle would be both memorable and miserable.

They crouched amid the thick brush at the base of the plateau wall until late in the morning. Sitting almost motionless under the rainforest canopy, they felt secure from any eyes that might be looking down from above. They were too far away to hear any sounds from the plateau rim, and Hanshee wanted to be sure that their pursuit would have long ago broken camp and moved on before he chanced any movement.

For Raymond the night had been akin to torture. Every exposed part of his body, and some parts not exposed, was repeatedly attacked by tiny ants, flies and unknown bloodsuckers; the real rulers of the jungle.

Both he and Hanshee still wore the clothes given them by King Moton of Cantor, made for the cooler temperatures that dominated the plains nations in late winter and early spring. The warm air of the jungle, even more stifling because of its humidity, made the clothing hot and uncomfortable next to their now sweaty skin. If not for the scant protection it provided against the insects, Raymond would have torn off his leggings, his tunic, and the long-sleeved shirt he wore beneath it.

They had gotten some sleep during the night; at least as much as the insects would allow. Once they made it to the forest floor and settled in among the darkness and vegetation, Raymond had been surprised at how tired he was. Thinking back, he considered that they had been on the move for almost two straight days with no sleep. Adrenaline had fueled most of their efforts, but their sprint to the plateau rim, and lengthy climb down the wall had pretty much used that up. Forced to remain still in the blackness of the jungle night, their exhaustion overtook them and they managed a fitful, but much needed, few hours

The sun was climbing ever higher in the morning sky and casting the rainforest floor in alternating patterns of shadow and light. The insects, though not as voracious in the daylight as in the darkness, still looked to get their fill from the moving buffets that had settled down amongst them. In the midst of such an unrelenting attack, even Hanshee was beginning to show signs of irritation.

"The climb back up is going to be a lot tougher than the climb down," Raymond said absently, as he slapped at a sudden sting on the back of his neck.

"Our way does not lie above," was Hanshee's reply.

Taking note of the position of the sun, Hanshee stood up and began brushing debris and bugs from his clothes. Seeing this, Raymond lept to his feet and began vigorously wiping down any part of himself that he could reach, even as he wrestled with what Hanshee had just said.

"We're not climbing back up?" Raymond asked as he continued to swat at his clothes, then at the surrounding air.

"They wait." Hanshee said, nodding his head toward the plateau. "Somewhere near, they wait."

Raymond started to protest, but Hanshee's raised hand cut him off.

"Think Way-mon. Think of the distance they have pursued us. When we lay their fellows low, still they pursued us. Though we hide our trail, they find it. No matter the cost in time, effort, treasure or lives, still they come."

Hanshee looked off into space, shaking his head in disgust before turning back to Raymond.

"There is something about these cursed people from these lands east of the Blue Towers. They expect to have their way with any they encounter, and will go to great lengths to do so. Nothing seems to give them pause!"

Raymond was taken aback by the frustration in Hanshee's words, and the description of people 'east of the Blue Towers' made him think back to what they endured in the city of Aggipoor. Though they entered that city with nothing but peaceful intentions, many lives had been lost at the end of a blade wielded by Hanshee of Clan Dula. Once they had escaped into the surrounding forest, the pursuit had come. Hanshee had laid false trails and changed directions, hoping to lose their pursuers. He had even engaged with them, leaving them dead, broken and bleeding, in hopes that they would relent. The pursuers had only regrouped and continued the chase, even into the Ursal Mountains. They only stopped when they were, to a man, cut down by elements of the Second Expeditionary Force under Galin's command.

Since their capture by the same force, Hanshee had stayed busy. He had killed at least six other men, all of which had been trying to kill them. Had any of this stopped their harassment and pursuit?

No.

And here they stood, in a rainforest at the bottom of a plateau, many hundreds of leagues from the Royal House of Pith and that damned Fourth Prophecy, still dodging the pursuit that had dogged their trail every step of the journey from Stronghold. What would it take to make it end?

Raymond thought back to words Hanshee had spoken as they huddled on a narrow ledge in the foothills of the Ursal Mountains.

"A warrior ever chooses the path leading to victory. Sometimes the moment calls not for killing. Sometimes it does. If it were called for, I would kill every one of those now camped at the river's edge."

These words were spoken about the initial pursuit from Aggipoor. Raymond remembered the chill that had enveloped him when Hanshee spoke them. He felt it now even as he reflected on them. At that time, back in those foothills, he had imagined Hanshee as little more than a cold-blooded killer. At that time, he had yet to come to terms with the savagery that this world could thrust upon you at any moment. He still wasn't sure that he had, even after being forced himself to take human life.

Raymond hung his head in shame for the thoughts that were now tumbling through his mind;

Killing them would make them stop.

Deep down Raymond knew these thoughts really weren't him; not who he was or wanted to become. He shook his head, attempting to clear his mind of whatever was leading him in this direction.

If we killed them, they couldn't hunt us anymore.

Ray cursed under his breath before looking up, straight into the eyes of Hanshee.

Hanshee had been watching Ray and wondered what thoughts caused him to shake his head in obvious disgust. As he continued to watch, he wondered if his own outburst had brought something deep in Raymond's mind to the surface; something Raymond may have been subconsciously wrestling with; something he had been able to subdue with the strength he took from Hanshee's unflappable focus and poise.

"In troubled times, a true warrior possesses a calm that he shares with those around him, leading them to find a calm of their own. Thus is panic contained, and the path to victory secured."

It was a lesson taught him long ago by his father; a lesson in how to discipline himself so that he could effectively lead others.

If this much is expected of the warrior, Hanshee thought, *how much more is expected of the Maiyochi?*

Hanshee took solace from this teaching, allowing it to settle him. He allowed Raymond time to watch him; see his calm return and a smile slowly reshaped his features. His frustration was now past, his demeanor was now one of focus and confidence. When he spoke, it was in recognition of how his words had affected his friend. It now fell upon him to help pull Raymond from the depths of his fear to a place of renewed strength.

"I forget myself, Way-mon," Hanshee said through his smile, "and speak of these men of the eastern nations as if they be demons. They are but men, and men can be bested. Yes, they never tire of tasking us, but have we not prevailed each time?"

Raymond searched Hanshee's face for any hint of deception; he searched Hanshee's words for any questions or doubts. In both cases he found only renewed confidence, strength, and commitment. Then it dawned on him what Hanshee had seen; how Hanshee's words, spoken in a moment of frustration, had quickly affected Raymond's own mind. And now Hanshee was pulling him back and rooting him in the here and now, so that they would be ready to face whatever came next...and prevail.

Hanshee watched as his words settled into Raymond's consciousness and was relieved to see the beginnings of a smile find the corners of Ray's mouth.

"Whatever thoughts are troubling you... they are but thoughts," Hanshee said. "Put them aside. Before us lies a new challenge," he waved his arm to take in the thick tangle of life that surrounded them, "survival... in a strange and foreign land."

Raymond cast his eyes around the dense jungle before looking back at Hanshee, his spirits somewhat restored.

"Survival," Raymond said, as he slapped at another stinging bug on his neck, "it's why we're here...it's what we do."

****

Captain Hendric was at his wits end, and everyone under his command was aware.

To remain undetected by their quarry, they had made camp the night before about half a league north of the crossing, building a small fire, and settling in for a good night's rest. The plan was to arise early and be in position to resume their pursuit by sunrise.

Ishmed's last report was that the two escapees had again mounted their horses and turned them east, onto the road leading to the southern nations that bordered the Great Inland Sea. The fact that one of them was attempting this escape on a lame animal was considered a testament to their desperation. Hendric knew they would not get far, and his whole command was alive with the prospect of one last swift push, culminating in the capture of the escapees.

Ishmed had taken up the trail where the hoof prints in the sand and dirt of the Merchant Way could plainly be seen by all. The prints led onto the flat rocks and gravel that was the bed of the road leading east-southeast to the southern nations. On this new road, the escapees sign was more feint due to the hard surface baring fewer and much less pronounced marks, but Ishmed was more than up to the task…for roughly a third of a league. Then the sign left by the two horses seemed to meander about, pausing, moving toward the side of the road and even into the brush, before reemerging and wandering into the brush on the other side. Finally, they started east again, but they still moved slowly and continued to veer back and forth across the road. At length Ishmed came to a place where the road showed more disturbances, most likely due to more horses he thought. The trail continued to the east and, a little further on, they found two discarded saddles bearing the mark of the nation of Cantor.

"Some of this I jess can't explain," Ishmed said to Hendric. "It looks like the two we're after might've met up with some others, and they all headed south toward Olmire."

Hendric wanted to reject this notion outright, but he had no better explanation than what his tracker offered. Still, some of the details failed to add up in his mind.

"When do you propose this happened Ishmed," Hendric asked "last night? We were closing in on them and had to halt due to darkness. Do you say that a mysterious group of riders came upon them in the black of night and took them south to Olmire?"

"Now, Captain, I can't swear to all that," Ishmed danced. "But we didn't find a campsite and I ain't seen the mark of a man's boot since we left the crossroads."

"What does that mean?" asked Lucius

"It means I can't say they ever got out the saddle on this stretch of road," said Ishmed. Everythin' points to them meetin' up with riders and pushin' on through the night…another night…on a lame horse… headed south to Olmire."

Hendric looked disgustedly at the scout, shaking his head in disbelief at the outlandish explanation he offered.

"They pushed on for another night without sleep?" Hendric asked. "According to your 'reading', they haven't laid their heads down in three days! And what of the saddles? Why would they abandon their saddles while traveling in the dark of night, down an unfamiliar road, on what you say is a lame horse? What kind of sense does any of that make, tracker?"

Ishmed could only shake his lowered head in befuddlement.

Now Hendric's frustration had spread to almost everyone in the pursuit party, and they stayed on the southern road for what seemed like another hour as Ishmed again took them from sign to sign, explaining what he saw, and why he thought what he thought. At one point, Seenio called Ishmed over to the side of the road to look at something. After a short while both shook their heads in agreement and Ishmed then took this new finding to Hendric.

"Captain, it looks like those other horses came out the woods to our left here," he said.

"What difference if they came from the woods or from down the road?" spat Hendric. "Do not all signs still point toward Olmire? Does this new finding change anything?"

Ishmed was quiet, as was everyone else save for grumbling and sighs as they waited for their captain to decide what all knew to be their next course of action.

"We have no choice," Hendric finally said. "We ride for the southern nations."

Except for his one question to Ishmed, Lucius had remained quiet during the whole of the morning search, taking in every clue that Ishmed had revealed and running it through his mind. Now, as the party turned their horses south toward Olmire, he could not help but look back in the direction of the crossroads and wonder.

As he turned back toward his companions, Lucius saw Seenio quietly sitting his horse and staring directly at him. Lucius paused in his saddle and the two exchanged stares for a moment, with Seenio briefly shifting his gaze toward the crossroads and then back to Lucius. After another moment, Seenio nudged his horse forward to join with Hendric and the others as they moved off toward the southeast.

Lucius fell in behind them.

CHAPTER 17

As Hendric and his small command pondered mysteries beyond the crossroads, Raymond and Hanshee made their way from beneath the walls of the southern plateau and further into the rainforest.

Further from the walls the trees grew slightly thicker, their canopies effectively blocking the sun. With less sunlight on the forest floor, many plants found it difficult to grow. This made for a less cluttered path and the occasional open clearing.

As they moved carefully along, Hanshee would periodically stop to examine a leaf that had caught his attention, perhaps reminding him of a similar plant that he had found useful in the past. Other times he would pause if he noticed a mark in the earth or on the bark of a tree, or some animal scat. Raymond watched as Hanshee attempted to familiarize himself with the different plant and animal life that inhabited the area, constantly scanning the ground around them, and even allowing his eyes to roam into the treetops. In this way he began to learn vital information about this new environment and to consider how this knowledge could be used to insure their survival.

In Hanshee's experience, almost every landscape had its share of large carnivores, and even some large herbivores, that could prove troublesome or dangerous. Being properly equipped could mean the difference between life and death; eating or being eaten. Though still valuable weapons, the bows that they carried were most effective for hunting in more open spaces. Hanshee insisted that they be carried unstrung on their backs for now. Swords could be used to fend off close quarter attacks by both man and beast, as long as the beast didn't have sharp horns and weigh half a ton.

Feeling that a better weapon would be required in this environment, Hanshee spent a good part of their journey searching until he found some downed saplings of the required length and strength. When they finally made camp, he set about carving, notching, and fashioning one into a clean straight lance about seven or eight feet in length. He then took a blade from his pouch and, using it as a guide, adjusted the notched end of his lance. He then inserted the handle of the blade into the notch and used the tough but supple roots that ran just under the forest floor to firmly secure the blade to the lance. As always, Raymond paid close attention to everything Hanshee did and was impressed with the end result; seven plus feet of hardened wood with eight inches of iron blade attached to one end.

"With this weapon," Hanshee explained, "I can pierce the hide of a large animal and pin it down. While I remain out of its reach, you can rush in with a knife or sword for the killing stroke."

Upon hearing this, Raymond looked sideways at his friend and both shared a good laugh.

"It would also work if *you* pinned the animal down," Hanshee conceded with a smile, as he reached for another of the saplings to fashion into a spear for Raymond.

Despite the damp conditions Raymond had managed to get a fire started and the smoke it produced gave them some relief against the hordes of flying insects. The crawling ones were a different matter, and so they spent their second night in the rainforest in much the same torment as the first.

In the morning they ate the last of the rations they carried in their pouches, drank some of their water, and prepared to move further into the forest. At Hanshee's suggestion they used ash from the fire to cover themselves and their remaining clothes. Hanshee explained that, until he could determine what plants were a safe deterrent, it was the only protection he could offer against bugs.

It was their second full day in the rainforest and Hanshee had come across the hoof prints of feral pigs not far from their campsite. Having planned to keep moving farther west every day, Hanshee now adjusted his thinking. Instead of spending the day scavenging their way through the forest, only to have to find and prepare another campsite, why not use this campsite at least one more night and spend their energy hunting this area?

That is what they did, and by nightfall the haunch of a fine young pig was roasting over their fire. Hanshee had prepared additional thinly cut pieces and placed them on sticks near the fire so they could dry out. In this way the meat would last for days and release them from the need to hunt again for some time.

With running water plentiful, and no pressure from the soldiers of Pith, Raymond was beginning to feel as though they had once again found a measure of the freedom he had not known since their early days in the Ursal Mountains.

Slap!

Now if only they could do something about these damn bugs!

"Thirteen," Raymond said as he completed the latest notch on his spear. "This will mark our thirteenth day in the rain forest."

Hanshee nodded in acknowledgement, not feeling that the moment required anything more.

Raymond only made a new notch while sitting around the evening fire. It was his way of saying that they had survived another day. Now he laid his spear to the side and looked around the camp with a feeling of satisfaction.

It had been a wise decision to spend an additional night in their first camp. Instead of blazing a trail through the undergrowth until they found a new place to camp, they had used that day to hunt. They had been successful, bagging a young boar pig which had fed them well over several days; days that Hanshee decided would be best spent at the same camp.

"Here we have water," Hanshee had explained, "and game. We are no longer hunted, so we can take our rest. As we remain here, I will explore and learn this new land. There are many useful things here. I know this because our Mother always provides. We have but to reach out with our eyes, our hands and our spirits. What is learned today will help us survive tomorrow."

It was good enough for Raymond, so they hunkered down in their initial camp and Hanshee 'reached out', roaming through the underbrush, along the streams, and even climbing into the lower canopy, to see and to learn all that he could about the rainforest and how best to survive here. Sometimes Raymond would accompany him, moving through the bush almost as quietly as Hanshee. He always carried his spear and his sword because one never knew what one might find. A day of exploration could turn into a foraging expedition or a successful hunt, depending on what was stumbled upon. In this new and challenging environment, the duo remained poised to take advantage of any opportunity that the jungle presented.

During the first days of Hanshee's excursions, Raymond had turned his mind and hand to how he could be useful in this new setting.

The ash from the fire was at least helpful in protecting them from the flying bloodsuckers that inhabited the jungle. So far, there had been no relief from those that crawled on the ground. They had been driving Raymond insane. Hanshee too, but his stoic nature allowed him to persevere with few outward signs of discomfort. After their fourth night in the jungle, Raymond shared with Hanshee his determination to do something about the torment they suffered while sleeping on the ground. Hanshee agreed and, while he was exploring their surroundings on day five, Raymond began to build.

Not really sure what it would take to protect themselves from the creepy crawlies, Raymond first envisioned a separate bed for each of them. After more thought on what building two beds would entail, he decided that a single bed, large enough for two, would be more efficient. And making this bed a sleeping platform, by raising it far off the ground, would be best of all. Thankfully, everything Ray needed was either in or very near the campsite.

It took two days to do it right but, when he finished, Raymond had constructed a platform approximately nine feet square, sitting about three feet above the jungle floor.

The foundation consisted of four young trees that formed a square in relation to one another. Ray didn't know what type of trees they were but, thankfully, their wood was soft. He only had his hand axe to cut the wood and, as usual with any construction, more wood was needed than first thought.

Raymond cut through the tree trucks until he could bend them down with just his strength and weight without separating from the stump. He was careful to ensure each tree was cut so it bent toward its neighbor. When he finished, each tree trunk was still firmly attached to its own stump, but also rested across the exposed portion of the stump of the next tree. Vines and roots were ever plentiful in the rain forest and Raymond used them to secure each trunk to the stump on which it lay. When he finished, the cut trees formed a square. This would be the foundation of the platform.

Ray then went further into the rainforest in search of several young saplings of a specific size. When found, he cut them to a length of about nine and one-half feet and carried the wood back to the campsite. The saplings were laid side by side across the entire width of the foundation formed by the trees he cut earlier. He again used the abundance of vines and roots to secure saplings to each other, and to the frame, before using his knife to whittle down anything on the young saplings that would protrude and cause them to be uncomfortable. Then he lay atop his platform to judge its comfort.

It's certainly strong enough, Ray thought, *but I could use some padding between the saplings and my back.*

Ray now gathered many of the smaller limbs he had cleared from both the trees and the saplings and, along with bundles of large leaves, grasses, and even bark, he lay down a cushion to soften the surface for a sleeping body. Atop this cushion, he placed their bedrolls.

When Hanshee returned from his explorations, he was genuinely impressed with Raymond's ingenuity and workmanship.

"I saw something like this on the discovery channel once," Raymond explained in modesty. Hanshee's blank stare reminded him that his references to TV shows were of no worth in this world.

Raymond heaped piles of ash from their fire around the bases of the supporting stumps to discourage ants and other biting crawlers from climbing them. Between the platform and the ash on their bodies, he and Hanshee enjoyed as near a bug free sleep as they could hope for. It was definitely their best night since entering this tropical rainforest.

Until the rain started, and it came pouring down in torrents!

Hanshee and Raymond awoke to the heavy drops striking the surrounding leaves so hard that the sound threatened to drown out any communication. Both had to shout in order to be heard.

"Way-mon! We must get underneath!"

"What?"

"The rain! Hanshee said while pointing toward the sky "We must get underneath!" he yelled, now pointing toward the ground.

Raymond was becoming overwhelmed by the crashing of the rain on the surrounding leaves and the stinging of the drops that found his flesh. In a panic he responded to Hanshee.

"Why don't we get underneath this thing!" Raymond shouted, as he launched his body over the side and crawled under the platform. He was soon joined by Hanshee who gave Ray a strange look as he pulled himself to the center of what cover the platform provided.

It rained off and on for the rest of the night as the two sat in the mud beneath the constant drip of the sleeping platform that Raymond had built with his own two hands.

The next day Raymond tied fresh cut saplings to the half-cut tree stumps and began work on a roof.

The rain on their fifth night in the jungle established a pattern that more or less held true over time. Every fourth or fifth night the rain would come. Sometimes it would start before night was fully upon them, but it would always end before daybreak. Raymond consoled himself with the thought that this was, after all, a rainforest.

They adapted to the weather patterns by improving their shelter. The saplings were attached to the stumps in such a way so that other saplings could be tied on to form a peak. By attaching a long sapling between the two peaks and filling in either side with saplings spaced about six inches apart, they constructed a solid frame for a roof. Several varieties of plants Raymond recognized as resembling elephant ears grew in the forest, some with spade-shaped leaves as long as three feet. They used these leaves to serve as shingles on the roof frame, laying layers of them from the bottom up to encourage runoff without leakage. When finished, the roof provided excellent protection from the rains.

Another idea of Raymond's was to dig a pit under the center of the platform in which they could burn a small fire. Care had to be taken with this since the platform above was extremely flammable. They kept this fire small, consisting mostly of hot coals. By maintaining a pit of hot coals, they always had the means to rekindle a larger fire outside the confines of the platform when the weather permitted. The heat from the coals could be used to dry out rain-soaked firewood and, as Hanshee discovered, certain green leaves could be added to the coals to create a thick, pungent smoke that did an excellent job of repelling the flying blood-suckers that attack them through the layers of ash on their skin.

And so, as the thirteenth day in the rainforest came to a close, they had a stockpile of roots, mushrooms and greens similar to some that Hanshee was familiar with, a supply of dried fish to go along with the dried pig, sufficient water and wood, and a viable shelter against the rains. And since the rains had come the night before, they anticipated a good nights' sleep.

Raymond looked around in satisfaction before laying his head down on his bedroll.

Surviving? Ray thought to himself as he drifted off. *If we keep 'surviving' like this, I might just gain some weight.*

The next day found Raymond emersed in what some would call "busy work".

The problem with having plenty was that, with no immediate need to hunt for meat, forage for other edibles, draw clean water, or gather firewood, Raymond found he had ample time to do nothing. As he was sharpening his hand axe, after already sharpening his sword blade and spear tip, he allowed his eyes to wander around the camp looking for what was next on the list to ease his boredom. He settled on the sleeping platform, which had become his go-to pet project.

Ray was understandably proud of his work, especially considering that he had never built anything remotely like it before finding himself lost in the wilderness with Hanshee. Now he often found himself considering the structure, what improvements could be made, and whether it would be worth the effort considering Hanshee could at any time decide that they should pick up and move on from this place.

Since finding Raymond, Hanshee's priority had always been to find a way to return to his people on the western slopes of the Blue Towers. Stopping in one place for any length of time was not something they had planned on, especially if that place was a rainforest. But here they were, forced by circumstance to seek shelter in one of the most aggressively inhospitable habitats in nature. What they discovered was that, despite its strangeness, it was possible to be surprisingly comfortable here.

Go figure.

As Raymond now looked at the platform, he envisioned ways to make it more like a real shelter. He had the basics of a raised sleeping area and a peaked and covered roof high above it. He had considered adding walls made from something light and strong, like bamboo, but quickly dismissed that idea. Walls were needed for protection against variations in heat and cold which was not an issue here. Walls were needed for privacy, another non issue. And since bamboo walls wouldn't even slow down the hordes of biting insects that lived here, there was really no need for them.

But what would be useful would be a hole in the floor!

A hole positioned right above the small fire pit they had dug below the platform. With a hole directly above the pit, they could service it without having to crawl underneath the platform. There would also be less chance of a fire if the wood of the platform directly above the pit were removed. The more he considered it, the more Raymond thought the idea had promise.

Cutting the hole would be no problem. The problem would be having a platform that supported their weight after removing its center. As it currently stood, the floor of the platform was made of individual saplings covering the nine-foot span from one side to the other. If the center was to be removed, some type of center support would be needed for the platform to continue to bear their weight. Two parallel support beams, running underneath and perpendicular to the saplings already in place, should work. And a couple of three-foot-high supports for their center should stabilize the whole thing.

Now Raymond was excited. He didn't look forward to the hours he would have to spend sharpening the blade of the hand axe again, but the idea of making another improvement to the platform was really starting to get his juices flowing.

Wandering the rainforest surrounding their campsite, Raymond had already marked the perfect piece to serve as a support when he was startled by a sound as if something was crashing through the branches a little farther ahead. He would have taken it for a falling limb if not for the scream that accompanied it; a scream that was cut short as quickly as it began.

To Ray's knowledge, he and Hanshee were the only people in the forest and he had not seen Hanshee since he left camp in the early morning. Ray had no idea where he could be, and his first thought was that it was Hanshee who had screamed. A moment's thought convinced him otherwise and he began moving quickly, but carefully, toward the sound. After a short run, he burst into a small clearing and immediately saw the source of the commotion.

An adolescent boy was lying motionless on the ground among the broken branches of a tree bearing a fruit that resembled a fig. It looked like the boy had been in the tree gathering the fruit when he lost his balance and fell. As Ray looked on Hanshee noiselessly appeared at the opposite side of the clearing.

After first looking around to see if someone else was near, Hanshee approached the boy, who was clearly dazed and injured. When Raymond followed Hanshee's lead, he saw the source of the boy's pain. His right lower leg was broken, the shattered tibia having torn through his copper-colored skin. The impact of the fall had knocked the wind out of him, but he had also struck his head and appeared only semi-conscious. As Raymond watched, the boy rolled his head slowly back and forth, his eyes fluttering and a soft moan drifting from his slightly parted lips.

"Find young bamboo," Hanshee said, as he reached into the pouch that was ever present on his left hip. When Raymond hesitated, Hanshee looked at him pointedly.

"Many…this long…" he said, using his hands to describe a length of about two feet, "…now."

By the time Raymond returned, Hanshee had mixed his potions and, holding the boy's upper body against his own, had managed to force a sufficient amount of the mixture down his throat. After again resting his torso on the forest floor, Hanshee stood careful watch over the boy until he determined that the mixture had done its job.

"He will remain unconscious while we set his leg," Hanshee said. "Still, he may thrash. You must lie across his body and control his shoulders and arms."

Raymond took a position lying across the boy's chest, placing one of the boy's arms through his crossed legs while holding the other in his hands. Once he saw that the boy was secure, Hanshee removed the sandal from the foot of the injured leg. Raymond kept his back to Hanshee, looking at the young face that presently showed no sign of distress. Soon he felt the boy's outstretched arms tense up, felt his body heave up from the forest floor, and saw his head thrash back and forth as his face twisted in pain. Then he relaxed, his arms going limp and his head laying still.

Raymond released the boy and watched as Hanshee cut the green bamboo into strips about one inch wide, trimming down the length as needed. Using one of the bamboo strips for reference, Hanshee determined how many strips it would take to encircle the lower leg. He then gathered the strips together and lined them up. Using slim, tough vines, he tied the strips together at both ends. When he had enough, he placed the outside of the tied bamboo strips against the skin of the boy's lower leg, wrapping it around the leg until the bamboo strips almost met. Pulling the whole thing tight around the leg, Hanshee used more thin vines to tie the ends together. He then used the remaining vines to reinforce the bamboo at its center, and again halfway between the center and the ends.

When Hanshee finally stood back, there was a sheath of bamboo surrounding the entire lower leg from just below the knee to below the heel; like a cast, but made from bamboo.

"We must move him to our campsite," Hanshee said, and Raymond began looking around for suitable young trees that could be cut down and fashioned into a litter.

Back at the campsite, they lay the still comatose adolescent comfortably on the sleeping platform and Hanshee went about preparing a broth the injured boy could easily get down. The broth, made with some of the contents of his pouch, would lessen the boy's pain and begin replenishing his strength for the healing to come. Only when this was finished did they begin to speculate as to how the boy came to be there, and where he arrived from.

Neither Hanshee nor Raymond had considered that they might not be alone in the forest. Hanshee had ranged out daily, exploring their surroundings and searching for whatever was needed to keep them alive. In all of his foraging, he had never spoken to Raymond about finding cut wood, a previously used campsite, a foot print in the mud, or anything to hint at the presence of others.

As late morning turned to late afternoon, the boy began to stir.

Hanshee was quick to tend to him, offering first water and then broth. The boy was still dazed from the initial medicines that Hanshee had administered and, though startled and surprised by the sight of two strangers, he was sufficiently pliable that Hanshee could get the liquids into him. After a few minutes the boy was again sleeping peacefully, the discomfort of his broken leg masked by the painkilling agents in the broth. Hanshee made sure to give him enough to keep him sedated through the night.

The next morning the cycle was repeated, this time with the boy more aware of the two strangers, the camp, and his predicament. Both Raymond and Hanshee tried to communicate with words and gestures. The boy would nod his head in response to offers of water and broth, but would not utter a word. This left Raymond with no basis from which to begin to exercise his extraordinary gift and learn the boys tongue. Following the morning broth, the boy once again fell into a deep sleep.

The others arrived late in the morning.

Raymond had been reclining on a part of the platform opposite the injured boy and pondering their current situation. Finding the injured boy, and assuming responsibility for his care, had surely thrown off any plans Hanshee might have had of leaving soon. With no idea who he was, who his people were, or where he was from, they had no alternative but to stay here and attempt to get the boy as fit as possible. They certainly couldn't leave him in this condition and expect him to survive on his own.

Ray looked over at Hanshee who was crouched beside the cook fire preparing a separate stew for himself and Raymond. He was using a broad piece of hardwood that he had shaped and scraped and hollowed out until it resembled a large bowl. After placing various wild vegetables, tubers, herbs, and bits of wild pig in the bowl, and covering them with water, he patiently heated several round stones which he took turns immersing in the water. After repeating this several times, a wisp of steam could be seen rising from the bowl. A few more times and the contents actually began to boil every time a hot stone was lowered into it.

Hanshee had just pulled the latest stone from the bowl, to be placed into the fire and reheated, when he suddenly stopped and trained his eyes on the forest directly in front of him. Raymond had been watching and, when Hanshee paused, allowed his eyes to follow Hanshee's gaze. He saw nothing but forest, but when he looked back at Hanshee he could see that the warrior's gaze had not wavered. Intrigued, Raymond sat up and prepared to question him, but was cut off as Hanshee spoke.

"They come."

Ray looked expectantly toward the thick brush before them and wondered if he had enough time to arm himself before whoever was out there made their presence known. His harness and spear were resting on the other side of the platform, beside the injured youth. Then he looked to Hanshee, and watched as the Maiyochi put away the knife he used to cut the ingredients for the stew. Seeing this, Raymond relaxed. If Hanshee did not feel the need to be armed, Raymond was certainly not going to arm himself. In matters such as these, his trust of Hanshee overruled any apprehension the situation might have caused.

Just as Raymond reached this conclusion, a figure appeared at the edge of the clearing, straddling the center of the path they used when they brought the injured boy in.

He was a man of average height, not short, but not as tall as Hanshee and Raymond. His complexion was a soft brown with golden hues and reminded Raymond of caramel taffy. His body was lithe and lean, free of fat or unneeded muscle, and reminded Raymond of a runner or a dancer. His jet-black hair covered his forehead and was cut short just above thin eyebrows. It grew uncut in the back and was tied with a strip of leather at the base of his skull. The only clue to his age lay in the wrinkles of his face. The lines were there but not too deep, and only because of them did Raymond guess this man to be somewhere close to middle age.

As Raymond continued to stare, others stepped forward through the greenery that formed the perimeter of the clearing. All wore their hair the same as the first and were naked but for a leather loincloth which tucked in between their legs almost like a diaper. Each carried a spear that was not quite as long as the ones Hanshee had fashioned. Some spears had metal heads while others had blades made of shell or rock that had been shaped and sharpened. Some carried pouches and implements attached to cords of leather or vine and strapped around their waists or across their shoulders.

Raymond looked around, trying to determine how many of these strange new people had descended upon them, and noticed that a good many of the shorter ones were actually children; male children about the age of the injured boy brought back to their camp. They were dressed as were the adults and even carried spears, some of which had blades of rock or shell, some of which were simply a wooden staff sharpened to a point. As they continued to step into the clearing from all directions, Raymond counted about ten adults with about twice as many children.

Hanshee stood up to his full height and, still facing the first of the strangers, extended his hands, spread his fingers, and turned them to and fro to show that he held no weapon. Then he walked over to the platform where the injured boy was sleeping, pointed down to him and beckoned the first stranger that appeared to come forward. As the others stood ready, the first took his time as he moved cautiously across the clearing to stand beside Hanshee and look down on the injured boy. A moment passed before he turned and motioned for another to join him.

This one had a large woven pouch slung across his shoulders which he set on the ground when he reached the platform. The first now spoke to him in a language neither Hanshee nor Raymond had ever heard before. Their speech was rapid and lively and accompanied by hand gestures toward both the injured boy and Hanshee, who stood quietly beside them.

Hanshee glanced at Raymond, a question in his eyes, but Ray could only shake his head, unable as yet to make out a word of the strange new tongue.

Now the second man pointed to the leg of the injured boy and spoke directly to Hanshee.

Unable to understand what was being said, Hanshee guessed that he was being asked what had happened to the child. He paused for a moment, deciding how best to try explaining what had happened, then he launched into a wordless description of what had occurred the prior morning, using only motion and facial expression.

First pointing to the boy, Hanshee then pointed high into the nearest tree before picking up a stick and throwing it overhead. When the stick struck the ground, Hanshee first pointed again at the stick, then at the injured boy. He then touched the boy's injured lower right leg before using his two hands to mimic something breaking. The men turned to each other and again spoke in their rapid manner before turning to Hanshee and nodding their heads in understanding.

Now Hanshee walked around the platform and over to Raymond. Pulling Ray to a standing position, he patted himself and Ray on the chest and again pointed to the injured boy. He then walked over and pointed to the litter that they had fashioned in the forests and grabbed one end while instructing Raymond to do the same with the other end. They then walked a few steps with the litter between them, stopping when they reached the boy. Then Hanshee pointed at the boy and at the litter.

Again, the two strangers chattered animatedly between themselves, finally turning to Hanshee and firing off a string of words so fast that he appeared overwhelmed just in the listening. When they finished and looked at him expectantly, Hanshee could only shrug his shoulders in the universal sign that he did not understand, before looking beseechingly at Raymond who again shook his head.

The 'First' and the 'Second' now looked at each other in frustration before the Second again turned to Hanshee and began firing off a jumble of words. They were obviously questions and the man was irritated by their inability to communicate. As his frustration grew, so did his voice, and soon he was gesturing toward the boy and toward the platform and to the air itself in a way that was starting to make Raymond feel uneasy.

And he wasn't alone.

Raymond glanced around the clearing and noticed that some of the adults, and a few of the children, adjusted their grips on their spears while looking around at one another. Some took tentative steps forward, unsure of what was about to happen.

The Second continued to question Hanshee, now yelling as if the act of talking louder would make him understood, while the other adults wondered if the time was right to move on these strange men who were obviously new to their forest. Before anyone could act, the First raised his hand, and the yelling and fidgeting stopped.

Ray had watched it all with growing apprehension. He had again been measuring the distance to his weapons, now located behind the two strangers, when the Second suddenly fell silent. Instead of bringing relief, this led to more confusion, and just when he was about to make a dash for his sword and spear, something inside his head clicked and he began to understand what was being said. Now he looked franticly from the Second to Hanshee and back to the Second, hoping he would again speak, but nothing happened.

His mind still in turmoil, Raymond turned to Hanshee.

"I understand," he said to his friend, but Hanshee only stared back with a look of confusion twisting his features.

Now Raymond was confused and he again looked to the Second, finding him rooted to the spot where he stood, looking wide eyed and open-mouthed at him. A quick glance around the clearing revealed similar expressions on the faces of most of the others gathered there.

Then it dawned on Raymond and he turned back to Hanshee.

"I understand them now," Raymond said in Hanshee's native tongue. He had been so caught up in the moment, he had first spoken to Hanshee in the language of the strangers.

Hanshee again marveled at Raymond's ability to learn a new language almost instantly but, knowing now was not the time to marvel, he spoke quickly, sensing that things were about to get out of hand unless there was some understanding.

"Way-mon, tell them you will answer their questions," Hanshee said.

Raymond quickly turned to the First and spoke, though much more halting and tentative than they did, as mastery of a new language did not come instantly to him.

"Pardons," Raymond said, still unsure how to address the obvious leader of the group. "Please let me to speak to you…and answer your questions."

The gathered tribesmen continued to look at Raymond in amazement, only looking away from him to make sure their brethren were hearing what they heard. Finally, the First spoke.

"You know our tongue?" he asked, his cadence slowed by the wonder in his voice.

"I do…now," was Raymond's reply and he instantly regretted the implication.

The First heard Raymond's words and made the connection.

"When first we spoke," the First said, motioning between himself and the Second, "you did not know our tongue?"

Raymond felt the heat rushing to his face and neck as he looked helplessly at Hanshee, who had no idea what was being said, then back at the first.

"It is my gift," Raymond finally said in explanation.

The First remained silent as he continued to look at Raymond in wonder and awe. The expressions on the others had hardly changed a whit, and the silence was beginning to take on an ominous quality before the First again spoke.

"I am Nuguro," he said as he touched his chest.

"I am Raymond and this is my master, Hanshee," Raymond said, falling into the comfortable lie that had carried him and Hanshee this far. My master is a wandering priest from beyond the Blue Towers…eh…the high mountains far to the west," Raymond looked to Hanshee and back to Nuguro, wondering if he was explaining this the right way or if, living in this rainforest, they even knew about the western mountains.

"What is a 'master'," Nuguro asked with a slight tilt of his head, again launching Raymond in to a confused explanation.

"*Master* may not be the right word… M'lord Hanshee is…Hanshee is my friend and my *teacher*," Raymond finally spoke truthfully. "I owe him a great debt. I follow him and in times like this," Raymond motioned around the clearing, "he speaks through me."

Another thoughtful pause followed, and then Nuguro pointed toward the makeshift cast on the leg of the sleeping boy.

"Did you do this?" he asked Raymond.

"No. My mast…Hanshee is a great healer. We found the boy in the forest. His leg was broken. Hanshee set the leg and made a brace to hold it in place so it can heal straight. He gave the boy medicines to ease the pain and help him sleep."

Nuguro again looked to the cast then raised his face to Hanshee. While locking eyes with him, he spoke to Raymond.

"Tell your master of my thanks," he said.

Raymond instantly conveyed the message, and then waited while Hanshee responded.

"My master is pleased with your thanks." Raymond said. "He says that he is of the People of the Earth, and it is their custom to offer food, drink, and rest to those who are invited into their camp. We have only a little stew, dried meat, and water, but you are invited to refresh yourselves."

Nuguro looked to Hanshee and saw the smile on his face as confirmation of the offer. He then waved a hand to encompass his fellows and turned back to Raymond with a smile of his own.

"We have been searching for this one since before the fall of darkness. Tell your master we will accept his offer."

CHAPTER 18

Nuguro and his people, who referred to themselves as 'Akinowatowa', stayed with Hanshee and Raymond until they felt Wahiya, the injured boy, was strong enough to travel. This was a period of several days, during which Hanshee and Raymond gained some knowledge of the tribe and the land they inhabited.

One of the first things they learned, to their great relief, was which jungle plants served as natural deterrents to the swarms of bloodsucking insects the duo had been tolerating since their arrival in the rainforest. Coming from a people who valued cleanliness, Hanshee was much relieved to wash off the ash that had provided what little relief they had found from the jungle bugs.

They were also able to do away with their other layer of protection; the heavy clothes they had continued to wear even in the jungle humidity. Now Hanshee stripped down to the leather skirt and loincloth that he wore when Raymond first saw him. Along with his weapons harness, his leather pouch, and his sandals, it was how he had first traversed the eastern lands and how he felt most comfortable. Raymond took off his leggings and shirt, opting to wear just his almost knee length tunic over his undergarment. His weapons harness was worn over the breathable fabric and his own canvas pouch was carried over his shoulder.

Along with a way to better control the insects, they also learned more about the variety of food available to them in the rainforest. Edible fungus, soft stemmed water plants, nuts, and even the sap from some trees, was now added to the tubers and limited greens that had formed the basis of their diet. New protein sources in the form of rodents, reptiles, insects and grubs, were also added to their diet, the latter over the quiet protests of Raymond.

All these new lessons were taught them by the twenty or so children who, it turned out, were the sole reason for the group being in this part of the rainforest at this time.

As in many tribal cultures, children are taught valuable lessons at the earliest opportunity. Daily life in a rainforest is filled with opportunities to learn how to recognize and utilize the many resources that nature provides. It is just as essential to learn how to recognize the many pitfalls of the harsh and demanding environment. These children, along with all the children of their tribe, had been learning these lessons since before they could walk.

But when a male child of the Akinowatowa reached a certain age, they were required to confirm their worth to their families and the tribe by proving how well they had learned their lessons. It would be considered a rite of passage into manhood in some cultures. Others would consider it a final exam of sorts. At around twelve years of age, sometimes a little older, the males are led by a group of seasoned adults into the forest. They might journey for many days, changing directions often, before the adults decide that they had placed enough time, distance and obstacles between themselves and the homes their charges had left behind.

When that time had come, the adults would step back and become observers as the adolescent's assumed responsibility for themselves and whichever adult they were bonded to for their time away from the tribe.

On this particular foray, there were two to three children for each adult. The boys had to work together to provide for themselves and their adult, with absolutely no aid from their adult or any of the other pairings of children. This sometimes put them in competition for resources with the others. This was encouraged, to a point, but was never allowed to escalate into open conflict. At other times they were allowed to join forces and work together as a group to accomplish a larger task. Whether in groups or as individuals the boys were expected to do their very best. Only when they were seen to have completed, or failed, a task was any teaching done by the adults.

There was no time limit to these jungle excursions and only when the adults were satisfied that their charges possessed the skills to survive alone, and the temperament to work together as a team of many, did they administer the final test of following the boys as they led the way back to the village.

It so happened that on the eve of their journey home, with their many trials behind them, Wahiya had gone missing.

Wahiya's injury meant several more days spent in the forest, which the Akinowatowa men took as an additional opportunity to test the maturity and resilience of their charges. The boys took the new circumstances in stride and, by nightfall of the first night with Hanshee and Raymond, had constructed several shelters against the now predictable rains. While some of the boys finished the shelters, others took the initiative to gather as a group and scour the nearby forest for sustenance, thus the abundance of new and exotic food for Raymond to choose from.

During this time, Raymond and Hanshee were asked to join with the other men around the fire and allow the youth to embrace the responsibilities they had been trained for. This was especially difficult for Hanshee. Although he recognized the ritual from a similar one that he had to endure to prove himself worthy as a hunter and provider, then as a warrior, he was used to providing for himself and Raymond. It felt *wrong* to merely sit in this strange place, surrounded by strange people, and be catered to.

What made it even more disconcerting for Hanshee was the relative quiet of the Akinowatowa men. Aside from performing basic maintenance on their weapons and tools, they merely sat quietly, sometimes speaking softly in pairs or small groups, sometimes smoking what Raymond recognized as a form of tobacco from hand carved pipes, but otherwise keeping to themselves, even as they cast silent curious glances at their hosts.

The *Second* - Raymond and Hanshee continued to refer to him in this way since none of the others had introduced themselves - was apparently their 'medic', or medicine man, and he followed Hanshee every time he arose to check on the boy. He never interfered, only watched, as Hanshee went about feeding and dosing Wahiya. He never asked what was in the stew given the boy that kept him sleeping for so long. When Hanshee undressed the broken leg to examine it, the Second looked over his shoulder intently, nodding his head in satisfaction at the healing and as Hanshee redressed the broken limb.

When Hanshee attempted to communicate with gestures, the Second was polite and attentive but did not reciprocate. Apparently having determined that they could not speak to one another, the Second had decided to shadow Hanshee only in matters that pertained to the wounded child. Having watched Hanshee care for the boy over the course of several days, he seemed satisfied with the care Wahiya received. Though he still followed and watched, the Second felt no need to contribute.

The little communication that occurred was only between Raymond and Nuguro. Clearly Raymond was capable of speaking to all of them, but only their leader approached him with questions or comments, and then returned to the others where they huddled up and he shared what he had learned. This struck both Raymond and Hanshee as strange.

In their adopted guise of wandering priest and faithful acolyte, Raymond always presented Hanshee as being in charge. When Nuguro asked general questions of Raymond, Ray always used the excuse of taking inquires to Hanshee, though he was capable of answering himself. In this way he kept Hanshee aware of all that was going on around him.

This was not always the case.

Usually, when Nuguro came to Raymond, it was to speak about Raymond. When a question was asked that allowed Raymond to reference Hanshee, Nuguro patiently listened, but instantly turned the conversation back to Raymond. Ray told Hanshee about these episodes but, aside from just being able to speak with him, neither of them could say why Nuguro found Raymond so fascinating.

And all the while the others simply looked on in silent curiosity, leaving Hanshee to sharpen his tools and weapons... yet again. If not for the care of the wounded boy, Raymond feared Hanshee would have sharpened his various blades down to nubs before the end of the second day.

Hanshee's potions worked amazingly well, as Raymond could attest, and by the end of the sixth day Wahiya was no longer in need of medicine for discomfort. Hanshee had removed the bamboo to check the leg and said the boy was healing well. He then replaced and reinforced it.

This time Raymond had watched. He had been astounded at how natural the broken leg looked; the wounds to the skin having already closed with only the swelling and discoloration to evidence the severe break that he had witnessed just days prior.

Looking to the next phase of his treatment, Hanshee carved a crutch that the boy could now use for short trips into the brush to relieve himself, at first only with another boy tagging along just in case.

Nuguro was also amazed at the speed with which Wahiya was recovering. Once he determined that the boy was alert and in good spirits, he began making plans for the group to make their way back to the main village. He insisted that Raymond and Hanshee accompany them and be guests among their people. It was up to the children to find the way back, but Nuguro intimated to Raymond that the main Akinowatowa village was several days journey to the west. After learning this, Hanshee readily agreed.

The next morning the boys gathered what provisions they had accumulated during their stay at the campsite, made Wahiya as comfortable as they could in the litter and, on Nuguro's word, wound their way into the forest, their backs to the rising sun.

The rain had fallen for most of the night, making it near impossible for Raymond to get any meaningful sleep. This was the second heavy rain since the journey to the Akinowatowa village had begun six days earlier. Raymond and Hanshee huddled in the brush beneath the spreading branches of a large tree. Here they could at least avoid the full force of the wind driven raindrops falling all around them. Of course, they were still soaked, just as if they had stood in an open field during the downpour, but there was really no way to avoid that.

The Akinowatowa had also taken shelter under many of the other trees surrounding them, usually with their knees to their chests and their heads toward the tree trunks. Raymond was amazed that, even in the heaviest rains, some of them actually appeared to find sleep in this position.

Ray lifted his head slightly and glanced at Hanshee huddled beside him. In the heavy rain, as in heat, cold, or even snow, Hanshee quietly endured. As still as he appeared, Ray was sure Hanshee was wide awake too. Now and then, when a lull in the downpour allowed, Ray would lean toward him and ask a question or make a comment. Hanshee always responded, though not always with enthusiasm.

Shortly before sunrise the intensity of the deluge began to trail off. When the first beams of the morning sun pierced the canopy, the only rainfall was water dripping from the leaves and limbs high above them. Once the young ones were formed up and accounted for, the procession continued on through the rainforest.

But this morning felt different to Raymond.

The boys now moved with an extra energy to their step and many of their faces bore silent smiles that they readily shared with one another. At midmorning they paused for their first nourishment of the day and the boys gathered together in small groups as they ate, whispering and laughing between mouthfuls.

The adult Akinowatowa seemed oblivious to the change in attitude that had overtaken their charges, but Hanshee and Raymond took note. Pondering on what could account for the difference, Hanshee sent Ray to ask Nuguro about it. Ray returned and told Hanshee what he had expected to hear.

"The young ones have recognized their surroundings," Ray said. "They now know they are half a day from their village."

Hanshee nodded in recognition that his conclusion had been affirmed, just as Nuguro signaled the boys to again form up for travel.

As before, the boys led the way; the men of their village following close behind. Nuguro walked with Hanshee and Raymond in the rear. This time, as the procession snaked its way through the still damp vegetation, a single voice could be heard chanting or singing seemingly in time to the footfalls of the group. After a while the single voice was joined by another, and another, and then a few more. Soon the entire formation of adolescents was chanting in unison as the adults followed behind, looking from one to another with smiles of their own.

This is how the group marched through the jungle for the next several hours. The volume of the chanting at times fell off, only to be lifted again as new voices took the lead, or a new chant was begun. When the sun was just about to dip below the western treetops, the procession was called to a halt. One last chorus of chanting was joined, at full volume, before Nuguro gave a signal and all chanting stopped.

Now the group stood still in the eerie silence. The sound of their chanting had become the norm, and the normal noises of the rainforest seemed subdued in the absence of their lifted voices. But, after a few moments, the sound of voices lifted in song could again be heard, this time from off to the west. As the group continued to stand in silence, the sound of the raised voices grew in volume as their source seemed to be growing ever closer.

The young men had paused among the trees on the eastern edge of what at one time had been a cultivated field. Now only knee-high plants of the jungle grew there, but they did little to hide the signs that, not long ago, man had beaten back the rainforest in this place.

Raymond and Hanshee listened as the distant chanting grew ever closer and were not surprised when people began to emerge from the trees on the opposite side of the field.

Still chanting as they presented themselves, the people; women and children adorned in brightly colored fabrics, men in elaborate headdress and carrying spears, lined up in what appeared to be family groups along the western border of the field. They were accompanied by several drummers whose skin covered instruments lent a rich cadence to the many voices singing and chanting in unison.

At the emergence of the families, the Akinowatowa adolescents drew themselves up to stand tall and proud, the earlier smiles now replaced by the stoic expressions of those ready to be welcomed as serious young men by those closest and most dear to them.

As Ray looked more closely at the families gathering across the field, he noted that each group carried an iron pot, a wooden tray, or sometimes both. Steam could be seen rising from many of the pots as the men carrying them set them on the ground. The women carrying the wooden trays stood proud and tall as the chanting and drumming climbed to a crescendo, before coming to an abrupt stop.

Now it was time for those who had been tested to be welcomed back by their families, not as children to be coddled and cared for, but as young men ready to carry their weight and the weight of those who depended upon them. The young men formed a line opposite their families. As the drummers again began to play, they crossed the field as one until they stood before their kin.

As they moved into position the drummers again stopped, a signal to the lead male, sometimes a father, sometimes an uncle or another relative, to step forward and welcome the tested back to the village by presenting to him a spear. These were not like the spears the boys put together in the first days of their trials in the wilderness. Neither were they ceremonial spears, fit only for display. These were true weapons, some being family heirlooms passed down from father to son for generations. Many bore ornate carvings and decorations identifying the family to whom they belonged, or recognizing the history of the weapon. All had razor sharp heads of good iron. All were a testament that their bearer was worthy to carry them and thereafter would be recognized as a young man of the tribe. As these spears were passed to the newly tested, their makeshift weapons were passed to their families and would also be cherished as recognition of their beginnings.

Now the smiles returned and the young men were welcomed back with hugs and laughter. In the pots and atop the trays were their favorite foods, prepared especially for their return by their family. After the time spent in the wild, making due with whatever could be found, it was one of the highlights of their return; a highly anticipated part of the ceremony and the reason for many smiles.

As Raymond and Hanshee looked on, some of the youngsters made a great show of waving off their favorite meals, fresh from their mother's pots. This too was part of the ceremony, though it was clear on some faces that this refusal was done with great reluctance.

Those who eschewed the meal now stepped back from their families. Turning to their left, they walked down the line to stand before a single Akinowatowa male who, by his dress and the many weapons that surrounded him, was representative of the warrior class. This lone warrior held before him a shallow pan. Upon reaching him, each of the tested reached in and withdrew several fat white grubs which still squirmed in their hands. Without hesitation, they forced the grubs into their mouths. Many struggled to chew and swallow, their expressions fairly screaming out their distaste, but all were able to finish this particular 'celebratory' meal. As they finished, they took their place in a line behind the warrior. When all were in line, the warrior began a chant which the young men quickly took up as he led them back into the western trees, away from the field, and away from their families.

These young men had chosen the way of the warrior.

CHAPTER 19

Raymond and Hanshee stood with Nuguro in the very back of the procession as it left the field and moved through the western trees toward the village. As it reached the village outskirts, it passed a platform on which sat an elderly woman surrounded by four guards.

The guards were all close to six feet; tall compared to the other Akinowatowa men Hanshee and Raymond had thus far seen. They were men in their prime, of stocky build and clothed in a course brown wrap that hung from their waist to just below the knee. Along with their sandals, it was the only clothing they wore. Their black hair hung loosely past their shoulders, with the front cut to keep from hanging in their eyes. Their naturally dark skin was tanned and oiled until it shown a rich copper color. No head dresses adorned these men and their only visible weapons were the almost identical spears they held. Seven feet in length, the last foot of the spears was a spade-shaped blade, curved along its base and with razor sharp edges tapering down to an almost stiletto-like point. They held their weapons upright beside them as their piercing eyes examined all who would approach the platform.

In the center of the four sat the tribal Chief, the leader of all Akinowatowa whether in this, the main village, or any of the several smaller villages that dotted the rainforest throughout the area. As the families filed past, the young men returning from the testing stepped forward to approach the Chief. One by one they paused before her to give their oath and receive her welcome.

When it was Wahiya's turn the Chief leaned forward in her seat and questioned the boy about his injury. She listened intently while he told of the climbing high in the tree in search of the ripest fruit, of losing his balance and falling to the ground. At some point in his description, he motioned toward the end of the line in the direction of Raymond and Hanshee. As the Chief turned her head in their direction, Nuguro raised a hand to that she could see those that had found the boy and rendered aid.

After the young men had passed through, Raymond and Hanshee found themselves standing before the Chief as she looked down on them with bewilderment and curiosity. Her guard went into a state of heightened alert at the approach of the two strangers, causing Raymond to silently question whether or not he and Hanshee had been led all this way for some reason other than Nuguro's feelings of appreciation. Still, all they could do was wait patiently while Nuguro approached the chief and whispered into her ear.

Raymond could not hear what was being shared, but the change that the whispered words brought to the Chief's placid expression was alarming. Her eyes grew wide with surprise and then narrowed into slits as her gaze darted between Raymond and Hanshee, while she tried to make sense of what she was being told. When she asked a question of Nuguro, he pointed towards Raymond. From that moment on, the Chief's eyes remained glued to Ray. When Nuguro finished, he backed away but maintained a position on the platform just beyond the Chief's farthest guard.

Now Hanshee and Raymond watched as the Chief extended her hand and a guard stepped forward to help her stand. Once she was steady on her feet, the guard withdrew and the Chief spoke in a voice much stronger than her somewhat frail appearance would suggest, and dripping with authority.

"Nuguro," she began with a nod toward the tribesman, "is a trusted and respected elder of the Akinowatowa, and his words have weight in every village. He tells his Chief of two strangers who found an injured boy in the forest and, without knowledge of him, rendered aid unto him. He tells of the same two strangers welcoming the Akinowatowa into their encampment and sharing what little they had with the many. Nuguro felt it proper to welcome these strangers to our lands and invite them to take refuge in this village so they could receive the gratitude of all Akinowatowa.

"I am Altua, High Chief of the Akinowatowa people. When I speak, it is as the people speak. For the kindness shown in the forest to those who were strangers, I extend the gratitude of the people unto you and ask that you remain among us to enjoy the kindness of the village. You are welcome to lodge here and refresh yourselves from our abundance."

Altua pause briefly and watched, paying close attention as Raymond translated all she said so that Hanshee understood. Then she continued.

"Other matters have been brought to the fore; matters that require wise council and careful deliberation. It is now near upon sunset, and these new matters will be discussed in the light of a new day. Even as I give you leave to partake of our kindness, I ask that you prepare yourselves for a questioning on the morrow."

It was not lost on Raymond that, through the entirety of her pronouncement, High Chief Altua had kept her eyes locked upon him. It was obvious to Ray, from the treatment he received in the forest and now from their Chief, that he had somehow become a focus of interest of the Akinowatowa.

Hanshee noticed it too, looking from Chief Altua to Raymond to Nuguro and back again to Altua. There was a mystery here that centered on Raymond. Until the Akinowatowa decided to share their knowledge, the two of them could only wonder what it was about Raymond that had drawn so much of their attention.

As Altua allowed her guard to help her descend from the platform, Nuguro stepped down and motioned for Raymond and Hanshee to follow him as he led the way toward the two tall wooden pillars that marked the entrance to the village. With the understanding that they would receive no enlightenment this day, the pair fell in behind him and passed through the threshold to the place where they expected to lay their heads for the next several days.

Beyond the pillars was a broad path of packed dirt that eventually led to the center of the village but, at this point, passed between several rows of small huts made from wood and grasses that looked to be set up as stalls for vendors and their wares. Though empty in the last hour of daylight, it was not hard to imagine the bustle of a marketplace where men and women, having scoured the rainforest for rare edible treats and useful items of all sorts, came together to peddle the literal fruits of their labors to those in the village who were bound to other work and could not forage for themselves.

As they moved beyond the market and further into the village, several paths - some wide and some narrow - trailed off from the central path. Most of the narrow paths led to clusters of huts that were visible from where the trio walked. These huts were also constructed of wood and grasses; the main sources of building material, being both plentiful and easy to acquire. These clusters of huts were somewhat larger than the marketplace stalls, and appeared to be homes for the villagers. Raymond could see cook fires before many of them, some with women stoking the flames and tending the pots that rested above them.

One thing that Ray was quick to notice was that the women dressed much more modestly than he would have thought.

This was, after all, a rainforest. Heat and humidity were a constant. With little need for protection against cold temperatures, one would think that head to toe clothing would be superfluous. It certainly was for the men, whose attire of soft leather loin coverings appeared to be almost universal.

Until now, the only women Ray had seen were those who had come to greet their sons on their return from testing in the forest. They had all worn colorful wraps that covered them from their armpits to the tops of their sandaled feet. Some of the men that accompanied them wore the same colorful wraps hanging from their waist.

The women inside the village had no need for colorful ceremonial dress and wore garments of soft leather, woven natural fibers, or plain cloth apparently obtained from the same source as their more colorful attire. These were worn in the form of skirts of various lengths which concealed their hips and legs while still hugging their womanly curves, and halters made to support, and possibly conceal, their breasts. Most midriffs were unadorned.

Among both the women and the men, bare feet seemed to be preferred in the village, though many more women than men were seen to wear sandals. This was different from the rainforest, where all of the Akinowatowa they encountered wore coverings on the soles of their feet.

The broader paths that deviated from the central path twisted deeper into the village in both directions, leading to parts of the village not visible from where they walked along the central path.

As they continued down the main path, Ray thought he saw what looked like the wooden roof of a large building up ahead.

Soon thereafter, upon rounding a curve on the path, they found themselves at the edge of a large circular clearing. Ray could only guess that this clearing was central to the village; a place for the villagers to hold important ceremonies and celebrations. The roof that he had spied earlier was the roof of a large shelter, raised slightly above the floor of the clearing and open on all four sides. It sat at the northern edge of the clearing, leaving plenty of space for any activities that may be held there.

Visible behind the shelter were what appeared to be several sheets of wood, about eight feet by five feet. They were constructed of tightly bound bamboo, and Raymond thought that they were probably used to wall the shelter when appropriate.

Nuguro led them through the clearing and down the main path that continued on its far side.

The first building Raymond noticed on this side of the village was an overly large hut which was on the main path but set back, so that one had to tread a long walkway to reach its entrance. The walkway ran in a straight line from the path and was flanked on either side by gardens abundantly stocked with several varieties of flowering and non-flowering plants, many appearing exotic even for a rainforest. The perfume they radiated was warm and delightful in the coming twilight, and Raymond could only wonder about the aroma in the full light of day when all the varied closed blossoms were open to the breeze.

In the doorway of the large hut, about forty paces from the road, the silhouette of a woman was visible, the soft light within highlighting her every curve as she stood with a hand raised high on each side of the narrow doorway. Raymond found himself looking back at the image she projected, three…maybe four times, only turning away for good when his sight was blocked by the exotic foliage along her path.

A little further on Nuguro led the pair to another hut built only a few steps off of the main path. It was not nearly so big as the one they had recently passed, but had a unique feature that was lacking in the other; it was vacant.

It was also clean.

Apparently Nuguro had sent one of the men ahead to make sure that this hut, not normally occupied, would be adequately prepared for their guests when they arrived.

Fresh sleeping mats lay on wooden floors that were freshly swept. There were no tables or chairs, but several low stools situated in the hut had been thoroughly dusted and cleaned. Two of them served as the base for two large clay bowls filled with water. There was also an assortment of smaller bowls and pieces of torn cloth, to be used however the need dictated. Nuguro explained that the large bowl of water placed farthest from the door was for washing while the other was to slake their thirst. There was a lamp beside the bowls that would give what little light the two would need until they acclimated to their new environment.

As they watched, Nuguro retrieved a hot coal from the small fire that had been burning outside in the yard, and lit the wick. Lifting the top, he showed them that the lamp was fueled with the oils from various plants, but could also use oils derived from animal fat. Since it could not produce the pleasing aromas of the plant oils, animal fat was used only when the oils from plants were not available.

As Nuguro was explaining this to Raymond, a young girl arrived carrying a large platter. She placed this on another of the short stools and, after receiving Nuguro's thanks, took her leave. Nuguro then uncovered the platter to reveal an assortment of fruits, meats, and flatbreads. Knowing how much he had just added to their feelings of welcome, Nuguro smiled broadly as he bid them goodnight and took his leave. Raymond and Hanshee looked after him as he moved toward the entrance and passed into the twilight.

When Nuguro's footsteps could no longer be heard, both Raymond and Hanshee turned their gaze to the platter overflowing with hot food, then to each other, both sporting happy grins.

CHAPTER 20

After shedding their bedrolls, pouches and weapons, and washing the remnants of their long journey from their bodies, Raymond and Hanshee fell upon the platter of food, truly enjoying the bounty bestowed upon them by the Akinowatowa people. Such were their appetites that the girl who came to remove the bamboo platter found nought but scraps and crusts to carry away. Following their meal, they again had to wash; this time due to the crumbs and juice's clinging to their hands, arms and faces. Afterwards, there was nothing left to do but spread their bedrolls on their respective mats, and settled in to discuss their excellent fortune.

Raymond was overjoyed to find that, though strangers, the villagers harbored no suspicions and welcomed them into their village with graciousness, good food, and comfort.

Hanshee acknowledged this but, being who he was, approached the situation with more caution than Ray.

"It is indeed rare for strangers to be welcome in any village," he said, "but perhaps these people do not see us as strangers. When they came upon us in the forest, had we not first shown goodwill by tending the boy, Wahiya? Perhaps our welcome would have been much different had proof of our good intentions not been there for all to see."

Ray recognized the truth in Hanshee's words, but still chose to sing the praises of the Akinowatowa.

"Of course, you are right, Hanshee, and you know much more about these things than I. But, to my thinking, they did not have to show us kindness. For all they knew, we could have been the cause of the broken leg. Coming upon us as they did, they chose to interpret the situation as our preforming a kindness, rather than a possible crime against one of their own. I believe these are good and generous people by nature, and we are supremely fortunate to have come upon them in so strange a place as this rainforest."

Hanshee raised his hands in mock submission.

"I have been taught to be naturally cautious at times such as this, but perhaps it is as you say."

"While we waited for Wahiya to heal, they taught us much about the rainforest. Having insured our continued survival, still they offered a place among them as they returned to their tribe, many days distant. Those who now shelter us are as the Dula; 'People of the earth'. If any were to show us kindness, it would be such as these.

"Still, I caution you Way-mon; we know too little to rest at ease. Though no schemes appear to be afoot, their High Chief spoke of a *questioning*. I would see what the morning brings before declaring the goodness of the Akinowatowa."

"Well, you be cautious," Raymond said, "for both of us... as you should... as maybe I should, too."

Ray sat up on his sleeping mat, the better to see Hanshee as he continued his thought.

"It's just that... when I think back over all that has happened to us since we met... hell, all that's happened just since I awoke from my arrow wound... fighting assassins within the Royal House... then choosing to flee into the cold of the night... the crazy chances we took on the sheer cliffs east of Stronghold... leaping into the treetops, just to shimmy down their trunks and walk on solid ground again... the journey to Cantor, on horseback... guided by a child... and trailed the whole way by soldiers of Pith who wanted to return us, or kill us… or maybe both, hell, I don't know…"

Ray could feel something changing within him as he thought back over their trials since leaving Stronghold. He sought out Hanshee's eyes, almost as a way to center his thoughts, and so continue to chronicle the highlights of their journey to this point.

"We finally reach what we thought was safety in Cantor, only to be caught up with 'the Robes', the Imperial Guard of King Moton IX… and then, to have the king himself help us escape the soldiers who had continued to trail us into the inner circles of Gunjunson."

Ray's voice lost its enthusiasm, taking on a bitter edge as he recalled the hardships of their journey to Rayine, then south on the Merchant Way.

"The escape from Cantor… the pleasure of meeting, and traveling with, the Menowin family… then, more danger… fighting… and killing…"

Ray's gaze lost its focused as he relived the terror and the turmoil of finding the slaughtered farmers, of tracking the murderous soldiers of Rayine, of taking up the bow given him by King Moton and personally adding to the toll of the dead as they saved the merchant family who had been so good to them on their journey south.

His voice was stilled as his mind confronted what had been asked of him, and what he had done… taking lives to save lives… the best reason for killing, if killing must be done. But he was still finding it difficult to justify the actions that he knew had to be taken. Unable to come to terms with the grim reality, he allowed his eyes to slowly regain their focus on Hanshee, who listened in silence as he attempted to purge himself of their recent past.

"Taken captive by the Rayine. Thank The One Spirit, they believed us when we told them what happened on the road south of the bridge…

"But then those damn soldiers from Pith... or from hell... show up in the middle of the Rayine garrison. And no matter how far or how fast we ride, they just kept showing up... they just kept coming...

"All that and more," Ray continued, trying to allay any concerns Hanshee might have for his state of mind by forcing a smile upon his face. "Much more... and now, here we are... comfortable, well fed, and safe... among a people who willingly took us in. No violence, no threats, no schemes."

Hanshee allowed Ray's last words to linger in the air for a moment before offering his thoughts.

"Our unfolding path, though fraught with peril, has led us to a place of shelter and safety," Hanshee said, as he stared forcefully into Ray's eyes. "For this we give thanks to The One; He who has guided out steps from our beginnings together. Is there any doubt that He will deliver is safely into the hands of the Elders of my people... to fulfill our destinies?"

It was Ray's turn to let the words linger in the air. When he again spoke, he was happy Hanshee's words allowed him to move on from their hardships. His question took him further away from the trauma of their recent flight.

"You really believe that our paths are preordained by The One Spirit? That no matter what we do or what we encounter, we are destined to reach the Blue Mountains... your homelands... and your people?"

"I do not know this 'preordained', Hanshee said. "I know only that within us lies all we need to accomplish our goal. If we remain true, focused, and stout of heart, we will prevail, for of such are those that receive the blessings of The One. We will never falter, nor will we allow others to hinder us from our course. We will reach my home, my friend, and with us will come the aid needed by the People of the Earth. We will succeed, no matter the challenges in our path.

"We have found solace among a people much like my own," Hanshee again pointed out. "Those who shelter us are a gift from The One; a gift to we who require respite. As we first took our rest in the rainforest, we will now take our rest here. We will replenish our strength and prepare for the battles that ever lay before us. This is His gift to us at this, our time of need."

Raymond quietly accepted the words of Hanshee of Clan Dula, nodding his head in appreciation as he again stretched out upon his sleeping mat and allowed his body, and his mind, to relax. Maybe it was their new surroundings… or maybe it was the fact that, for the first time in many moons, Ray saw no fight for survival, no pressing mysteries to unravel, no pursuit to outdistance, and no hidden agendas to consider.

And no death waiting to fall upon them from every shadow.

As Raymond slowly drifted toward sleep, he marveled at his and Hanshee's unexpected good fortune. For the first time in a very long time they found themselves in the bosom of safety, and fully expecting the new day to bring more of the same.

EPILOGUE

The usefulness of their guise as mercenaries for hire was swiftly passing.

Seenio could see no further benefit to be gained from he and Nola remaining with Hendric's command.

They had joined with the Pithians as they hunted what many of them thought were two prisoners who had escaped from the dungeons of the Citadel, the Pithian capital. Only Captain Galin, his sergeant Lucius, and the Priest Petri, knew the importance of their quarry; that the two escapees were actually the Harbinger of the Fourth Prophecy and his acolyte. No one from Hendrics command knew that Seenio and Nola had also been on the trail of the same two men since well before joining up with them.

The temporary alliance had been a benefit.

It had placed Seenio squarely on the trail of the men he sought, while allowing him a firsthand look at those who unknowingly competed with him for the prize. On the whole he thought the group competent, but not worthy of note. When the trail was lost at the end of the Merchant Way, Seenio knew their partnership was close to an end.

Over the last several days, the Pithan soldiers had been frantically searching every settlement they came upon for any sign the two had passed this way. In this manner, they worked south along the Southern Road eventually coming to the shores of the Great Inland Sea. Through various crossroads, fishing villages, towns and small cities, Hendric and his command traveled its eastern coast as they sought information that would again put them on the trail of their quarry.

They worked their way south until they crossed the northern borders of the nation of Olmire, eventually entering its capital city of Maestell.

They searched the city as best they could, concentrating most of their efforts on the vast docks of the port that serviced the whole of the nation and by extension, all the lands above the Great Plateau and east of the mountain range known as the Blue Towers.

After many days and nights of searching the capital city, Hendric reached the conclusion that their quarry had yet to pass this way, most likely being somewhere north of the city, holding up in a place as yet unsearched.

And so, Hendric led his contingent out of Maestell to begin working their way back up the eastern coast of the great sea, hoping fortune would favor them with a sign.

Three days had passed, and the command found itself several leagues north of Maestell. As night approached, the soldiers, tired and frustrated from another day of fruitless searching, found a secluded place in a patch of woods east of the main road. It was here they decided to make camp.

As had become her custom when camp was made, Nola spread her bedroll behind Seenio's. Anyone coming awake during the night would glance around their encampment, see the hulking form of her father, and figure she lay to his far side, as always.

This night was different.

On this night, after everyone was deeply asleep, Nola quietly slipped from her bedroll. Moving with the stealth that was her specialty, she approached the line of horses tethered to a rope strung between two trees and situated well downwind of the encampment. Carefully she separated the two horsed belonging to Seenio and herself. After saddling the pair, she slowly walked them through the woods toward the Southern Road, the road connecting the nations of the eastern coast of the sea to the Merchant Way.

Following their plan, Nola continued to walk their horses north along the road, to place about half a league from the camp. There she awaited her father. When he arrived, the pair mounted up and continued north at a fast clip, intentionally leaving a trail that would be easy for Ishmel to follow.

When passing this way many days earlier, Seenio had made note of a rock outcropping that intercepted the road about a league north of the camp. The hard solid surface meant that it would be difficult to track anything over the rock and gravel. Once the pair reached it, they brought their mounts to a halt. Leaving the saddles, they slowly and carefully led their animals into the dense woods to the east of the road, being careful to cover any sign left by their boots and the horses' hooves. By dawn, Seenio had found a good spot to make camp. After quartering the horses, he and Nola settled in to catch up on the sleep they had earlier forfeit.

As usual, Jared was the first to rise, and was stoking the fire back to life as the slowly rising sun gradually turned the eastern sky a pale shade of blue. Caught up in his task, it took him a while to notice that Seenio and Nola were not where they bedded down the night before. Only when his still groggy brain understood that not only were the mercenaries absent, but their bedrolls were also missing, did he think something was possibly amiss.

"Captain… captain," Jared whispered softly, as Hendric began showing signs of awakening. When Hendric turned his eyes in Jared's direction, the soldier pointed with his chin to the place where Seenio and Nola had bedded. Turning his face in the direction Jared indicated, Hendric immediately saw the problem.

"Dammit!" he spat without thinking.

"What "Dammit"?"

It was Blige, one of the two soldiers foisted upon Hendric at the crossroad to Strongholds Gate. He had come awake just in time to hear his captain cursing to the wind. Now he looked around the campsite with the slightly confused eyes of the newly awakened, first finding Jared, whose blank expression was indecipherable, before focusing on Hendric.

Hendric resisted the urge to send another curse into the morning air, before resigning himself to speaking the words he knew he could not avoid.

"Seenio and Nola appear to have awakened early" he said, hoping by his nonchalant manner to the keep the morning calm intact. It was a futile attempt.

"Awakened early?" Blige said, loud enough to get a reaction from Sergil who, until that time had been curled in the fetal position on his own bedroll.

"Are they about?... Where'd they go?" the questions were now pouring out of Blige. "Where's Pitri?" he asked, before fully rising and stumbling menacingly toward the sleeping priest. Two steps from Pitri, Blige was caught by the arm and spun around.

"Leave the priest be for now."

It was Lucius. No one had noticed the sergeant as he approached from the trees beside Sergil. Hendric glanced over to see Lucius' bedroll still in place before speaking up.

"Keep your wits, Blige. We'll question Pitri if need be. For now, wake Ishmed and have him find a trail for our two missing mercenaries… if one exists."

Hendric said this last to Lucius who released Blige and walked over to the still sleeping Ishmed.

Blige stood speechless, looking first to the retreating Lucius, then to the sleeping priest, and finally to Hendric, not knowing in what direction to vent his frustration first.

"What the hell's this about?"

It was Sergel, now fully awake and pushed up to a seated position atop his bedroll. He looked from one to the other, searching for an explanation for the early morning tension already thick in the campsite.

"The Priests' pet mercenary is gone," Blige said quickly, a gleam now come to his eyes, "and he took with him the woman Nola, who beat your arse and made you bleed."

"God damn you!" Sergel spat as he heaved himself up from his bedroll and glared across the camp at Blige. "You know that bitch can't outfight me!"

"But you wouldn't be namin'er a bitch if she was still here," Blige chuckled, then darted toward Hendric as Sergil started in his direction.

"That's enough!" shouted Hendric, as he stepped between the two.

"Blige, you and Jared prepare the morning meal! Ishmed!" he shouted toward the tracker just rising from his bed, "wake up! We need you to tell us in which direction the mercenaries have taken off! Sergel, by the spirit of The One… you busy yourself at something!"

Now Hendric took a moment to calm himself.

"Once we hear from Ish, and get a biscuit and some bacon in our bellies, then we'll have a talk with Pitri."

Pitri only snorted, still lost in sleep.

THE END OF BOOK IV

ABOUT THE AUTHOR

Phillip Johnson is a retired analyst living in Columbia, South Carolina. A graduate of the University of South Carolina, he and his wife Louise have raised two sons and are surrounded by family and friends. He loves music and nature, follows South Carolina Gamecocks Women's basketball, smokes the best St. Louis cut ribs you've ever tasted, and really appreciates a good bourbon.

After spending a career in the private sector, he now has the time to do what he really wanted to be doing all those years behind a desk, write stories of excitement and adventure.

NOTE FROM PHILLIP L. JOHNSON

Word-of-mouth is crucial for any author to succeed. If you enjoyed *Along the Merchant Way*, please leave a review online — anywhere you are able. Even if it's just a sentence or two. It would make all the difference and would be very much appreciated.

Thanks!
Phillip L. Johnson

We hope you enjoyed reading this title from:

www.blackrosewriting.com

Subscribe to our mailing list – *The Rosevine* – and receive **FREE** books, daily
deals, and stay current with news about upcoming
releases and our hottest authors.
Scan the QR code below to sign up.

Already a subscriber? Please accept a sincere thank you for being a fan of
Black Rose Writing authors.

View other Black Rose Writing titles at
www.blackrosewriting.com/books and use promo code
PRINT to receive a **20% discount** when purchasing.